# Zippin Pippin

ALSO BY

BENJAMIN GRANT MITCHELL

BOOKS

*The Last Great Day*

ALBUMS (as 'Ben Mitchell')

*The Stars Can See*

# Zippin Pippin

Benjamin Grant Mitchell

Zippin Pippin

Copyright © 2012 Benjamin Grant Mitchell
Published by Benjamin Grant Mitchell
All rights reserved 2012.

ISBN 978-0-9873803-0-2 (eBook)
ISBN 978-0-9873803-1-9 (Paperback)

Original publication date: 16th August 2012
Recommended Retail Price $24.95
www.benjamingrantmitchell.com

# ACKNOWLEDGMENTS

Thanks to Pauli for endless love, encouragement and belief and for taking care of our gorgeous girls when important author obligations like Twitter call.

Thanks to Glenn and Sharna for sharing in the best research trip any writer could dream of having. Thanks to Kate Moon for inspired artwork and to Marika Webb-Pullman for meticulous editing.

Thanks to Angela and Richard for believing in me, and to everyone who bought a copy of my first novel for giving me the confidence to write a second one.

And finally, thanks to Elvis, someone I never met, but whose music and spirit inspired me to sing and dream—and buy that motorbike I had when I was a teenager.

You all rock!

For Cherry Jasmine

# CONTENTS

Introduction iv

PART I The Orphan 1

PART II Doin' As You Please 99

PART III The King 181

PART IV Santa Claus is Coming 261

# INTRODUCTION

First, I'd like to tell you something nobody knows.

Or at least not many.

It's not like I want to give the whole story away but if you've come this far—I mean you're reading the introduction, aren't you?—you've probably already heard the rumors:

Elvis had a son.

That's right. The royal heir to the rock n' roll throne, the only male offspring of the legend millions of us grew up with, discovered as teenagers or fell in love with retrospectively (and adored ironically—as it seems everything deemed to belong to another generation must be) is alive and well and living down under.

And yes, I know what you're thinking now:

*Wow! What a story that'll be. What's the son of the king of rock n' roll doing living in a land of dingoes, dags and drongos?*

I'm glad you asked. Because that's why I decided to share this tale. To answer that very question:

How did Elvis Presley *Junior* end up in Australia?

So now, please allow me the pleasure of sharing with you the whole story and nothing but the story so help me Zippin Pippin.

Man, it's a doozy!

Angus Pippin Flynn
*Melbourne, Australia*

# PART I:
# The Orphan

# DON'T CRY DADDY

It was the dream I didn't tell anyone.

Not the dream where I help Jennifer Aniston and Angelina Jolie work out their differences—by the three of us sharing a skinny dip in my bath—but another dream: the one where I grow up to be just like my country mega-star singer father; the dream I'd always imagined would have made my Mum proud; the dream I have where she doesn't die just after my seventh birthday.

And the three of us live happily ever after.

"Where's your head, Angus?" asked Hank. "You look like you're off with the fairies?" I pushed my Buddy-Holly-rimmed prescription glasses back onto my face, my fringe out of my eyes, and looked up from the brass sundial between us.

"I'm right here," I said. "Just tired from staying up all night." Breathing in the fragrant smell of ripe tomatoes, I looked around at the oasis of vegetables growing in our backyard farm patch. I never bothered telling Hank about my dream. What was the point? I was never going to be a singer. My nerves made sure of that. Besides, Hank's fading star was a good reminder that anything you might achieve in this life wouldn't last for long; whatever you get is just something you're going to lose.

And I'd lost enough already. So had Hank.

I watched Hank flick his long grey ponytail over his shoulder and adjust his trademark red bandana headband. With such a distinct look, and even if Hank reckons he was wearing his long hair tied back and held in place with the bandana a year before his country-singing nemesis had adopted the near identical look, there was no getting away from how much my father looked like Willy Nelson. Hank and Willy were a very close vintage, right down to the tough-as-a-dried-snakeskin wrinkly skin.

Wiping sweat from his lip with a sweep of his forearm, Hank then pulled his T-shirt out of his old jeans, shaping it into an improvised veggie basket.

"You stayed up all night, hey?" he said. "Don't suppose you been recording any of those songs I've caught you scribbling lately?"

"Matter of fact I was."

"Do you think you'll ever let your old man take a listen to your songs? You got me intrigued, boy." Hank plucked a few tomatoes from a section of the veggie garden underneath a hand painted sign saying 'April's Garden'. "How's that eight-track working?"

"Fine," I said. "It works perfect. Not like me. I'm not cut out for recording. I don't know why I bother. It's not like I'm ever going to play those songs outside of my shack. You know it's just a hobby for me. You're the pro, Hank."

"Don't compare yourself to me, son. Don't ever compare yourself to anyone. There might be some more famous than you but that don't make 'em better. Popular ain't good—just popular." I wondered if Hank was maybe referring to Willy, whose 'Blue Eyes Crying in The Rain' had kept Hank's hit song, 'Killer', out of the country top position back in '75, a couple years before I was born. "Plenty of talented songwriters never get a hit," continued Hank. "So forget whether a song's gonna be popular, just write what you like. You'll know whether it's good or not. Good's good."

"Good's good, hey?" I said, holding up a bunch of white roses I'd bought earlier. "See what I mean. You're the wordsmith in this family, Dad," I added with a wink, "not me."

"I never tried to be Shakespeare, I just tried to be honest." Hank sniffed the roses, nodding his appreciation. "And you can do that too, I know you can."

"Doubt it," I said.

"It's all about being yourself," said Hank. "Don't try and please anyone else or *be* anyone else other than who you are."

"Maybe that's my problem?" I said. "Maybe I don't really know who I am?"

"Well now you're getting a bit *deep*, boy. Is your mother's anniversary making you ask these big questions, or has something else got you all philosophical? Like a girl, maybe?"

"There's no girl, Hank."

"Not since Honey Rose," he said knowingly.

"Exactly." I took another big breath of country air, grateful as always for living on the outskirts of the city. Trying to delay the inevitable of what I had to tell Hank— something I knew he wouldn't like—I looked around our property: from the weatherboard house with wraparound decking where Hank lived by himself, to the granny flat shack (Hank built for my sixteenth birthday) behind me. In the near distance, beyond our property fence, I searched for the kangaroos which often gathered in the open fields come dusk.

"I don't know how to tell you this," I said, turning back to Hank. "But I…I won't be going with you to the Elvis festival this year. It's time for a me to make a change and Franny has offered me a full-time job." Hank looked up.

"You're not coming to the festival?"

"No," I said.

"You're going to work full-time at the bar?"

"Yeah." Hank ran his spare hand down his ponytail, a habit he had when thinking over anything possibly upsetting. I steeled myself for him to try and convince me music was the only life for me, and even if my stage-fright stopped me singing like him, life on the road was in my blood and I didn't have to sell my soul to 'Tick-Tock' as he called the world of nine-to-fivers and peak-hour sheep.

"Fair enough," he said. "You've been talking about it for a while. I know how hard the road can get. Believe me."

"You're not disappointed?"

"Of course I am," said Hank. "Not many old farts like me get to have their son—*and* the best guitar tech around—with them for every show. I was doubly blessed for a long time but I also knew you'd have to spread your wings one day. I'm glad you're takin' off."

"Becoming a Bar Manager is hardly a stratospheric flight."

"Might lead to something," said Hank encouragingly. "Anyway, we had a good run together, you and me. Didn't we?"

"Yeah," I said.

"Gotta be getting on ten years, ain't it?"

"And the rest. The first time I roadied for you was at Parkes in '89. When they first started promoting you as 'Elvis Presley's *best friend*'. I was twelve."

"So it's what? Fifteen? Sixteen years we been on the road together then? Like I said, that's a pretty good stretch."

"And I'm sad to see it end too but, you know. Things do."

"I know," said Hank, falling silent for a long moment after. "What's that in your other hand?" he said, pointing.

"It's Mum," I said, holding up my favorite framed photo of her. "And me. You know the one."

"Your favorite? The picture she signed for you. Let me see it." I passed the postcard-sized frame across the sundial we'd brought out from Memphis. Along with April's ashes, which now lay bricked up underneath, we hadn't brought much more. Hank read the inscribed autograph.

"To my little Pipsqueak, with all my love, your guiding star, Ma xxx." Hank handed the photo back and adjusted his T-shirt-as-a-basket to stop the tomatoes from falling out as he stood. It was his turn to look around Flynn Station.

The nearby hills were dark, with the setting sun behind them. A kookaburra swooped down from a tall gum tree to land gracefully on an electric wire connecting Hank's house with my shack. "April would have loved Australia," said Hank. "So would the rest of our gang," he added, a tad more upbeat. "I'd love to know what Roy and Doris and Ginger—especially Ginger—are up to these days."

"Why don't you go visit them?" I said.

"I don't want to know *that* bad," said Hank. "When I left Tennessee, I left for good. Too many reminders of your mother. But I'd be very happy if those guys ever made it all the way down here."

"You never know," I said. "They might surprise you one day?"

"Maybe," said Hank, with no real sign of hope.

"Look, I just want you to know again how I'm really sorry I won't be going with you to Parkes," I said. "I know it's always a big one for you but I think the time's come to throw in my guitar tuner."

"No problemo, kid. If you say your days of sharpening axes backstage are through—no problemo." Hank's acceptance of my decision *not* to go to the Elvis festival with him brought up in me a desire to go one more time. There was always such a great spirit of fun at Parkes, where Hank was seen as rock n' roll royalty for having been the last support act to share the stage with the King; they loved Elvis so much up there the local council was even considering plans to build a replica of Elvis's favorite roller-coaster, the Zippin Pippin.

"As much as I love doing that gig I haven't had a year off from it since we came to Australia," I said. "Before I started working for you, you dragged me up there every summer just to watch. Remember? That's like twenty-seven years straight." Hank snapped off some beans, adding them to the other pickings in his tattered T-shirt.

"I wasn't gonna leave a young teenage boy alone on his holidays," said Hank. "I thought you liked it?"

"I did," I said. "I do. But I just gotta do something more regular now. Normal."

"I understand," said Hank. "You've come to a fork in the road and you're picking up the spoon." I smiled.

"Franny offered me the management position," I said, "but only if I 'can assure her' I won't be going on the road again." Hank looked me in the eyes.

"Got a contract for ya, does she? God, seems even bartenders gotta sign their lives away these days."

"Yeah, there's a contract. But don't worry, I know how you feel about that." I looked down to the brass marker casting a shadow past six-o-clock.

"Yeah, well, I'm sure you know what you're doing. You wouldn't be as foolish as your old man to sign away your future," said Hank. "Not many would." Hank beats himself up over this all the time. When he was starting out he signed over most of his publishing rights. He ended up losing almost all earnings to his biggest hit, 'My Best Present Ever', a song still considered a country Christmas classic.

"Lots of songwriters lost out with dodgy dealings back then," I said, trying to encourage him out of his funk.

"It was my own fault—signing that song over to the Colonel—I was too eager."

"You had no way of knowing Elvis would be dead before he could record it. It would have been a great deal to even get ten per cent of an Elvis hit, even if you actually wrote the whole song."

"But I didn't have to go and make it my big breakthrough, did I? I should have pushed my other songs, the ones I still owned." Hank's share of the royalties from 'My Best Present Ever' was miniscule, his lack of income or savings the reason the old guy still had to play live. I paid the food and utility bills and Hank handled the mortgage repayments; we didn't have much spare cash but we got by.

"Who can predict what song will be a hit?" I said. "At least you get everything from your live shows. And you don't even have a manager taking twenty per cent anymore."

"Yeah, well those gigs are dryin' up quicker than our driveway," said Hank, pointing to a mini-twister swirling dust towards the front gate. "Now, Angus," he said, turning to face me directly, "you really sure you wanna spend the rest of your life workin' for the man? Before you settle into full time Tick-Tock—and since you're throwing in the towel on show business—maybe you oughta travel some."

"I've seen most of the world, Dad."

"You ain't seen your home. You've never been back to Memphis, not once."

"*This* is home," I said, looking down at Mum's sundial.

"Not where you were born," said Hank.

"Where I ended up though." I shrugged. Hank nodded.

"Me too," he said. "Me too."

I placed the roses down then briefly rested my open hand on the sundial. Despite the cool, country air the brass felt warm, the heat from the sun still alive in Mum's grave marker. Bending down, I read the inscription on the plaque.

"May the sun never set on the memory of April Flynn. Loving wife and much-loved mother. 1949-1984."

"It's hard to believe it's almost three decades since April died," said Hank.

"Yeah, but unlike us," I said, holding up my picture of Mum, "she never ages. In my mind she'll always be the same elementary school teacher by day and sometimes country singer by night."

"Yeah, your mother was something alright," said Hank. "But you know, as special as she was, one day you're gonna have to let her go, son. You gotta make room in your heart for a gal of your own."

"My heart's fine, Hank."

"Probably," he agreed.

"It's yours we've got to keep an eye on," I said.

"Right again," said Hank, putting his arm around my shoulder. "Another good reason for you to hang around, I guess."

"This is home," I said.

"Best one I've ever had," said Hank. A beam of sunlight reflected off the sundial across both our faces as the whole of Flynn Station seemed to fall silent.

"Love you, Mum," I said.

"Love you, April," said Hank. He bent down and kissed the sundial and our ritual was complete. As he stood up, Hank pulled a sweet potato from his shirt-basket.

"You having another meat-free day?" I asked. "The doctors will be happy."

"Fuck them," said Hank. "I don't care how high my blood pressure or cholesterol level is. Right now I'd kill for a sausage. Even one measly chipolata."

"You don't mean that, *Killer*," I said. "You wouldn't harm a fly. Otherwise you'd use some pesticides out here instead of losing so many carrots to the rabbits." Hank smiled, then followed my hand as I pointed to the kangaroos bounding across the field to come to a rest at the foot of the nearby hills. We watched the majestic marsupials bounce, prop and bounce again before I started back to my shack.

"How about I cook up some of my famous Yam Pie? For when you get home tonight, or maybe tomorrow for breakfast? You know you want to try it some day, don't ya?" I smiled and kept walking, waving away his offer.

"And you know I think that down-home desert's disgusting," I said. "I'll never know how you eat a vegetable as a sweet."

"Some things ya just gotta try, Angus. At least once. You might love it?"

"No thanks," I said, running up the stairs of my shack and opening the door. "I may be Memphis-born but I'm Australian-raised. I guess I left some things behind in Tennessee? Especially the taste for potato pie."

"It's *sweet* potato!" yelled Hank. I closed the door and took a clean handkerchief to wipe the blood from my finger where a rose thorn had punctured it. Then, as I placed April's picture back on the dresser, I faintly overheard the last thing Hank said, something I wasn't sure he was directing at me or April's sundial. "Some things you never leave behind." Listening for more, I heard Hank say, even softer, "No matter how far away you go."

Already running late for work, I flipped the lid on my turntable and put an old Elvis record on, to hear the song I always listened to on the anniversary of Mum's passing. I was getting a bit old for it now but 'Don't Cry Daddy' had always comforted me. The classic Elvis song about a father and son getting on with life after losing their wife and mother also reminded me what a magical gift music was; a gift I'd deeply wished had been granted to me, ever since my mother had died.

At seven years old, I'd thought maybe I could have even sung Mum back to life.

# NOT ANOTHER COUNTRY SONG

After a quick tidy up—putting my acoustic on its stand, a vinyl copy of Elvis's *The Memphis Sessions* back in its sleeve, and my songbook journal into a sock drawer—I grabbed the keys to my van and headed off to work.

On the way I retuned my car radio from an FM indie station to a national AM one playing golden oldies. I'm pretty nostalgic at the best of times but on Mum's anniversary I indulge my fondness for a bygone time guilt-free. To my pleasant surprise they were playing a cover of 'Hey Jude' Hank had suggested Elvis record for *The Memphis Sessions*. It was actually my least favorite song on my favorite Elvis album but that meant I still preferred to listen to it more than almost anything else on the radio; I guess you'd be right in calling me a big Elvis fan.

When Elvis finished butchering The Beatles I thought about yet another connection to Elvis—besides Hank writing a song *almost* recorded by the King, and Hank being his last support act a few weeks before Elvis died: on 16th August 1977, minutes after Elvis took his last breath in the bathroom of his Memphis mansion I took my *first* breath in a Memphis hospital. Over the years Hank had often told me how Mum had said it was at once the happiest and saddest day of her life; evidently, and as with millions of other fans around the world, Elvis had held a very special place in my mother's heart.

After the ten-minute drive I arrived at Green Onions as the house band (an indie four-piece who played obscure blues and soul songs) finished setting up for their early Saturday night start. Heading to the bar I noticed we were pretty empty but a few people were starting to settle in for the night.

With the seventies light fittings—tall lamps with big shades, silver balls suspended from curved arms—and retro furniture, Green Onions looked like any of the supposedly cooler inner-city bars about an hour's drive away. Our regular clientele was a mixture of local artists and musicians who'd moved away from the city for cheaper rent and fresher air. Hank had been ahead of his time moving us to the edge of town and working at the bar I rarely missed the few years I'd spent house-sharing in the city.

"Where you been, partner?" said Oli, as I tossed my keys onto the counter behind the bar. "Thought you were meant to mosey on behind this here bar *before* sundown?" Oli McGregor's company, not to mention his habit of speaking like a character in an old Hollywood western, always made my shifts at the bar that much more fun. Oli and I had become friends about a decade ago after a harrowing night in Thailand when I'd ended up too drunk to tell the difference between a legitimate taxi driver and, what Oli later told me was, an organ trader. And not the sort of organ with ebony and ivory keys; Oli reckons he probably saved my kidneys.

"What are you? My mother?" I said. "I march to my own drum Anyway, I get enough clock-watching when I'm out doing gigs with Hank. That's why I like working here—it's more relaxed. Fancy another, or are you having a night off?" Oli frowned, sliding his glass forward.

"Yeah, right. A night off? I've told you before my drinking is not for fun, it's…"

"Medicinal. Yeah, you're too sensitive, I know." I smiled and took Oli's empty glass for a refill, one of the idiosyncrasies of his Scottish heritage being a fondness to nurse the same unwashed glass all night.

"You know me, partner," said Oli. "It's on account of my over empathetic state I gotta drink. If I don't drink I feel everything."

"Me too," I said with a wink. "The weight of the world is likewise on my shoulders until I get off my trolley." Oli nodded.

"Then it rolls right off. Exactly. We're classic romantics, you and I. Besides, and as I've also told you before, that's where our similarities end. I don't have the benefit of having a famous father to help get me laid."

"Hank's not that famous."

"He opened for Elvis! It doesn't get much bigger than that."

"There you go," I said, handing Oli his refill.

"Cheers, partner! This here saloon ain't the same without you," he said. "I had to order me my first thirst quencher from Fanny. And you know me and Fanny are like a horse and a pig. We weren't made to ride each other. We're different animals, me and her."

"Her name's *Franny*, not Fanny," I said. "I would have thought for the sake of harmony at my workplace you'd get it right occasionally."

"What'd be the fun in that, Sheriff? Don't tell me you're gonna run me outta town 'cause I done gone insulted your girlfriend?" Oli turned to the door as it opened, his sixth sense for attractive newcomers always active. We watched a group of hen's party girls, with an unmistakeable air of 'come and get it boys', find a table in between the bar and the stage. One girl, in a sexy bride's outfit, looked especially ready for action. Two of the others wore french maid costumes, yet another was dressed as a sexy hillbilly, and the rest were similarly styled for maximum exposure. The Green Onion Players (as the band had imaginatively called themselves) noticed the girls too, deciding then was the perfect time to casually fire up their instruments and bohemian hipster charm.

"I wish you and Franny would sort out your playground problems, Oli," I said. "And besides, she's not my girlfriend." Oli grinned.

"Well, what do you call someone you sleep with on a semi-regular basis but don't give the keys to your shack to then, Mr?"

"Boss," said Franny, popping up from a hole in the floor leading to the cellar. "He calls me boss, cowboy." Franny's blue tank-top showed off her best assets: hard-working arms and her gym-toned chest. Although a natural blond she died her hair lighter and her eyebrows darker, such was her habit of self-improvement for art's sake (which included an addiction to tattoos; Franny had two full sleeves and was working up from her lower back with more ink).

"Everything alright, Franny?" I asked, stepping up to take an order from one of the hens, a gorgeous brunette with fake freckles and two pigtails.

"Yeah," said Franny, standing in the middle of the bar—*her* bar— with her hands on her hips, and giving Oli daggers. "Just changed a keg. Luckily the last beer I poured was for some dumb drunk who couldn't tell his stale lager from his stale ale." Oli looked mortally wounded. Beer being his life's study and all.

"I did think it tasted a bit funny actually," he said, losing all the bravado he'd had when Franny was out of sight. "Maybe the next one should be on the house, Miss?" he said more confidently, clawing back ground.

"My ass," said Franny.

"If I have to," said Oli, back in full flight.

"Get fucked," said Franny.

"If I have to," said Oli, with a wink to me. "But only if you strap it on tight. I buck like a mule." Not everyone got Oli's sense of humor but he made me laugh. Franny hated that.

"So where's these demos you needed last night off to record," said Franny, ignoring Oli's ribbing.

"Yeah," said Oli, "you've gotta have at least one song you're ready to share. What in darnnation have you been doing all these years?"

"I've told you both before I'm not happy with any of my songs yet."

"They're just demos aren't they, partner?" said Oli. "They don't have to be perfect. If you wait for perfection you'll never do anything." He turned to Franny. "Or anyone," he added, rising from his stool and indicating the hen's party. "Now if you'll excuse me, Mrs Franny, I've spotted *another* damsel in need of a good rogering."

"Charming," said Franny. "And, Oli—it's *Miss* Franny to you. There's no ring on this finger yet." Franny waved her hand my way. It was my turn to pretend not to notice. Oli headed in for the hen-party kill, his aim set on the drunk girl dressed as a bride. Franny's aim set on me.

"Tell me again why that twenty-something teenager is your only friend?"

"Not 'only'," I replied. "'Best'. Better than bringing back an exotic disease from my Asian expeditions."

"I'm not so sure," said Franny. "The amount of time you've spent bumming around Thailand and Bali—and anywhere else you can buy a beer for a buck—you'd think you might have returned with something more to show for it than a free-loading sex maniac. Something nicer maybe? Like say a hand-carved Thai wedding chair?"

*Wedding chair?* I thought. *Is she kidding? Fuck-buddy stool maybe? Do they make one of those?*

"You sure you're ready to put down some roots?" asked Franny, flamboyantly pulling out some stapled papers and placing them on the bar in front of me. "It's not only my love life that needs sorting. This place needs someone reliable too."

"And I need a regular paycheck," I said. "Yes, I am ready to be rooted to one place. I told Hank my years of skulking around backstage waiting for the next guitar string to break are over. I'm done with the road."

"Your dad's cool with that?"

"Cool enough."

"Good," said Franny triumphantly. "Then the job's yours." She handed me a pen. Before I could sign the employment agreement, The Green Onion Players came to a screeching halt. Franny and I looked up to see what was going on. Mick, the singer, took a swig from a bottle of scotch, the drummer was already rolling a new cigarette and the bass player sipped a piña colada as Joe, the guitarist, looked down at his broken string, an apparent welcome excuse for an unscheduled band break.

"I'll sign it later," I said, folding up and pocketing the contract. Guitar Joe made an announcement over the PA.

"Hey Angus, you got a sec? We need a fast string-change up here." I smiled at Franny.

"I'll give this to you later," I said. "Guess my roadie days aren't quite finished."

Five minutes later, having re-strung and tuned Joe's guitar, I came to collect the band, who were stubbing out cigarettes and binning empty beer bottles underneath a graffitied 'Stage Door' sign in the alley outside.

"All done, guys," I said. "Ready to go?"

"Sure, Angus," said Joe, his long hair matted thick, one wash shy of dreads. "Just having some trouble agreeing what song to kick off the next set with."

"What about some Elvis?" I said. "Something from *The Memphis Sessions* maybe." Mick considered my suggestion, puffing on the last of a joint. He had slits where his eyes should have been, his fringe falling like an eye-patch over one.

"Naa," slurred Mick. "None of that old country shit."

"Elvis was rock," I said. "And soul. He started out country but he ended up rock."

"Elvis was shit," said Mick. "He just ripped off the black man's music and called it his own. Besides, Elvis has been done to death. What we need is some original songs.

19

Unfortunately none of us can write for shit." Mick took a final toke on his joint. "'Cause of this shit, man."

"Come on, let's go," I said. "Show time!" Guitar Joe had an idea.

"How about *you* open the next set?" he said. "We could blues up an old Hank Flynn classic? None of us have ever heard you sing, Angus. And you got it in your blood, man."

"I told you," said Mick angrily, and with a dope hound's paranoid authority, "this band doesn't play *country*. Country. Is. Shit. " Mick turned to me apologetically. "No offence."

"None taken," I said. Mick handed me his joint, a peace offering. I took his whiskey bottle instead.

"This is my drug of preference," I said, downing a mouthful.

"What about one of yours then, Angus?" said Joe. "If you won't do your father's songs, why don't you join us and do one of your own instead?"

"Firstly," I said, "I'd never compare my songwriting to my father's—I'm not in the same league as him. And secondly, I'm not a performer. I can't get anywhere near a stage. I have a phobia. But none of that matters because you know what? Franny doesn't pay me to sing, she pays you guys. Let's go!" The band slumped off to finish their set with singer Mick dragging his feet and gesturing to the bottle of scotch in my hand as he passed.

"Take good care of that for me, won't ya?" he said.

And I did. Over the next few hours I managed to drink almost as many as I served. Though I normally didn't drink when I worked, one night of the year I made an exception to my rule. Whether I was touring with Hank, pulling beers, or home alone, every year on the anniversary of my Mum's death I drank to her memory. I never forgot.

At the end of the night Franny even joined me in a couple of shots and by chucking-out time Mick's scotch was all gone. By way of apology for knocking off his rider, I helped him and the other guys lug out their gear. By the time we were done bumping out all four of them had hooked up with girls from the hen's party and they headed off to someone's house for more rock n' roll.

While Franny finished closing up shop, I joined Oli at his table where he and the bride-to-be hen were watching the hillbilly—the fake-freckled cute girl with lustrous brunette pigtails—attempting to hold a jug of beer between her breasts.

"That's pretty impressive," I said.

"Thanks," she said, guiding the jug onto the table with her chin. "Angus, isn't it?"

"Who told you?" I said.

"Oli. He told me *lots* about you, handsome."

"Did he? All good, I hope?"

"All great."

"So what's your name then, Freckles?" I said, pointing to her nose and cheeks, adorned with fake spots.

"That'll do," she said flirtily. "Call me Freckles Girl."

"I was just joking," I said. "What's your real name?"

"Freckles is fine. Now what's this business Oli was telling me about your dad writing a song Elvis sang? Is that true?"

"Almost," I said, frowning at Oli, who smiled back 'you're welcome'. "Elvis never got to record it. Dad did write a song for him but it never happened."

"That's a shame, but still—wow! I never thought I'd meet someone who knew the King personally. Not in my life."

"Are you a fan?"

"Not really," said Freckles Girl, with no hint of irony. "But I *know* him. Everyone knows Elvis."

"What are you into?"

"Country. I like Johnny Cash. Have you seen the movie?"

"You mean *Walk The Line*?"

"Yeah. It's great, isn't it?"

"I guess," I said. Oli took a break from groping the bride and leaned over to us.

"Angus is a singer himself," he said. "Why don't you ask him to play you a song? He won't even let his best friend hear anything he's written."

"That's a great idea, Oli," said Freckles. "A private show just for us."

"I haven't got a guitar," I said, opting for the easiest excuse rather than the truth—that I was shit-scared of singing in public.

"Use that one," said Freckles, pointing to the stage. I looked up to see the battered old acoustic hung on the back wall as a prop.

"It"s no good," I said. "It doesn't even have all the strings."

"You can fix that," said Oli proudly. "He can fix that."

"Will you?" asked Freckles. "Please? For me?"

I looked around the room. The only other person left was Franny, giving me the evil eye for flirting with Freckles. Whether it was the booze, the thought of the Tick-Tock life I was about to commit to, or just my party-night horniness, some hitherto unexperienced courage powered me to stand and walk to the stage. I pulled down the old guitar, dug out some strings from behind the sound desk, and tuned it up best I could before holding it protectively against my chest.

*I was standing center stage*; the alcohol had done the trick. *I was ready to give singing a shot*; my first shot. For a moment I thought I was going to throw up on the fold-back monitor. My glasses fogged up with perspiration. Yellow, red and pink spotlights still set for the band blazed hot rays like lasers on my face.

"You sure we're closed?" I drunkenly mumbled. Oli nodded.

"Go for it, Angus," he said.

Even though it was my song, and even though I'd written every word, opening my mouth to sing I was sure I'd forget them all. But I was wrong. My words came. And, for an audience of four, I began my first ever public performance with a song of all country words and all country chords:

'Not Another Country Song'

*Never gonna write a country song*
*About being done wrong*
*Waitin' for love to find me*
*Never gonna play my guitar*
*In some forgotten bar*
*Waitin' for love to find me*

Franny came out from behind the bar, noticing Oli and the two girls sitting up front. Sensing the competition for my attention Freckles Girl moved up to sit on the stage, at my feet. I could barely make out Franny's resigned expression but we all knew who was going home with whom that night.

*Never gonna lose all my hope*
*Even at the end of my rope*
*Waitin' for love to find me*
*Never gonna forget my dream*
*No matter how bad it seems*
*Waitin' for love to find me*

Freckles Girl smiled and tapped her feet. Through the silent courtship ritual I kept singing my song of denial.

*Ain't nothin' wrong, and this is not another country song*

When I finished singing, Franny stepped onto the stage and handed me the keys.

"You can lock up, lover boy. I'm going home." Before my eyes had adjusted from the spotlights, Franny was gone.

"I don't feel like going home yet," said Freckles, jumping up to take Franny's place. "Maybe you can show me the band room? If you've got one?"

"We've got one," I said. 'And I'd love to show you, sure." Freckles smiled and wrapped her arms around my neck, running her fingers through my short hair, twirling my sideburns, and kissing me with all the grace of a salty-lipped giraffe. But I didn't care.

"Where's Oli and your friend?" I said. "They were just here a minute ago."

"Gone," said Freckles. "Let's go too." She dragged me towards the band room as though she'd been there many times before and, slightly disappointed, for the first time it occurred to me maybe she had.

But whatever. Maybe I was happy to play along.

24

## THE LONELY MORNING LIGHT

The next morning Freckles Girl left without asking for my number.

I guess she hadn't been as impressed by my Elvis connection as she'd made out. Or maybe she'd just been looking for a bit of fun and having found it moved on? Honestly, I didn't know and I didn't mind. I wasn't looking for a lifetime companion and not having to awkwardly extricate myself from our sexual encounter, by the eye-scorching light of sober day, was just fine by me. Being single was how I liked it.

Ever since Honey Rose.

Sitting hungover in my van, outside my shack out back of Flynn Station, I thought about my childhood sweetheart and the first song I'd ever written, a song with her name as the title. After mustering the nerve to sing for Honey (solo on my acoustic guitar) at her sixteenth birthday, she'd dumped me right there in front of her frosted three-tiered birthday cake, and all our high-school friends. I guess

Honey had been embarrassed by my public declaration of love. Or something.

But whether it was just teenage awkwardness or peer-provoked jealous school-girl cruelty, one thing I'm sure of is nothing was ever the same for me again. Not school, not my relationship with my friends and most of all not my music.

I'd never written—or at least finished—another song again. Not until 'Not Another Country Song'.

The twenty-seventh anniversary of my mother's death the previous day had also marked the day of my first completed song since 'Honey Rose'. I'd finally finished, and now performed, my second song ever. For years, Hank had been trying to get me to come on stage and sing with him but I'd never had the nerve. Even at Green Onions the night before it took me getting drunk before even considering performing—but I'd done it.

I was practically on a roll.

Though I was still pretty sure I'd never write another *love* song. Not for anyone. Love hadn't worked out for my widower dad and it hadn't worked out for me. As the son of a country-music legend, I was starting to think maybe I should accept a fact of life shared in so many country songs: you never end up with the girl. Not for long anyway. And certainly not forever.

On the drive home from the bar that morning some new lyrics had started to form. Before I forgot—and before I went inside to shower and prepare for my next shift at Green Onions—I had to get the words down. From my glovebox I pulled out my Moleskine. Over the years on the road, following Hank around from one town, one gig and one hotel room to the next, I'd filled up dozens of them.

*'The Lonely Morning Light'.*

I didn't always get the title first.

*There ain't no room in this lonely old shack*
*For someone to love and to love me right back*
*I've been alone for too long I know*
*That's how I'll stay—so on with the show*
*Leave me alone to my lonely life*
*It's not so bad, I've grown to like*
*The solitude and the silent night*
*And the lonely morning light*

Inspired by my solitude, I chipped away at a song I sensed lay whole within, waiting now for me to transcribe it from the ether into pen-on-paper and melody-in-mind existence. But before I could get to the chorus I was startled out of my muse meditation by the violent sound of a jumbo jet crash-landing behind me. Turning around I watched a long line of bikers coming along the gravel road and roaring down our dirt driveway. Flynn Station was under attack.

I thought of a snake—or a mythical serpent—breathing smoke and fumes. Twisting back in my seat I watched the serpent's head pass the front of my van, between it and my shack. Wearing an open-face helmet, the biker I assumed was the leader of the motley pack had uneven scars across both cheeks, no doubt the result of a jailhouse fight or a bar-room brawl. He led the rest, a seemingly-connected body, in a circle around April's Garden. From the backdoor of the main house, Hank emerged with a shotgun.

*But we don't have any guns*, I thought as Hank loaded both barrels. I dropped my notepad and jumped out to see what the fuck was going on.

"Don't worry 'bout it, kid," yelled Hank, striding down the stairs, "I'll handle this." Confidently, like Clint Eastwood might have in one of his old movies, Hank cocked his weapon, running to meet the invading herd. The bikers rounded Hank and me up, each mongrel shouting and hollering like a cross between a Hollywood Indian savage and Frankenstein's monster on his first full moon. *Who were these guys?*

Some of the bikers wore leather vests, others had dirty denim jackets with multiple patches; only a few wore full leather protective jackets. Whatever their outerwear, though, I noticed most of them had the same T-shirt underneath: a white round-neck with 'Growling Harleys' written in a dripping-blood font. For a second I wondered if the lettering was *real* blood?

"Woo-hoo!" A leather-gloved fist punched the side panel of my van.

"Watch out for the 'Killer'!" screamed another biker, spinning up dirt onto my porch.

"Fuckin' Yankees!" yelled the scar-faced guy who'd been first down our drive, as he skidded his Harley into Hank's feet. Hank stood tall but the shotgun in his hands might as well have been a bouquet of roses for all the intimidation it appeared to present to the chubby biker boss.

"That for me, Hank?" he said.

*Why does this pock skinned, pot-bellied dirty-goatee-wearing mug know Dad's name?* I thought.

"It might be," said Hank, lowering the pointy end of his gun. "What are you doing here? It's not even six a.m., Max."

*Why does Hank know THIS guy's name?*

"What can I say?" said Max. "My boys like to ride through the night. Less pigs—more fun." A few of Max's tattooed followers grunted n' chuckled as Max got off his bike. One guy spat into the dirt—too close to Hank's feet for my liking. I pushed my way through to get to Dad's side, feeling an anonymous slap over the back of my head as I did. "So, what have you got for me then?" said Max.

"You told me I had until the end of the month," said Hank, looking worried.

"Changed my mind," said Max. "Just like you did when you decided to miss your last payment."

"What's he talking about, Hank?" I said, following Hank's gaze to the biker emerging from the back door of the main house, the stranger to me—if not Hank—carrying a bottle of wine in one hand and Hank's favorite painting of Mum in the other.

"What are you doing with that?" I yelled. "Give me that!" Before I could get close enough to claim back what normally hung above Hank's bed, Max stepped forward, coming between me and the thief.

"Debt collection, Angus," he said. "We're simply professionals—doing our job." *How the shit does Max know MY name?* I thought. Hank put his hand on my shoulder.

"Angus…" he said calmly, "I've got myself into some trouble."

"No trouble if you pay," said Max, signaling for his minion to bring him the wine. Hank turned angry.

"Where am I going to get a lump-sum hundred thousand dollars? That's a helluva chunk of cash for anyone, let alone a washed up old muso like me."

"That's why we let you give it to us in installments, Mr Flynn." Max sounded calm and reasonable. "And it's why we encourage you to stay on the road working and why we haven't broken your fingers. Yet. How much did you get from that theme park show you just did?"

"Hank got sick," I said. "He didn't play out the two hours they contracted him for, so they wouldn't pay him." In his long career Hank had never cut a show short before that one. He normally played too *long*. The theme park manager wasn't the only one surprised when Hank finished early that day; afterwards I'd realized maybe Hank's heart was worse than I'd thought.

"I heard about what happened," said Max knowingly. "That's why we're concerned. We want to make sure you're feeling up to your next gig in Parkes. It's a big payer, innit?"

"My biggest all year," said Hank. Max grabbed the shotgun, easily wrenching it from Hank's hands, and turned it against Hank's forehead. I stopped breathing, the shock of seeing a shotgun aimed at my father's head knocking the wind out of me. Max started laughing wildly, tossing the shotgun on the ground. "Then make sure you fuckin' do it. Otherwise we'll be taking more than a bit of booze from your kitchen." He took the wine bottle and read the label. "Pinot Grigio? I fuckin' hate Pinot Grigio."

I laughed—I couldn't help myself. *Is this guy for real?* Max looked to me.

"Yeah, I fuckin' hate this wine your daddy drinks, Angus—but I fuckin' *love* real estate. And though it would pain me to see you and your old man with nowhere to fuckin' live, it would give me great fuckin' pleasure to have the keys to that old homestead and that fuckin' shack."

"It fuckin' would, would it?" I said. Max appeared ready—he was visibly twitching—for his morning brawl. But before I did something I would have no doubt been made to regret Hank stepped between us.

"It's not Angus's problem, Max," said Hank. "I'll sort it out." Max smiled.

"I know you will, mate. That's what I'm here to tell ya. You're going to do that gig in Parkes and you're going to put on the best show of your fuckin' life. Or else. See, I got showbiz contacts comin' to check you out. They're ready to give you a whopper gig back in the States, one that'll make you enough to pay me everything you owe me—plus interest. All you've got to do is play your biggest hit—what was it called?"

"'My Best Present Ever'," said the biker holding the painting of April.

"'My Best Present Ever', that's it. All you've got to do is play that fuckin' song Elvis was meant to sing. Play that for all those crazy Elvis fans and, if my people like what they see, you've got yourself a headline gig in Hollywood." Hank frowned; Max smiled. "That's right old Hank, you're goin' on tour again."

"Dad doesn't go overseas anymore," I said. "He just does the odd one-off show now." Max scowled.

"Then one more 'one-off' won't hurt. Will it? Unless you don't want to have a fuckin' home to polish your glasses in, four-eyes?"

"It's okay, Angus," said Hank, making peace again. "I'll do it, Max. Whoever these contacts of yours are, if they can pay my way back to America—I'll do it." Max nodded, then took a mouthful of wine, grimacing as he spat it out.

"Slade Gaitlin's his name. The guy who's comin' to blind audition ya. He's a record producer and music promoter from Los Angeles." Another biker standing in the middle of the vegetable garden unzipped his jeans and starting pissing all over a bountiful lettuce patch. Hank's face turned red.

"I don't care what his name is or what he does for a fuckin' living," said Hank, "but if he's gonna pay me to go back for a gig, then like I just said—I'll do it. Now would you please ask your friends to leave my beans alone?" Max laughed, chucked the full bottle of wine into the garden (where it shattered on a rock edging a patch of cucumbers), and got back on his bike.

"Pleasure, as always," said Max.

"As always," said Hank.

Max signaled to the biker still holding April's painting to bring it to him. I stepped forward to claim the painting back. Hank put his hand on my chest, stopping me. With a subtle flick of his eyes Hank indicated two bikers either side of Max, a couple of the roughest looking ghouls who'd ever leathered up, choosing that moment to check the aims of their semi-automatic pistols—by setting us in their sights. Hank and I watched helplessly as Max took the painting, punched through Mum's face, then tore the canvas away from the frame, tossing the remains into the dirt. He started his bike and roared off as Hank fell to the ground to pick up what was left of April.

The Growling Harleys slithered fast out of our property. Dust rose into a cloud, and, in a blink of my hungover eyes, Hank and I were alone again. I ran to the front gate and picked up a 'Flynn Station' signpost I'd painted when I was twelve, resting it against a tree as I watched to make sure Max wasn't coming back for round two. Then I rushed back to Hank, and over to April's sundial to pick off the empty beer cans our visitors had left on our vegetable garden's central piece.

"Sorry you had to find out like this," said Hank.

"Do you really owe them a hundred thousand bucks?" I asked, bending down to fetch out the jagged bits of glass scattered amongst the greens from the wine bottle Max had smashed. Hank nodded.

"Plus some change."

"Right," I said. "Then I'm coming with you to Parkes."

"What about Franny?" said Hank. "What about your job at Green Onion?" I shrugged.

"It's only one more gig," I said. "Franny will understand."

"Will she?" asked Hank. "I wouldn't want you to lose your new job over it."

"I'd rather lose my job than my home," I said.

"Because of your old man's foolishness, you might end up losing both."

"There's no way that's going to happen," I said. But for the first time in my life I felt like it might. If Hank didn't impress the promoters Max wanted to hook him up with, I could find myself without a home. Then, as I picked up yet another bit of glass, I decided there was no way on earth anyone was taking April's Garden from Hank and me.

And I was sure Franny would understand.

# THE ORPHAN

"Fuck you, Angus! You promised me you were finished working for your dad! You were meant to start working for me *today*!"

"'I do work for you," I said. "But I just can't take the managing job yet. I'm sorry. There's nothing I can do."

"But I thought we had a fucking deal?" screamed Franny, pouring a bag of coins into the till and slamming it shut. "Why can't your dad get one of the local guys up there to hand him his fucking guitars? Jeez, it's not like he's playing a stadium or anything. Does he even need a roadie?" I'd waited until the end of my shift to tell Franny the news but delaying the inevitable hadn't lessened her fury.

"We did have a deal," I conceded, squirming on my stool on the punter's side of the bar. "But things change. I didn't know my home was about to be repossessed." Franny took a deep breath and, to my relief, a slightly more reasonable tone.

"All the more reason to give up following your father around and take control of your own life, Angus. If your very home's on the line isn't it about time you started living in the real world?"

*Ahh, the 'real world'*, I thought, and my failure to engage fully with it being the worst abuse any girlfriend had ever been able to hurl my way. *There's another reason to stay single*, I thought. *Who wants to let people down just by being yourself?*

Franny huffed and puffed, considering her next argument as to why I should abandon Hank in his hour of need. Oli, who as usual had kept me company all shift—and who enjoyed nothing more than a chance to stir up Franny—returned from the loo and chimed in with his two cents worth.

"Yeah, barkeep," said Oli, jabbing my arm. "Get back behind this here bar. Keep yer' sorry dumb roadie asshole where it belongs." Franny stared at him, daggers and ice.

"I didn't mean anything *derogative*, Oli. Yes, Angus has other skills besides bar-tending too. I know he is a very talented 'guitar technician' but those skills are not always in demand, are they? I offered your friend to manage this joint—permanently." Franny turned to me. "You can't just up and leave whenever you want to anymore."

"Yeah, imagine if you did that," said Oli sarcastically, downing the rest of his beer. "Going where you want, when you want? You might start to think you've been born to experience life on your own terms instead of accepting your fate as some other person's shit-kicker." Franny stared disbelievingly at him.

"Managing Green Onions would be a reliable income for the first time in his life," she said, before turning to me. "Shit your friend's a *wanker*." Before I could defend Oli's right to be one he came to his own rescue.

"While it's true I do milk myself from time to time, *Mrs* Franny, it does not follow that I am completely defined by my nocturnal emissionary habits." I smiled and joined in with the fun.

"I thought you tossed-off in the morning, Oli?" I said.

"Du jour—ce soir? My old fella follows his own clock."

"Your cock's not on the clock."

"Exactly."

Franny wasn't amused near as much as Oli and me. I got up to go.

"I'm really sorry, Franny. I don't want to let anyone down but right now I've gotta be looking out for Hank. These guys hounding him aren't mucking around." Despite herself Franny seemed to finally understand.

"Is Hank gonna be alright?" she asked. "How's his heart?"

"I'm not sure. That's why I've got to be there for him in Parkes." Franny smiled. She'd always been a big fan of Hanks, and not just his music. Hank was a bit of a father figure too.

"He doesn't do one of those tacky Elvis tributes, does he? I can't imagine Hank getting his long grey locks up into a quiff."

"Na. This gig's on the back of Hank being the last guy to support Elvis. And the last guy to write a song for the King too."

"Those die-hard Elvis fans will do gosh darn anything to keep their hero's memory alive," said Oli. "If their love was enough to resuscitate him the old jumpsuit jerry'd be poppin' out of a seven-eleven every day." Distracted, Oli turned to watch a trio of gorgeous girls walking into the bar. Judging from their appearance the objects of his attention were either Californian surfer chicks or Nordic backpackers—or, if Oli was lucky, some combination of both. A cheeky grin came over Oli's boyish face.

"Speaking of being brought back to life," he said. "I think that bunch has just jump-started my heart. I love Australia." Oli got up from his stool. "Who'd ever want to leave a place every hot and bored twenty-something from around the world comes to get naughty in? And often straight out of high school!" Franny hung her head in disgust. I headed off. Oli called out for back-up.

"Hey, partner?" he said, pulling a John Wayne stance and raising a couple of invisible six-shooters. "You got my back?"

"Not today, Oli," I said. "You're gonna have to handle this one by yourself." The girls noticed Oli and me talking about them, but rather than being offended at being objectified, they seemed very pleased they'd caught our attention. Franny had seen it all before. Finding a misplaced twenty-dollar bag of coinage she unceremoniously—and as noisily as possible—dumped it into the till.

"Do you want me to call you later then?" asked Oli. "I might not be able to handle all of them by my lonesome."

"Nah, that's okay," I said, not wanting to upset Franny any more and eager to get home to check on Hank. "You know I don't have a phone anyway. You'd have to contact me by smoke signals."

"Why do you refuse to join modern man?" said Oli, pulling out his mobile 'smart' phone. "Did you know you can video yourself having sex with these?"

"Survived alright 'til now," I said. "I'll look out for you on YouTube. Make sure the girls get your best angle." I waved back to Franny and sent her a 'thanks for understanding' smile. The last thing I saw as I closed the door behind me was Oli checking out his butt, wondering which of his cheeks was most photogenic.

Driving home after another long shift at the end of a long couple of days I thought about how it would only be a couple of weeks and I'd be back at Green Onions, starting my new life as a full-time bar manager. With the financial shit Hank was in, it was more important than ever for me to make a go of my life. I'd drifted around long enough. Franny was right. It was time to join the real world.

As I got closer to home I began thinking more about Hank. I thought about his life before becoming a father and how even though I missed out on having a mother, at least I'd had a dad. And I still had one parent. It was more than Hank ever had.

Then, without thinking about what I was doing, I pulled my van over and grabbed my notepad out of the glovebox.

I started to write.

*I had no one to call 'momma'*
*No one ever called me 'son'*
*I knew no name other*
*Than 'The Orphan'*

A dog walking by on the gravel path next to the road stopped and looked up to my open window. I nodded my acknowledgement, but apart from noticing there was no collar on the old mutt, kept on writing. My first song for Hank. Maybe a bit for me too.

*Where are you from*
*Kids often asked me*
*I'd tell them I did not know*

*Someplace that I never did see*
*Someplace that I'll never go*

Taking a break from transcribing lyrics I looked out the window at the dog now down the road, rummaging through a knocked over rubbish bin. I pressed play on my CD player and smiled wryly at the Elvis song, my favorite from my favorite album: 'Only The Strong Survive' from *The Memphis Sessions*. It told a story about a young man—a boy—who's had his heart broken but is lovingly consoled by an understanding and supportive mother whose wise words give him comfort that love will come again and how he shouldn't give up on finding that perfect somebody for him.

When the song finished I started thinking about Franny and my love life and how maybe I really should have been considering settling down. Even if I didn't think Franny was 'the one'—even if she wasn't the love of my life— maybe it would be enough for me just to have someone to call my own.

Nobody wants to be alone forever.

# MY BEST PRESENT EVER

It was a game I'd played ever since I was a kid. From the age of eight, when Hank did his first Elvis festival in Parkes, I'd look forward to returning to the New South Wales country town every year just to play it. But this time would be the last time Hank and I would ever play:

*How Many Elvises Are There?*

As night fell on a stinking hot summer's day, Hank and I waited for his show time while watching the outside action from inside my van.

There's *one* Elvis, walking into a public toilet on the main street. From the urgency in that white-suited one's doubled-over shuffle, the King really needed to go.

There's *two* Elvises. That one's leaning against a stop sign, chatting up a girl in a puffed up fifties dress. The 'girl' looked at least forty though. Hank gave a wry smile.

"Guess Pretzel's taste in women is finally maturing," he said.

There's *three* Elvises. A dead ringer for the King cruised by on a Triumph motorcycle, waving to the barefoot Aboriginal kids all grinning back at the funny man wearing gold-framed sunglasses, fake sideburns and a stiff white jumpsuit.

Elvis was everywhere. Parkes was Elvis heaven.

"Looks like more than ever this year," I said, pointing to a busload of tourists alighting from a bus parked outside Graceland Three (Parkes' latest tourist attraction, a replica of the original Memphis mansion most of the crowd had probably paid pilgrimage to already). Watching the excited fans from around Australia and all over the world pouring into Parkes, I was feeling a little sad knowing it would be my last time there with Hank.

"Don't know where this Slade Gaitlin friend of Max's is," said Hank, winding up his passenger side window. "Nobody introduced themselves at soundcheck." We often used my van as Hank's green room. It was a good thing, too, since Hank's gig that day was on the back of yet another truck. "Max said there was supposed to be a representative from the American touring company coming to check out my show."

"If they can afford to pay you a hundred thousand dollars for one performance they must have some clout," I said. "I guess Max is more connected than you'd think— just from looking at him anyway." Hank shrugged.

"Fuckin' bikers are in bed with everyone these days," he said. "In my day it was just the drugs they pushed. Now it's fuckin' credit too." Reminded by the amount of money Hank owed Max's gang I shook my head in disbelief.

"Why didn't you go to the banks?" I said.

"I did. They turned me down. Seven times. Fuckin' banks."

"Seven times? Really?"

Hank nodded. "It was either Max's gang or move out—and I wasn't about to leave your Ma behind."

"It's just her ashes buried there," I said. Not that he needed reminding. "Who knows where Mum's spirit is? She's wherever we go isn't she?" Hank looked at me warily.

"Yeah, well, before we both find religion how 'bout we leave the spirituality chat-show for Oprah and go get this gig done." Hank climbed out. I followed. "Let's see if we can find these money men before show time." Striding purposefully through the crowd Hank kept his head down. He was always friendly with genuine fans but tried to avoid autograph hounds and photo-opportunity-seeking Elvis impersonators who loved to pose with 'The Last Man To Support Elvis'.

Over the years a few naysayers had criticized the fact there weren't any photos of Hank and Elvis together at the final Presley gig—on 26th June, 1977—but since The Colonel (Elvis's all powerful manager) had a strict policy of not allowing support acts to be filmed, recorded or photographed, the only proof of Hank doing that show in Indianapolis was a collectible poster with Hank listed as the opening act. These days those posters fetch a few hundred bucks on eBay; many people still happy to pay big for even the smallest piece of the King.

Backstage, after a brief ask around for anyone asking around for Hank, Hank and I split up so he could have a chat to the band about his set list and I could go to work fine-tuning his guitars. Another hour passed with no sign of the guys Max was supposed to be sending. Whoever they were I doubted they had plans to pay for an extra flight for me to accompany Hank to Los Angeles, but I was keen to make sure Hank wasn't getting mixed up in anything dodgy.

"Don't worry about me," said Hank in reply to my observation he was looking a little grey. "Just make sure my weapons are loaded, cocked and ready to go. Have you brought your acoustic with us?"

"Yeah, of course," I said. "But it's in the van. I didn't know you wanted to use it today."

"Would you mind fetching it for me," said Hank. "I fee like doing a couple more laid back numbers today. Your guitar plays nicer than any of mine."

"Do we have enough time? The stage manager just gave us the five-minute call."

"They can't start without me, boy. Would you mind?" I nodded and ran off to get the guitar. When I returned, out of breath, Hank too was struggling to breathe, sprawled flat on his back across the stairs leading up to the stage. I dropped the guitar case and bent down to lift up his head, seeing the drool down one side of his mouth as Hank let out a guttural moan.

"Dad, this isn't funny," I said. Hank had played this kind of trick on me before so I tried not to panic straight away.

"Probably not," Hank managed to say before contorting uncontrollably and thrusting the gold Telecaster around his neck into the stairs. Something cracked. I hoped it was only the priceless guitar.

"What's wrong? Where does it hurt?" I took his guitar, haphazardly casting it aside.

"My heart," wheezed Hank, clutching at his chest.

"You'll be alright," I said, signaling for the stage manager. "We need an ambulance here!" She was already dialing on her mobile phone. "I turned back to Hank. "Just hang on. Help will be here soon."

"It already is," said Hank, pushing himself up onto one elbow and wiping frothy saliva from his chin. 'You can save us both."

"What are you talking about?" I said.

"You've gotta go on for me, Angus. You've got to give them what they want."

"Out there?" I said, pointing to the stage on a truck in front of a capacity crowd. "No way!" Immediately I felt every organ inside my body constrict. Like Hank, it became even harder to breathe.

"You have to," said Hank. "Think about our home, about Flynn Station—about your mother's resting place." The sick feeling of dread moved through my stomach, spreading out to my limbs.

"Of course I want to keep our home but I can't do it, Dad! I can't suddenly be you. I'm a mess on stage. You know that? They'd eat me alive."

"Then I'll have to do it," said Hank. "We're not going to lose April's Garden." He gasped for air, struggling to his feet. "Not while I've got one breath left in this old body. I've gotta go on." Not quite standing, Hank fell on his face.

"Dad!" I yelled, helping him up. I thought about my shack, about April's Garden and about the now very real possibility that everything we owned could soon belong to a bunch of biker bankers.

"Looks like this is it for me, boy. The big producer in the sky is pullin' the curtains closed. This is my final call."

"Bullshit," I said, helping Hank to his knees. "You're going to be okay. Who cares about this goddamn show?

We've got to get you to a hospital." The stage manager stepped forward, helping me lift Hank.

"The ambulance is on its way," she said. "A couple of minutes, tops. You need to lie down until they get here."

"They're probably on stand-by for a thousand pill-popping Presleys," joked Hank. "But don't worry, Miss. There's no point takin' me off to hospital," he said, turning to me. "Life ain't worth livin' if I don't have April's Garden. I don't have nothin' to live for if I got no home. I got nothin' if I don't have April, boy."

"Then you'll have her, Hank," I said. "I won't let that Max fucker take what's ours." I flung open the case, took out my acoustic guitar, slung it over my neck and gave it a quick tune.

"What are you doing, kid?" said Hank. "I know. You're right. You can't go out there. You even fainted collecting your high school certificate. Remember?"

Looking around the tent I found what I badly needed: a bottle of scotch. I took a big slug. And another. The spirit burned my throat but I drank more.

"I remember," I said. "Honey Rose laughed. But I'll be alright now, Hank. I just need a minute." I took another mouthful. "And some more of this." I looked into Hank's watery, glazed eyes. "I know every song you ever sang, Dad."

"You think you can save April's Garden?"

"I'm gonna try."

"Then take this." Hank grimaced with the effort of removing his red bandana and placing it on my head, knocking off my prescription glasses as he did. "And take these too." Hank handed me his mirrored glasses. I took another swig of scotch then put them on. It seemed after all the years of watching Hank ignore colds, flus, hangovers and even a broken toe once, I'd learned something about show business. The show must go on. And I was about to make sure it did.

"Hank Flynn Junior!" announced Hank proudly, as two ambulance men arrived and began lifting him onto a stretcher. I bent down and kissed him on the cheek. *"Hank Flynn Junior,"* he said again, reverently, as if he'd seen a vision.

"I love you, Dad." I said. "See you after the show." Hank winked my way as the ambulance guys wheeled him off.

Walking up onto the stage I felt like I was having an out of body experience. The crowd was a blur; my heart in my throat. Behind me the band looked to each other for a clue, *what's going on?* The Elvis impersonator MC, having just introduced "The songwriter to the King, Hank Flynn!", passed me on his way backstage, looking confused. I took center stage. My lips touched the microphone and I jerked backwards at the electric shock. Not enough to knock me out but enough to knock my eyes wide open.

"Good evening," I said, in no discernible accent. "There's been a slight change in plans." I turned to the band and gave them a forced casual nod for them to begin. Back facing the audience I kept talking over the intro. "My Dad's been taken sick but….don't you good folk worry." I noticed I sounded more American than I normally did, more like Hank now. "I'm Hank Flynn Junior," I said in Dad's confident drawl. "Tonight, it's my honor to perform for you my Pa's biggest hit. The song he wrote especially for Elvis Presley—the King, the legend, the man and the reason we're all here tonight." My gut turned. Nerves fought with booze for the right to control my heart. The booze was winning. But, even if I suddenly found myself too drunk to walk I could probably still play every song Hank Flynn had ever recorded. I looked down to his set-list gaffer-taped to the stage:

'My Best Present Ever', Hank's breakthrough Christmas hit of 1977.

"We'll never know what it would have sounded like if Elvis had gotten the chance to record this and we'll never know what it sounded like when Elvis joined my father on stage at that last gig in Indianapolis. But I bet it would have been like everything Elvis touched: magic!"

The audience cheered; Elvis turned to Elvis turned to Elvis. 'Uh huh, uh huh, uh huh.' Hundreds of clones nodded affirmatively, thousands of fans likewise. I continued to tell my version of a well-known—especially around these parts—myth: the song never sung; the songwriter so close, and Hank Flynn—the last guy to open a show for the King of rock n' roll.

The band played on and I realized I'd already missed the first verse. The professional musos showed no sign of anything wrong though, vamping along until I found my place. I took a deep breath and turned away from the microphone. I couldn't do it.

*You have to*, I told myself, as underneath the drums, bass, electric and lap steel guitar music, I heard the ambulance siren disappearing into the distance. Hank was on his way to hospital; he was counting on me. I turned around and began to sing.

*All my Christmases have come at once,*
*Now I have you in my arms*
*All my loneliness has disappeared,*
*Now I have you here*

*Oh, I thank the heavens, for my best present ever*

Hank wrote this song for Elvis but it was about Mum.
And like the King's spirit, I could feel April's with me too.
Trying to ignore my racing mind—which was tormenting
me with negative thoughts about *what would happen if I forgot
the lyrics* and how *nobody had paid to hear me sing*—I forced
myself not to stop, not to give up now. I had to go on: for
Hank, and for what was left of Mum, and the garden she
lay at rest in at Flynn Station.

*All my Christmases have come at once,*
*Now I have my lucky charm*
*All my happiness is alive,*
*Now I have you by my side*
*Oh I thank the heavens, for my best present ever*

Between singing each line I sucked in air hoping
maybe, just maybe, my nerves weren't showing too much.
From the reaction of the thousands of music lovers in front
of me, maybe they weren't? They sounded like they were
loving it. It seemed Hank Flynn Junior was a hit.

But as relieved as I was not to have thrown up from
fear all over the stage, I could hardly relax. I didn't know
what had happened to Hank. For all I knew he might not
even have made it to the hospital. And, as horrible a
thought as that was, all I could do was take strength from
the fact that if Hank had died at least I'd had a chance to
tell him how much I loved him.

It was more than I'd ever got to do with Mum.

# KILLER

After the gig I was a mess. My emotions were all over the place.

I'd felt proud I'd pulled off the gig, perversely embarrassed—by the tacky costume I'd done it in (wearing Hank's mirrored glasses and red-bandana only at his insistence)—and unexpectedly inspired to get back to Melbourne and maybe finish my own album one day. But overriding everything was my need to get to Hank and make sure he was alright. Whatever other feelings my performance stirred in me, most of all I was worried sick about my father.

*Was Hank alright? Was he even alive?*

The unbearable thought Hank hadn't survived the trip to the hospital was only made worse by my intoxicated state; I was so obviously inebriated the stage manager wouldn't let me drive. She did call a taxi for me, though, which took me straight to Parkes hospital where I found out Hank was no longer a patient. My heart sank until I deciphered what the very patient nurse had to tell my drunken self three times:

"Hank has gone to Sydney. We had to transfer him to a bigger hospital."

"He's gone to Sydney? *Shit!*"

But it was better than gone to God. By the time I ran back to my van I thought myself sober enough to drive—though I'm sure I wasn't—and I arrived at the Sydney hospital around eleven that night. They let me in to see him but Hank was sedated, and hooked up to a bunch of life support and monitoring machines, so we didn't get a chance to chat. I waited around for another couple hours until taking the suggestion of another kind nurse who advised me to get some sleep at a local hotel.

After a restless night's sleep, on the drive to the hospital the next morning I listened to a tribute segment to Hank on the radio. News of his heart attack had already reached the media and at least one FM station had, somewhat inappropriately I felt, decided to play the title track to Hank's breakthrough album in "honor of the adopted Australian singer".

Did those radio people really think, out of the hundreds of songs he'd recorded, the best song to play for Hank—as he lay near death in hospital—was 'Killer'?

*I've played cards with cheating men*
*who look you in the eyes*
*Tell you my God's honest truth I ain't gonna lie*
*So when I heard you tellin' me "Nothin's going on"*
*I knew, because what you deny, is what you become*
*Killer—it ain't right*
*Killer—to take my life*

Hank's song told the story of a man's wife who'd been cheating on him, and how when the man discovers the truth—despite her denials—his sense of betrayal almost kills him.

*When I came home and found you in*
*The arms of my best friend*
*I couldn't think how it began*
*But I knew how it would end*
*Though I am not a violent man*
*I've never shot a gun*
*I can no longer deny*
*What I have become*
*Killer—it ain't right*
*Killer—to take my life*

Arriving at Hank's floor, I waved to a couple of nurses I'd met the previous night, busy at their station with an older nurse I hadn't met. Walking by, I noticed the older nurse proudly showing off her vintage copy of *Killer*, the nonplussed expressions on her younger co-workers faces making me wonder if they'd ever seen a vinyl record before, let alone one by a faded eighties country superstar.

Closer to Hank's room, the almost jovial atmosphere in the ward turned to panic. A doctor ran past me, followed by a nurse moving just as quick and pushing an expensive-looking medical contraption in need of a power socket.

"What's happening?" I said, firmly grabbing the doctor's arm. He was built like a rugby player and hardly noticed. "What's wrong with Dad?"

"Mr Flynn's had another attack." The doctor opened the door to Hank's room and I let go of my grip to follow him in. Doc abruptly turned, putting his hand firm on my chest. "You can't come in right now."

"Is he going to be alright?" Through the open door behind the doctor, and between the privacy curtain frantically opening and closing, I could see Hank being attended to by another doctor and a flurry of nurses.

"We're not sure," said the doc. "He shouldn't be having business meetings in a hospital though, I know that much."

"Meetings? What meetings?" I said. Doc shook his head.

"Apparently, when he had this relapse, your father was in the middle of a heated conversation with someone who described himself as a 'business associate'. Look, I need to get in there and help." I heard Dad splutter and groan loudly. I tried to push past Doc Rugby Arms but he wouldn't budge. He was a virtual wall separating me and Hank.

"Can I just see him quickly? I've got to tell him the show went fine. Please!"

"Not now. I'm sorry. I'll let you know when." The Doc disappeared into the room, the door self-latching behind him. I put my hand on the handle but thought better of attempting to force myself in. I decided I should let the medical staff do what they knew how to. I felt a stranger's hand on my shoulder and turned around, half-expecting hospital security coming to throw me out.

"Hello, Hank Flynn *Junior*."

The stranger before me wasn't a security guard, or another doctor, but he had the same sense of belonging as both—an authority. A man about my age—thirty, thirty-five—smiled broadly, his perfect teeth evoking a sense of, if not insincerity, then an obsessive preoccupation with appearance. His suit looked Italian or something else expensive. Underneath his unbuttoned jacket he wore a red T-shirt; his urban player outfit finished off with *orange* designer sneakers.

"Do I know you?" I said, taking my glasses off for a quick polish.

"No, but I'm a friend of your father's." Tired, as I was, from lack of sleep, the stranger's American accent didn't straight away indicate to me who he might be. "I was with Hank when he had his incident," he said.

*Incident?* I thought. *Who is this guy?*

"Are you the promoter who was supposed to met us in Parkes?" I said, getting my senses back. "Are you the 'business associate' that crazy biker Max is trying to hook Dad up with?"

"Yes, I'm a music promoter," he said. "I also work as a record producer and an entertainment lawyer—among other things." I nodded.

"They probably complement each other," I said, making no effort to hide my sarcasm. "I'm sure a thorough knowledge of the law helps you stitch up—sorry, 'sign up'—any act you think worthy of exploiting."

"You don't seem to have a very high opinion of my line of work."

"Sorry. Did I say 'exploiting'? I meant to say 'promoting'. That's what you said you do, right?"

"I work for the company who've offered to back the Hank Flynn homecoming tour," he said simply.

"Well, I'm sorry but I don't feel like talking business with you right now. I want to know what happened with Dad—what were you doing in there with him, anyway?"

"It went down pretty quickly—Angus, isn't it? We'd only been chatting for a few minutes when your father grabbed his chest and arched his back in pain. I called the nurse immediately. Actually, it was lucky I *was* with him."

"Yeah, real lucky," I said. "But I guess not so lucky for you. Hank won't be able to go anywhere now. You'll have to cancel the gig you had planned."

"I agree. It is unfortunate. We really wanted the Hank Flynn brand to be part of our next push. And, of course, it goes without saying I'm not only sorry for this hurdle to my company's aspirations; I'm also very sorry for your father. He was telling me about your home and how it's about to be repossessed. You still live at home right? Where will you two head next?" Being homeless was something I'd tried not to think too much about. I didn't feel like thinking about it then either.

"We'll sort something out," I said. "Right now all I want to do is see Hank." Promoter guy smirked. I wanted to punch him on the chin. "Don't worry yourself about Hank and me," I said. "I've got a promotion at the pub where I work. Maybe we'll move in there? We'll figure something out." I hated that I was explaining myself to this twit but something about him intimidated me. I hated that, too.

"Do you really think Hank wants to spend his remaining years living in a pub? Though we only spoke briefly Hank seemed very concerned about losing his home. I gather your mother is even buried on the property?"

"It's not like we've got a choice, is it? Sorry, I don't know *your* name."

"Excuse me. Where are my manners? Slade is my name. Slade Gaitlin. And I'm here to offer you an opportunity." *This should be good,* I thought.

"Really?" I said. "What's that?"

"Your father and I discussed how you took over for him last night for that gig in Parkes. I'd intended on being there myself but got tied up in a meeting here in Sydney. I heard it went pretty well, though? From all accounts the audience lapped up your performance."

"Don't ask me," I said. "I was half-tanked."

"However you got through it, my sources informed me you got a great reception."

"Your 'sources' hey? That's nice for you." *Where is that fucking doctor?* I wondered.

"Let me explain," said Slade. "My company is releasing a country Christmas classics compilation and your father's hit, 'My Best Present Ever', is the lead track. Since Hank's obviously in no shape now to perform for the launch we're planning…"

"And, like I told Max, Hank doesn't tour anymore, anyway. His health's not up to it."

"And that's another reason why we've come up with a mutually beneficial solution. We'd like to offer *you* your father's gig. My associates and I have already seen the video footage from your show last night, and we've decided we want you to do the same tribute you did in Parkes in Los Angeles."

"What? You're kidding. That's not going to happen." *No way,* I thought. "No way!" I said.

"Oh, that's a shame. A real shame. The show we've got lined up, combined with an advance on the Christmas album, would give you more than enough to pay off those pissed-off bikers your dad is so worried about."

"Your friends, you mean? Max and his Growling Harley hounds?"

"Max isn't my 'friend'," said Slade, his tone implying 'as if'. "I'd describe Max more as a 'sometime business associate'. But I do know when it comes to calling in debts owed to him, Max really means business. A loan's a loan, I guess."

*How could I do another bloody show?* I thought, unable to believe I was even entertaining the idea of torturing myself again.

"That gig last night was a fluke," I said. "I was lucky they didn't hurl bottles and abuse me off the stage."

"Nothing to do with luck," said Slade. "Talent's in your blood. And you can't grow up in a family like yours without learning a performer's trick or two." Slade watched a pretty nurse walk by. I looked to the closed door of Hank's room. "Look," said Slade, "if you agree to do it you'll get a first-class flight to LA, accommodation at the world famous Chateau Marmont in West Hollywood and you'll only have to do *one* show. You're a natural and we think America will love one of her prodigal sons returning to her welcoming arms."

"I'm more Australian than I am American," I said. "I've lived here most of my life."

"Even better," said Slade. "How many of your countrymen have mine embraced? We fuckin' love you Ozzies." I shook my head.

"I can't do it. Thanks for the offer but I'm no good performing in front of people. It makes me sick. Physically sick."

"Well, I'm sorry you feel that way. I know your dad's gonna be very sad to hear it too."

"What do you mean? Why would he be sad? Did you already tell him you wanted me to do it?" As if sensing my growing anger at his boss, Slade's African-American chauffeur-cum-bodyguard appeared in the hallway behind him.

"Sir?" he said menacingly. "Phone. It's the New York office." The guy looked like a Hollywood movie hit-man. I imagined in Slade's business he liked nothing more than ordering, if not an actual 'hit', a whole lot of hitting. Slade hardly turned his head, acknowledging his man-servant with the slightest nod.

"It was Hank's idea," explained Slade. "Like me, he thinks you're a natural." Slade handed me a business card. "If you change your mind I left all the details with your father. Have a look at the contract, it's all very straightforward."

"Me and the stage don't get along," I said. "I wish it wasn't that way but it is." Slade nodded as he moved off, taking his mobile phone from his muscle-bound employee.

"Good luck sorting out your home situation," said Slade loudly. "And please, when he comes around again, pass on my best wishes to Hank. Your old man was a real player once."

Slade put the phone to his ear as he disappeared out of the hospital. Standing alone in the hallway, I noticed the ward was strangely free of nurses, doctors or any other patients. For a moment I was completely alone. Outside Hank's room I sat down on a single chair, closing my eyes, trying to think of how I could come up with all the money we needed. I didn't know what to do.

A few hours later I was finally by Hank's side. He looked weak; the tubes sticking in and out of his arms emphasizing his helplessness. Sitting next to him I tried to make Hank as comfortable as possible. He hated the public seeing him without his trademark costume so, when he came around enough to start making sense, I helped him put his red bandana back on and offered him his mirrored glasses. He asked me to put the glasses aside. Placing them on the bedside table I picked up Slade's contract.

"Just take a look," wheezed Hank. "That's all I ask."

"You are a great performer, Dad. But I'm shit. I can't even step on a stage without getting blind drunk first." Hank smiled.

"Everyone gets high on something, sometime. Man, you should try the drugs they got me on, boy. Talk about calming your nerves. Look, it's only one show, son."

"It was almost impossible for me to get through one *song*."

"But you did. And you got through a whole set. So you can do it again. Take one gig at a time. That's what I always did." The older nurse—the one I'd spotted showing off her *Killer* album—decided then would be a good time to interrupt our father-and-son chat.

"Sorry, but it's time to go, Mr Flynn," she said. "I need to give this to your father." Holding up a freakily serious needle, she smiled Hank's way. "In here it's not illegal but it's still pretty good shit." Hank smiled back.

"I knew I liked you for a reason," he said, rolling over and giving her a half-moon.

"Not there," she said, smiling. "Here." The nurse jabbed the needle into an intravenous feeder, then, after checking for a good flow, tucked Hank in. She twinkled a wave his way before heading out the open doorway, a path she indicated I should have been taking too.

"We'll find another way out of this mess," I said encouragingly. Hank let out a low, long groan. I watched his eyes flicker back in his head then forward again as the drugs kicked in. In seconds he looked positively serene. *'Good shit' alright*, I thought.

"Man, it's a shame you won't go back to the States," said Hank. "It's a perfect chance for you to meet some of your mother's and my old friends—maybe visit where you were born. You really should know the truth about your family before it's too late too." Rising to my feet, I stopped where I stood.

"What are you talking about, Dad?"

"*Dad.* That's right. *I'm* your *father.* Don't matter who got your Ma pregnant. I'm the one who raised ya." I glanced towards the impatient old drug-pushing nurse standing just outside the door and barely out of earshot. Rubbing the tiredness from my face I turned back to Hank, then bent over, leaning in to whisper into his ear.

"What did you say, Hank? Are you a bit delirious or something? What are you saying about Mum?" Slowly but deliberately, Hank picked up his mirrored glasses from the bedside table and put them on. He smiled creepily, like a coke dealer who'd just tried the best merchandise ever black-marketed.

"All's I'm saying is—though I was the lucky one to marry that wonderful woman, I was not the only man fortunate enough to have sexual relations with her. The knockout bombshell April Devine was my best friend and the love of my life, but she was not big on exclusivity." I shook my head. Dad was talking crazy.

"I think those drugs are messing with you, Dad. I'll see you later."

"I love you, Angus, but I'm not your daddy. That man died the day you were born." I laughed and bent down close enough to see my whole face reflected in Hank's glasses.

"He died the day I was born, hey?" I said, smiling, sure Hank was higher than a Rastafarian skydiver. "Yeah, so did Elvis." Grabbing both my hands with both of his, Hank managed a final sentence before falling into a drug-induced sleep, his words weighted as though they might be his last.

"Yeah," he said. "So did Elvis."

## ROUSTABOUT

Waiting at Melbourne International Airport to check in for my flight to Los Angeles, I thought back over the couple of months it had taken me to commit to Slade's offer to reprise my role of Hank Flynn Junior.

After the drugs had worn off and Hank's health had stabilized enough to get him home to Melbourne, I took more time off from Green Onions in order to play nurse. At first Franny had been understanding, but when I told her I was heading to America for what could be up to a month she'd spat it again. But I had a bigger concern than upsetting Franny and jeopardizing my bar manager job. If we wanted to keep our home, Max needed his money and there was only one place I was going to get that kind of dough: wherever Slade wanted me.

"It's not coming up," said the check-in girl. "I'm sorry but no first class ticket has been purchased in your name."

"Are you sure?" I asked.

"Yes," she said with a smile. "Are you sure you've been correctly informed?" The first thought of how much Slade

Gaitlin may have *ill*-informed me crossed my mind. I wondered what I might have gotten myself into with the contract I'd signed, sealed and delivered two months before Slade sent me my flight details.

"No," I said. "Though I'm not sure of much at the moment. The guy who booked my flight said it was a first class ticket, see." I showed her my print-out and she shrugged 'sorry' before printing off my boarding pass and handing me an economy ticket. I smiled and thanked her as I felt a tap on my shoulder.

"Hey partner, thought you'd leave town without your best buddy riding by your side did ya?" Oli grinned.

"What the fuck are you doing here?" I said. 'Where are your Swedish girlfriends and their beat-up van?"

"There's plenty more volleyball players on the beach," said Oli. "Besides, I've done me plenty of miles over the land down under. Never been to 'The States' though, partner. So, here I am!" I picked up my passport and papers from the counter.

"Well, I'll see you in California," I said. "I've been taking up too much of this very helpful lady's time already and now I'm running late."

"Not at all," said the check-in girl. "We could chat all day." Oli smiled and punched me playfully in the shoulder.

"Hey, Pipsqueak," he said, "we're on the same plane. I'll meet you at the saloon onboard." I returned Oli's smile and slap on the back, leaving him to apologize to the people behind us for line-jumping. One couple looked particularly miffed.

"Sorry," said Oli as I walked away. "He's my partner. We're headed for the Wild West. You don't mind, do you?"

"I don't mind," replied a bookish-looking girl, "but my boyfriend does." I kept walking, glancing over my shoulder to see Oli face up to a near seven-foot dude in a tracksuit, a man mountain easily mistakable for a weight-bearing column. I could just hear Oli's timid response as he contritely backed away to the back of the line.

"I'll just mosey on back here," said Oli. "Don't mean to cause no trouble, Mister. There's no use me being a dead hero." For the first time since agreeing to the tribute show I had a new thought about my LA trip:

*Maybe this'll be fun?*

Ten minutes later, though, it was anything but. On my ass on the airport floor, with security guards seemingly everywhere around me, I was struggling to remove my footwear—as I had humorlessly been requested to do, working up a sweat as I did. The guards accusatory eyes watched me pull and push at the new pair of black cowboy boots Hank had given me to complete the Hank Flynn Junior makeover. They were shiny and stiff and glued to my feet and calves. I was pretty sure I was about to pull a muscle in my back before I got either foot out of the damn things.

Eventually though, and with much puffing and grunting, the first boot came free and, spurred on by my success, I focused my complete attention on the second. Just as I was sure I was going to burst a blood vessel in my temple I showed the second boot who was boss too, the sheer force of my efforts sending the hard, leather, wooden-heeled missile flying out of my hands. It landed on another traveler's toes, pretty feet in flip-flops, nails painted with orange polish. *Shit*, I thought. I'd gone and booted a girl.

"Ow! Fuck!" said a female voice. "Look out. Terrorist on aisle nine."

Looking up, I saw a beautiful girl in her mid- to late-twenties. She had green eyes and curly brown shoulder-length hair. Her lime-colored V-neck T-shirt showed off a little cleavage and her jeans were tight enough to show off her slim, but not crazy skinny, figure. Despite the pretty girl's undoubtedly sore toe, she looked a lot more comfortable standing there than I felt on the floor.

"Sorry," I said, scrambling to my feet and trying to regain some composure. I smiled apologetically at the guards too. "Sorry," I said again. The girl handed me my boot. Submissively, I lay it, and the other on the x-ray conveyor belt. Then I took a moment and a calming breath before walking through the metal detector. No bells or alarms sounded. On the other side I breathed out.

Too soon.

A beady-eyed, uniformed guard stepped forward and put his big hand on my chest. Fluorescent airport lights reflected off his shaved head. Strangely, given his intimidating appearance, he spoke softly—gently even.

"Stop here, please. There's a problem." The girl had followed me through and I noticed her expression was serious too.

"Clearly," she said, nodding to the gladiator-guard.

"What?" I said to both of them. "What have I done?" *I really hate these fucking security checks*, I thought. Gladiator's stern mouth cracked a quarter of a smile. He winked at the girl with the boot-bruised toe. They both pointed down towards the airport floor and to where, contrasting harshly with the bland, nondescript patterned carpet, were my two footsies—in bright pink socks. Except for me, everyone started laughing.

"We'll let you off with a warning," said Gladiator.

"I wouldn't, Mister," said the girl. This time I noticed her American accent. "He looks like all kinds of trouble." She flashed me a smile and a quick wink. I felt electricity up my spine, as though she'd shot me with a taser gun. Gladiator got serious again.

"Perhaps you're right, Miss." He said, turning to me. "Sir, I'll ask you to move to the side and…put your boots back on." He smiled as I felt my cheeks flush with embarrassment, and a strong urge to explain my absentminded habit of washing colors with whites. I plonked back down on my ass to wrestle my stiff boots back on. The girl smiled again. She was even more gorgeous.

"I guess it's moments like these when someone like you is hoping there's no paparazzi hiding behind an escalator somewhere," she said.

"No one would want a photo of me," I said. "I'm hardly famous. What makes you think I am?"

"Well, with the way you're dressed I just took you for a rock star, Cowboy."

"Well, I'm neither. My name's Angus, actually."

"And mine's Cherry, *actually*," she said, offering her hand. "As in the fruit not the sexually inexperienced state." I shook her hand as I stood up. With our boots and flip-flops back on we stood motionless, facing each other at the end of the conveyor belt. Time may not quite have stopped but the x-ray conveyor belt did.

"If Mr and Mrs Actually could keep moving?" said Gladiator, motioning for us to move off. "I've got a long line of people to intimidate."

"Where are you headed?" I asked, as we did as requested.

"Souvenirs. I've got a habit." Cherry pointed to the duty-free shopping plaza opening out in front of us.

"Nasty," I said. "Can't you go cold turkey?" Cherry shook her head.

"Kookaburra, maybe? Koala—sure. But Australia's not known for her turkeys. I'm not sure Mum would appreciate a green and gold gobbler."

"That's nice. You getting something for your mum?" We stopped in front of a shop loaded with Australiana. Stuffed kangaroos, Aboriginal prints and didgeridoos filled every available high-rent space.

"Yeah," said Cherry. "I don't see her as much as either of us would like, but like me, she appreciates knick-knacks of unique origin." I picked up a decent-sized but travel-friendly boomerang.

"What about this for your Mum, then?" I asked. "You've got to take a boomerang home to…?"

"California," said Cherry. "Same place you're headed." I stopped pretending to peruse postcards.

"How did you know that?" I asked before handing Cherry the boomerang.

"Umm…just a guess. Aren't you flying into LA? I assumed we were probably headed for the same flight."

"Yeah, I am." I said, picking up and putting back an 'I Love Melbourne' sticker with a ten-dollar price tag. Cherry caught me staring at her. I took the boomerang back for closer inspection. "Oh, no! Sorry. It's no good. You can't buy this one."

"Why not?" asked Cherry.

"It's made in China," I explained, turning it over in her hands. "See." Cherry smiled again. More gorgeous.

"Perfect," she said. "I only buy souvenirs made in foreign countries."

"Huh?"

"I've got an American flag made in Russia," explained Cherry, "and a Nepalese hand-crafted 'I Love Paris' beret." I picked up a soft-toy koala.

"You better get this one too then," I said, handing it to her. Cherry took the koala and lifted the tag.

"Made in Taiwan. Perfect. I love bears—so cuddly. This is like finding treasure for me." I knew what she meant about finding treasure. I'd just met the girl and I was already acting like a lovesick teenager. A perfectly-timed announcement came over the public address, filling the natural pause in our flirty banter.

"This is the final call for passengers Charlene Stephanie Ockham and Angus Pippin Flynn. Your flight is waiting to depart. Please make your way to gate forty-two immediately." We both looked at each other in pretend shock horror. Cherry rushed to pay for her goods.

"Hey, that's us," she said.

"Charlene? I thought you said your name was Cherry?"

"I did. It is. Cherry is my nickname, Angus. Or should I call you Pippin?"

"You can call me Pipsqueak if you like. That's the only nickname I've ever had."

"Okay, Pipsqueak. Let's fly."

"I'm right…in front of you." I said, running off and leaving Cherry gathering her carry-on luggage and bags of new purchases. After disappearing around a corner I came rushing back to help her, and was rewarded with another one of those smiles.

Much to my disappointment though, fate had not conspired to seat me next to Cherry on the plane. Many hours later, as I removed my headphones, deciding against yet another scotch and coke in a plastic cup, I got up to stretch my legs and seek out Oli—and, maybe, Cherry too. The video map of our plane's position indicated we were almost halfway to our destination. Walking along the aisles I noticed the long flight had sent many to sleep. But apart from the random light from dozens of flickering movies (and a seemingly endless choice of video games) spilling into the aisles, the cabin was dark.

Next to the middle food-preparation station I bent over and touched my toes, wondering if I'd be able to get my cowboy boots back on at the other end of the ankle-swelling journey. Standing up, I noticed Oli on the other side of the mini-kitchen, moving in on a sexy stewardess. She smiled politely and pulled the curtain shut in his face. From my vantage point I could see her giggle—obviously enjoying teasing my friend. I wondered if Oli was going to take no for an answer. I doubted it.

Looking around and spotting Cherry, I sock-slid along the carpeted aisle up by her side. She was watching an Elvis movie I'd just finished with.

"Elvis fan too, hey?" I said, kneeling next to her. Cherry pulled her headphones aside.

"Yeah, I love Elvis. Ever since I was a kid. Mum used to take me to an old movie-house in Los Angeles that used to play all his films. *Roustabout* is a classic."

"I love that movie too. Poor guy knocked off his motorbike has to go to work at the circus."

"Where he falls in love…"

"…and sings and swoons."

"What Elvis does best," said Cherry, taking her earphones all the way down. "Another fairytale love story. Are you a big Elvis fan?"

"Sure. Especially his later stuff."

"*The Memphis Sessions* is when he really came alive," said Cherry.

"You're kidding?" I said. "That's my favorite album."

"Mine too. I even forgive him that cover of 'Hey Jude'."

"Hey, it's not so bad," I said. "He was only human." Cherry shrugged. *Was he?*

"I've often thought about visiting Memphis some day," she said. "I'd love to see where the King was born."

"Elvis was born in Tupelo," I said. "He only moved to Memphis when he was a teenager."

"That's right," said Cherry. "I did know that," she added with a smile. "Anyway, I'll definitely go to Graceland eventually. I'd like to check out Sun Studios too. You know, where rock and roll began."

"That would be good," I said. "But I don't think any of that tourist stuff is on the cards for me this trip. Though I would love nothing more than to see Sun—where Elvis started it all. My dad actually wrote a song for Elvis. And my parents were kind of friends of his."

"Really?" said Cherry, impressed. "That's amazing. How close were they? Your parents and Elvis?" *Closer than I thought*, I wanted to say.

"That's a good question," I said. Cherry looked confused. "I mean, we left Memphis when I was a kid. I don't remember much about my family's life there."

"Were you born in America?" asked Cherry. I nodded.

"The day Elvis died," I said. "So, obviously, unlike my parents, I never met him."

"You must be excited about visiting the country you were born in?"

"Sure. Though I'm mainly going for work."

"Oh, really? What do you do?"

"Well, I've been a roadie most of my life but I write songs too. Believe it or not though I'm going to California to sing my dad's greatest hits." Cherry looked impressed.

"He must be proud? Your dad."

"He's pretty sick, actually."

"What about your mum? Is she happy her son is following in his father's footsteps?"

"She's not around anymore. My mother died when I was seven. It's been just Hank and me since." Cherry put a hand on her heart.

"I'm sorry," she said. I shrugged.

"Don't worry." Cherry wrapped up her headphones and stowed them in the seat flap. "Well, if you've got any spare time and you'd like a personal tour guide I'd be happy to show you around LA. How long do you have?"

"Not long. I'm not sure exactly? The promoter didn't specify a date on my return ticket. But yeah, I'd love to hook up for a while. That'd be great." Oli strutted up, still scouting for feminine company. Noticing the same sexy stewardess from before delivering a drink a few rows in front of us, he elbowed me in the ribs.

"Wonder what *her* name is?" he said. "Wouldn't mind rustlin' up a little somethin' with that fine filly. Do you think she could handle my complimentary nuts?"

"Hello, Oli," I replied before making the introduction. "Oli, this is Cherry. Cherry, Oli." Oli took Cherry's hand for an old-fashioned gentleman's kiss.

"Delighted," he said. "I'm Pipsqueak's road manager."

"Pleasure," said Cherry. "Are you really?" She looked to me for confirmation. I shrugged—*guess so*. Cherry nodded. "Penelope," she said, pointing to the stewardess.

"What?" said Oli. "You *know* that fair lady with the long blonde hair?"

"Yep. We're friends. We're so close she even hooked me up with these spare seats either side of me, so I can take a stretched-out nap."

"That's right fortunate for me then, isn't it?" said Oli. "Do you reckon you might like to introduce my fine self to her extra fine self?" Oli looked puppy-dog hopeful. Cherry smiled.

"Maybe? Know anyone who can vouch for your character?" I smiled and played along.

"He's not a terrorist," I said. Oli jumped at his chance.

"No, I'm not. But I am the *bomb*!" A concerned old lady raised her grey eyebrows. Oli winked at her. Then blew her a kiss.

"I'll see what I can do," said Cherry. "But right now, I'm going to catch some shut-eye." Cherry pulled out a paper sick-bag and wrote down her name and number. I pointed to her private screen, where Elvis was kissing a pink-sweatered babe swooning in his arms.

"What about *Roustabout*?" I asked.

"I know how it ends," said Cherry. "All good comedies end the same way. Happily—believe it or not."

"Elvis always gets the girl," I said.

"Of course," said Cherry, handing me her number. "He's the King."

# TREASURE

The Chateau Marmont hotel looked cool. Very cool.

When Slade had first mentioned, back in Melbourne, where I'd be staying in Los Angeles I'd tried not to let myself be impressed by the history of rock stars and Hollywood legends who'd stayed at the famous hotel before me—but I couldn't help it. Especially when I got there. I mean, everyone from Howard Hughes to Jim Morrison had stayed at the Marmont; it had even inspired 'Hotel California', one of America's biggest bands', The Eagles, biggest hits.

When I arrived at check-in, however, I was far from impressed. In fact, when I found out Slade had broken his word for the second time I was pissed off good. Not only had Slade failed to book the first class flight he'd promised me, now I discovered he'd also stuffed up my hotel booking. Tired and disheveled after a fourteen hour flight—and well more than twenty-four hours in transit from Melbourne, Oli and I then had to find last-minute accommodation for both of us.

But we weren't alone.

While Oli checked us in to the Saharan hotel—a slightly run-down joint down the road from where I'd expected we'd be staying—I loaded our gear out of the people-mover taxi we'd shared from the airport into LA town proper with Cherry and Penelope.

"I'm sorry about dragging you around Hollywood," I said, pocketing Slade's fictional itinerary. "And thanks so much for finding this place for us."

"Don't be silly," said Cherry. "There's nothing to apologize for. This is fun." Pulling out my last bag, I placed it with my guitar and Oli's back-pack.

"It's just I felt like a dickhead making you guys wait," I said. "I shouldn't have argued with the receptionist back there either, but I was definitely told my room was booked at the Chateau Marmont." Penelope shrugged, unimpressed.

"It's not everything they say it is," she said. "Unless you go in for all that old-Hollywood mystique…or you happen to enjoy a bit of luxury?" Cherry squeezed Penelope's knee, *don't rub it in.*

"It's lucky we decided to share a taxi," said Cherry. "That way we could deliver you to the swankiest of alternative accommodation." Cherry rolled her eyes ironically, gesturing to a broken window in the reception area. Oli returned to the car with a satisfied grin.

"Have they got a room?" I asked.

"Yeah, partner," said Oli, leaning on the open sliding door of our taxi, making sure his suggestive look met its mark—namely Penelope, the sexy stewardess. "Do we need one room or *two?*" he asked. Penelope smiled and reached for the door handle.

"One room, cowboy," she said. "For you and your 'partner'."

"Well, Missy, it ain't like me and him are joined at the hip," said Oli. "Mr Angus and I encourage the other to have adventures of our own. We often wander the range solo." Both girls smiled.

"Then I'll leave you to *wonder*," said Penelope.

"Glad to hear Angus is free to explore," said Cherry, signaling to the driver to wait another moment. "You still want to hook up sometime, Angus?"

"Sure," I said. "I've got a rehearsal with a pick-up band in the morning but my afternoon's free. Then I was hoping to get in a bit of tourist action, check out an old Elvis haunt—his last home in Beverly Hills."

"Sounds like fun," said Cherry. "Count me in." Oli wanted some fun too.

"And how about us, Miss Penelope? Do you fancy showing this free-roaming gentleman the best of these Hollywood Hills? "

"Sorry, Oli. I've got an early flight in the morning."

"Oh well," said Oli. "But if there's a change in plans I'd be much obliged to make your acquaintance again. You know where I am."

"Yes, I do," replied Penelope dryly, as she closed the door.

"So, where do you live, Cherry?" I said. "Have you got far to go?"

"I'm staying at Penelope's flat in Santa Monica at the moment. I've been doing so many writing gigs interstate and overseas I haven't had my own place for a while."

"You like living on the road?"

"Don't mind it at all," said Cherry. "Not forever though. One day I'll probably shack up in the burbs. Until then though…"

"Wild and free?"

"Exactly."

"See you tomorrow," I said. Oli wanted in with Penelope on some of the flirting action Cherry and I had going.

"See you…whenever, Penny," said Oli suggestively.

"*Penelope*," she said, correcting him. "Whenever," she added bluntly, and nodded to the driver. As the door clicked shut, the van pulled out and away down Sunset Boulevard.

"She'll be back," said Oli confidently, as we watched them go. "They always come back."

"Just like a boomerang, hey?" I said, picking up my luggage.

"If you throw it right," said Oli. I looked at him curiously.

"Have you ever thrown a boomerang?" I asked. "Ever?" Oli smiled.

"Never."

We grabbed our bags and I went off to pay for our room. With most of my savings used up covering Hank and mine's living expenses while I was nursing him—not to mention the recent engine overhaul my old van had eaten up a couple of grand on)—I didn't have much cash to spare. Luckily, I wasn't going to be in LA for long, and as I handed over some freshly-exchanged American bills I consoled myself about the unforeseen expense by thinking about the money Slade's gig would give me and Hank: enough to pay off Flynn Station and my credit cards too.

It wouldn't be long and both Slade and Max would be a memory, an unexpected hiccup in the Flynn mens' normally cruisy lives.

A few hours later, Oli and I were in our room and it was getting dark outside. Through our hotel window the lights of The Strip (as Sunset Boulevard is known) were tempting me out. But as I'd informed a very disappointed Oli, I'd decided to stay in. I'd spent all afternoon practicing and brushing up on Hank's back catalogue but I still wasn't finished. I had my guitar in hand as I opened the door for Oli to head out into the night on the hunt for local wild life.

"Try not to wake me when you come in," I said. "I need to get some rest. I've got a big day tomorrow." Oli had spent most of my practice time trying to convince me to join him on the prowl but I was focused on preparing for the gig. A lot was riding on me doing a good show: Hank's financial future, Flynn Station staying in the family and everything I cherished back home was on the line.

"You're really not coming, partner?" asked Oli sulkily. "Who'm I gonna hitch my wagon to?"

"Sorry," I said. "You have fun though." I gestured for Oli to get going.

"Damn. Oh well, guess I'll have to rely on my own charms—considerable as they may be—to wreak some Hollywood havoc."

"Knock 'em dead," I said. "Just don't wake me when you come in. Cool?"

"Cool." It took another nudge to convince Oli to go it alone, but when he finally left (with a skip in his step) I closed the door behind him and got back to work. Sitting on the bed I opened my little lyric book. The airplane sick-bag with Cherry's number on it slid out. Unfolding it, I placed it on the bed and picked up my guitar. I started finger-picking a run-down, a slow, soulful ballad feel in the key of A. At least I think it was in A—I'd never done music at school and everything I learned was either from ear or Hank.

As my guitar-playing busied the part of my brain that needs order, rules and all that jazz, the other part, the part that thrives on chaos and spontaneous creativity came to life. I started to sing.

*Take my hand, I'll give you all I can*
*Stand by me, this love I believe*
*Will last forever*
*You're my treasure*

It wasn't just chords and words on my mind though. Cherry was there too. Her love of stuffed bears made in foreign countries made me smile. Momentarily stalling on inspiration for another verse, I remembered Cherry talking about her souvenirs being like treasures to her, and the title of my song—the first I'd ever written in the country of my birth—chose itself:

'Treasure'.

And though it sounded to me very much like a soul love ballad, I knew it couldn't possibly be a genuine love song. After all, after Honey Rose I'd promised myself I'd never write one of those again. Not for anyone. Ever.

# GINGER

The next day I was still thinking about the lyrics to 'Treasure'—the love song I was yet to finish—as Cherry drove us from Santa Monica Pier to our next offbeat tourist attraction in her beat-up yellow Kombi. We'd picked up a couple of milk shakes at the beach and I'd almost finished mine by the time we arrived at the street of our destination.

"So your rehearsal went well then?" asked Cherry, turning her van into a wide, tree-lined Beverly Hills street. Sipping on my shake, I noticed expensive cars parked behind security gates: Mercedes, late model BMWs, one red Ferrari and a sparkling Bentley sports. *These people are loaded*, I thought.

"Pretty good, yeah," I said. "The band was awesome, that's for sure. You'd have thought they've been playing Hank's stuff all their lives."

"Must make you confident the gig will go well?"

"I wouldn't go that far," I said. "But I was very happy about one thing. The promoter—Slade, the guy I need to have words with about my flight and accommodation mix-up—didn't show up. At first I was pissed off he didn't show but then I realized it was probably a good thing. Left us to get on with making music."

"Sounds like you don't think much of this Slade guy?"

"I try not to think about him at all actually." I counted off the house numbers then pointed to our destination. Cherry pulled up against the curb and turned off the ignition.

"I haven't had a milkshake for years," I said, slurping down the remains.

"Me neither," said Cherry, taking a sip from her shake. 'That's wrong. They're good."

"So was that hot-dog," I said, turning to face Cherry and yawning and stretching out my arms like a cartoon bear as I did. "And I can't believe I fell asleep on the beach. Sorry." Cherry shrugged, pulling out her smart phone to show me some video she'd taken of our recent sand castle building.

"Seen one Santa Monica Pier ya seen 'em all," she said wryly. Cherry fast-forwarded to some artistic footage she must have taken while I'd been sleeping on the beach. Seawater lapped around the wooden uprights of the pier; sunlight bounced off the ocean, illuminating gulls resting on beams underneath.

"That's beautiful," I said. "You've got a great eye."

"Only one?" said Cherry, smiling.

"I mean you've got good taste. I like how you caught the light on the water."

"Thank you," said Cherry, pocketing her camera. I yawned again.

"Sorry I'm so tired," I said. "Oli woke me up when he came in last night. He was pissed up to his eyeballs. I think my jetlag is still lagging."

"You look alright to me," said Cherry with a smile. I felt like kissing her but sober as I was, didn't have my normal late-night inflated confidence. I think it was the first daytime date I'd ever been on.

"You look alright to me too," I repeated back. *Brilliant.* The ghosts of Lothario's past should all hang their heads in shame. Errol Flynn'd be rolling over in his grave. I imagined if Elvis was watching he was hanging his head at my feeble romancing.

"I'm really glad you called me," said Cherry, before turning away to stare blankly at the dashboard. *Maybe she's nervous?* I thought. "But unfortunately I won't be able to show you much more. The day after tomorrow I'm going on a bit of a road-trip and I'm not sure how long I'll be gone."

"Where are you going? And what sort of writing did you say you did again?"

"I freelance doing a bunch of stuff. Lately I've been paying the rent with my travel blog. I guess you could call me a photo-journalist-cum-travel writer."

"Cum-professional-souvenir-collector," I added. Cherry flashed me her killer smile.

"I always bring something of my adventures home with me," she said, "to remember the fun times." The way she said 'remember' sounded to me like Cherry was already assigning our brief encounter to memory. I didn't like how that made me feel.

"Where are you headed on this trip of yours?" I asked.

"East," said Cherry. "From Santa Monica to…I don't know? New York?"

"Go with the flow of the road, hey?"

"Exactly," said Cherry, putting both hands on the steering wheel. "Wherever it leads. How would you like to come along?"

"Really?"

"Sure. There's plenty of room."

"That sounds cool," I said, un-coolly. "Unfortunately, though, I've got to stay in LA for at least a couple of weeks. Slade has me down to do a recording after the gig, the son's version of the father's hit—or something. I'm not looking forward to that, I can tell you."

"It was just a thought," said Cherry. "The best way to see any country is by road. I always think, anyway."

I agree," I said. *Fuck*, I thought. I wished I could go with her.

"Are you ready to go in?" Cherry pointed to the house we'd come to visit.

"Yeah," I said. "Shall we?"

"Let's." In unison we climbed out and walked up to a shoulder-height gate blocking the driveway. Cherry pointed to a security intercom on the wall. I headed over and looked around for—I wasn't sure what, eventually pressing a 'SPEAK' button.

"Hello…excuse me…," I said. "I'm looking for Mr Roy Watts."

Cherry smiled. Nothing came back from the little speaker box. I adjusted my glasses, as though being able to see better would help me hear better.

"Try again," she said. "Maybe he's getting a bit deaf? He'd be pushing seventy, wouldn't he? I mean if he played in a band with your dad before you moved to Australia?"

"Yeah," I said. "You're right. He would be pretty old." I went to try again but before I could say anything more a woman's voice responded.

"Roy ain't no longer here." The woman sounded feisty but I couldn't tell how old she was.

"Ummm…hello again," I said. "Sorry to bother you but do you possibly know where I might find Mr Watts?" Cherry gave me a thumbs up. *Progress.*

"Who's askin'?" said the unseen lady. "You a pig?" Cherry and I smirked at her melodramatic tone.

"My name's Angus Flynn. My father, Hank Flynn, used to play in a band with Roy Watts and I wanted to ask him about something." I waited for her response but nothing came back. I tried again. "This is the last address Dad had for him. It's a bit of a long shot but I don't know where else to start. Dad said Roy knew my mother too." Cherry smiled encouragingly. But still nothing. I shrugged and started back to the Kombi.

As I opened the passenger door, Cherry pointed behind me to a hidden door in the wall opening up. A woman of about sixty-five (maybe more) popped out. She was made up to the nines (as they used to say in old Hollywood) and her long legs looked like they belonged to a former dancer or perhaps model. Her sheer black stockings and high heels seemed at odds with the Californian sunlight, but completely in tune with the wealthy, playboy-esque surroundings.

"April Devine? You're talking about April. You must be April's little boy, Angus?"

"Yes," I said. "My name is Angus Flynn."

"Angus. That's right!" said the woman, standing with one hand on her hip, the other holding what I could smell was a joint. "April always had a thing for *bulls*." She looked suggestively to Cherry. "If you know what I mean?"

"Were you friends with Angus's mother?" asked Cherry.

"Honey, April was like my sister." The old broad turned to me. "Your Ma and I followed those Pretzel players around for years, until eventually—they started following us." She flicked her red hair back and, as she did, I remembered a photo Hank kept from a holiday he and I took before leaving America for good. The woman who'd accompanied us on that trip to California, the striking figure my seven-year-old self begrudgingly played mini-golf with, was standing right in front of me.

*Ginger.* The woman who'd tried to convince Hank to stay in Tennessee after Mum died.

"Is your name Ginger?"

"Mmm-hmm. Hank still talk about me, does he?"

"Once or twice. Maybe?" I said. "You're definitely in some of our family photos."

"Well, I hope I am," said Ginger, taking mock offence—which might have been real.

"This is great," I said excitedly. "The main reason I wanted to meet with Roy was to find out about my parents. It probably sounds crazy but I heard a rumor Mum might have had a bit of a…thing for Elvis back then?" Ginger smiled and nodded, though both actions were a little wary. Ginger had the same quality Ann Margret, who starred opposite the King in some of his most successful films, had: positively feline.

"We *all* had a thing for Pretzel, Honey," said Ginger. "He was *the King* and we were his little princesses."

"So, is it true?" I asked, forgetting the fact I hadn't told Cherry anything about Hank's crazy claims. "Did my mother have a fling with Elvis?" Ginger took a long drag on her joint.

"It was a crazy time. I remember driving April around to Pretzel's near the end. She was pretty nervous but wouldn't say why." Ginger suddenly stood up straight: the cat stretched her back. "All I know is, after your Ma—God bless her soul—passed away, Hank couldn't bear to live in Memphis anymore. No matter what I said, or *did*, to convince him otherwise. Hank said April was on every corner and in every face of all our old friends. We were all sad to see him—and you—leave, especially me, but we understood." Ginger's gaze turned distant, faraway. Maybe she went back to playing mini-golf with Hank and me, back to trying to convince him to stay in Memphis?

"Then Mum *did* have a relationship with Elvis?" I said.

"We *all* did, honey. Pretzel was either a lover, a friend, a brother or a big daddy to everyone." Ginger sounded emotional now. I thought she was about to cry. "We loved him." Cherry put her hand on my shoulder. Ginger's eyes, frozen somewhere back in time now, suggested to me that maybe I wouldn't get the direct answer I was seeking. Not then anyway.

"I'm a big Elvis fan," Cherry said buoyantly. "My mother played Elvis to me all the time growing up."

"I still play him every day," said Ginger perkily. "That's why I bought this pad off Roy. When Pretzel moved to Hollywood to make his movies we all had such great times here. I never wanted those days to end." A pool maintenance van pulled up in Ginger's driveway, almost knocking Ginger over. But to both Cherry's and my surprise, Ginger didn't hiss. She simply walked over and, through the driver's window, laid a passionate kiss on the driver's lips. Then, she waltzed seductively over to the security panel, punched in the code and watched her gates swing open with a ding.

"If you still want to find Roy head to Palm Springs," said a completely invigorated Ginger. "Roy's got a residency there at the big Mexican place on the main street. He probably knows even more than me about how serious your mother's 'fling' with Pretzel got. April and Roy really hit it off. April always had lots of male friends. She loved opening up to the boys." Ginger winked at Cherry again. "If you know what I mean?"

The idea that Mum was at all 'easy' didn't rest well with me but before I could say 'What choo talkin' about, Ginger?', Ginger was waving her pool man in and following him on her high-heeled feet.

"Of course I'm not one to judge," announced Ginger, as the gate began to close behind her and her beau. "I don't even have a pool. But I sure need me some 'maintenance'." Behind the now-closed gate, Ginger signed off with a shoulder-high kick. "Come back and see me *anytime.*"

"Angus," said Cherry, coming to my side, "do you really think your Mum had an affair with Elvis? Who told you that?

"My dad," I said. "Well, I think Hank's my dad, though apparently he's not so sure. Hank reckons Elvis is my birth father. You may well be looking at the only living son of the King." Cherry gave me a look. Before deciding whether it was derisive or impressed, I chuckled away the seriousness of my claim. I didn't want her thinking I was crazy.

But maybe I was too late?

# NEVER LOVE YOU LESS

Cherry wasn't at all fazed by my claim to be the son of the King.

In fact, she actually took the news of my possible Presley paternity very well. To her, the evidence added up. My mother's close relationship with Elvis near the end of his life; the timing of my birth, and even Hank's need to get out of the country made the fact Elvis could be my father highly possible. At least in Cherry's eyes. Her gorgeous green eyes. Maybe, Cherry had pointed out on the way back to the Saharan Hotel from Ginger's Beverly Hills home, mine and Hank's move to Australia hadn't been motivated purely from grief? Maybe Hank had been trying to escape something else too?

"When you take off those Buddy Holly glasses you actually look quite a bit like the old hound dog," said Cherry. "There's a definite resemblance to Elvis there." Arriving at my hotel I hated the thought I wouldn't see Cherry again. But with my Hank Flynn Junior commitments and her road-trip starting the next day, it seemed life was pulling us in two different directions. I tried to stay philosophical. What else could I do?

"Thanks for a lovely day at the beach," I said, getting out of the Kombi. "And for showing me around a bit. I really hope you don't think I'm a nut for telling you what I did about Elvis and my mum?"

"No way," said Cherry. "Like I told you, sounds plausible to me. I hope you find out whatever you need to, Angus. And I hope your gig goes great too."

"Yeah, thanks. If I wasn't so batshit nervous I'd invite you along. But I just want it over with. I'm really only here for the money. For Hank."

"And I'm sure he's very glad you *are* here. Sounds like a nice place you two have back in Oz. It'd be a shame to lose your family home."

"It would," I said.

We made a little more small talk. I told Cherry that, before I flew back to Australia, I might give her a call to see how her trip was going. She said that would be great. I wanted to kiss her goodbye but we ended up instead with an awkward goodbye cuddle through the window.

And then she was gone.

That night as I waited for the approaching showtime inside a cinema-sized ballroom in Slade's Beverly Hills mansion, I did my best to put Cherry out of my mind. Standing with Oli next to the temporary stage, and without the protection of any wings to hide me from the expectant stares of doubtful-looking music execs, I tried not to think too much about Hank either; in a brief phone call with him I'd just found out he was on extra pills to keep his heart from turning on itself again. Hank had wished me well but all I'd taken away from our conversation was how much was riding on my performance.

I knew I had big shoes to fill but when I looked up to the enormous screen behind and above the waiting band, and saw my transformed image the size of a movie screen, I understood just how big those shoes really were. Huge.

*Hank Flynn Junior*, Hank and Slade's Frankenstein creation, cut an imposing image, the still slide projected onto the screen being the main point of focus for the couple hundred or so selected few invited to the private party. Cowboy-hatted record company executives flown in from Nashville mingled with Hollywood elite and urban rock n'roll riff-raff. Impossibly attractive waiting staff (models and actors all, no doubt) weaved through the crowd, carrying trays of canapés and drinks. French champagne, fine wine and expensive spirits flowed as the lights dimmed and the silver-screen image of me dressed as Hank took on an even brighter glow.

Nervously, I laughed to myself. While it's a well-known fact pretty much everybody who comes to Hollywood comes looking for fame, here I was, fresh off the plane and already a virtual movie star. The thirty-foot still-life of me wearing Hank's mirror sunglasses, Hank's red bandana (around my neck rather than head, as Hank wore it)—and even Hank's 'I've seen it all before' half-grin—looked like it was promoting the latest summer blockbuster; the text on the single 35mm frame evoked an old wanted poster. In a Western-style font it read: *Hank Flynn Junior—Rides Again!*

You could hardly read 'Junior' though; Slade was obviously pushing the '*Hank Flynn* riding again' angle. On the raised stage set up below the big screen, Slade took to the microphone.

"Good evening and welcome to a very special event," announced Slade. My stomach did a back-flip, the nerves kicking in like a bucking mule. I wanted this over quick. Fidgety and anxious, I looked around at the lush surroundings, all a bit fuzzy after replacing my prescription glasses with Hank's mirrored ones. How Slade—who was about the same age as me—had amassed such wealth and influence (I lost count of how many older suits had lowered their heads submissively as they shook Slade's hand) perplexed me. In truth, it pissed me off. And it always had.

Why the people *behind* the talent got so much of the talent's money had always baffled me. I thought about Slade's broken promises of my first-class flight and the just as non-existent Chateau Marmont booking. For years I'd watched Hank getting ripped off by better business-minded players (parasites, he called them) and I hated the thought I was about to continue the family tradition of being an exploited talent. But I just tried to think about the money.

*It's just ONE gig*, I reminded myself. *One gig.*

"We've all grown up," continued Slade, in a voice worthy of any Academy Award presenter, "listening to the songs of the man who put the 'outlaw' into country and helped turn what was once considered 'hick' music 'hip'." It had been a couple of months since I'd first met Slade but he was proving exactly how I remembered him: full of it. Although blurry, as close as I was I could make out Slade's facial features—his smarmy, over-confident grin, his clean shaven corporate lawyer chin—and I decided he looked like a cross between Christian Bale (from *Batman*) and Bradley Cooper (from the *Hangover* films). Though Slade was even less endearing than those bad-guy-specialist actors. Colder. But what could I say? The guy was paying the bills and the bill on Flynn Station needed paying.

Checking my bandana was tight enough around my neck not to fall off, and loose enough not to accentuate the growing throb in my head, I looked down at my black jeans and western shirt, thinking how if not for the red bandana and the spill of the spotlights catching Hank's glasses I'd be just as invisible as I normally was in my roadie gear. Though I was no longer hiding in the wings. Not that there were any.

Noticing my discomfort, Oli put his arm around my shoulder.

"Where's your Cherry pie?" asked Oli with a wink. "Why didn't you bring her to your big-time showcase? She might even have brought her friend, Penelope Perfect." Slade gestured to a projectionist in a booth at the other end of the room to begin the slideshow proper.

"I didn't want her to see me dressed up like this," I said. "I feel stupid."

At Slade's instruction the show began. Hank Flynn Junior morphed back into the original, my old man, Hank. The hair was longer and the skin aged and wrinkled, but anyone would have been convinced those two guys digitally swirling into one were the same man across time. Behind Slade, the band took up their instruments. My stomach twisted. My tongue went dirt-driveway dry. I grabbed another drink, a beer chaser for the four straight scotches I'd already downed. To the growing delight of the cash-hungry record execs, Slade kept building the hype of their latest pedigree stud.

"Hank Flynn had some amazing career highlights, including being the last performer to grace the stage with the original country kid outlaw, the kid who became the King of Rock n' Roll himself, Elvis Presley." The next slide showed a bloated Elvis with his arm around a young, slim Hank. It was dated June 26, 1977—just under two months before Elvis died and I was born.

"You going to see Cherry again?" asked Oli, loading two beer bottles in each jacket pocket. Oli loved an open bar more than me.

"I want to," I said, feeling like throwing up. "But she's hitting the road tomorrow and Slade has got more for me to do in LA." As if sensing my wondering mind Slade shot me a look: *get ready*.

"After Elvis's untimely passing," continued Slade, "Hank Flynn went on to have two of the biggest hits in country music. One of those songs gave Hank his name. I am, of course, talking about 'Killer'." The audience, heavy on ambitious musos and undiscovered starlets, cheered and hollered. Even the suits made some noise. Another slide showed Hank in a bejewelled country suit receiving a gold record from his old image nemesis, Willy Nelson.

"Have you done the recording Slade wanted you to?" asked Oli.

"Not yet. Some time next week, maybe." *Where's a bucket?*, I thought, sure I was going to spew my guts. I wanted another drink but there was no time. Slade's show was in full flight and I was due to take off.

"The other song," said Slade, "was arguably an even bigger hit for Hank, and has a truly amazing story behind it. Originally written by Hank for his good friend, Elvis, this song is the reason we are all here tonight. This song will forever be regarded as *the* country Christmas classic. On its first release in 1978 it became the longest number one in popular music history." More cheers and applause. I wiped the sweat from my upper lip. Slade eyeballed me, *ready?*

"Now, due to popular demand, I am pleased to announce the great Flynn dynasty continues today. Here to perform his dad's greatest hit, 'My Best Present Ever', is the one...the only...Hank Flynn *JUNIOR!*" Oli nudged me. I stumbled forward.

"That's you!" said Oli. "Go get 'em, 'Killer'." The band kicked in but for a moment I couldn't move any further. Slade stepped down from the stage and grabbed my shoulders, appearing to everyone as though he was being friendly, bigging me up with a manly embrace. He whispered menacingly in my ear.

"Remember your mother's garden, Pipsqueak. You don't want those nasty bikers to tear it all up, now do you?" I turned to Slade, willing myself to chuck my churning guts all over his expensive suit. No such luck.

"Killer! Killer! Killer!" The audience's chant got louder. I pushed past Slade to grab one of Oli's beers. I took both. I stepped up onto the stage drinking from one and raising the other as a toast. "Killer! Killer! Killer!" The crowd seemed to approve of my outlaw antics. I played along, keeping everyone waiting as I finished my beers. Then, with a swagger I walked to the mic. I put down the empty bottles and stood up dizzy. Decades of listening and watching Hank perform did some magic though and my drunken state proved no obstacle to me completing the transformation. In costume, song and voice, Hank Flynn Junior came to life in Beverly Hills.

*All my Christmases have come at once,*
*Now I have you in my arms*

*All my loneliness has disappeared,*
*Now I have you here*
*Oh, I thank the heavens, for my best present ever*

Side-stage I noticed something. It was, like everything, blurry but I thought I saw Slade smiling. Realizing the whole charade would all be over soon brought a smile to my face too. I turned to the audience and gave 'em everything all us Flynns had.

Afterwards, the party kept going into the night, spilling out and around Slade's super-sized pool. Bikini girls outnumbered buff boys three to one; Oli had cornered a Playboy bunny waitress by a ten-foot statue of Cupid, and a couple of topless girls were in a jacuzzi. Everyone was partying hard.

As Slade told me some of the other acts featuring on the Christmas album—including Gil Teaman, the hottest country act in the country (and therefore world)—the consensus was I'd put on quite a show. Having taken off the red bandana and replaced Hank's mirrors with my own glasses, I got a few confused looks from the various partygoers who came up to congratulate me on an 'awesome' show and a 'brilliant tribute', but Slade seemed happy enough, despite my reluctance to stay in character all night as he'd earlier requested.

"I've got something special for you," said Slade, handing me an official-looking stack of stapled paper. "It's an updated itinerary with all your live dates and venues—all your shows before we hit New York. Congratulations, Pipsqueak!"

"What do you mean?" I said. "I've done the show. Now we've just got to record my version of Dad's song and we're done. Isn't that right?" Slade shook his head.

"Not quite. As originally stipulated, you are required to perform all reasonable promotional activities ahead of the release of the *Christmas Country Classics* album. Since tonight went so well we're going through with a couple more promotional shows we've lined up for you."

"But you told me one show?"

"Yeah," said Slade, as though I should know his word obviously meant nothing. "To see if they liked you—and they do, which is great. Now, we capitalize."

*But hold on*, I thought. *That wasn't what I'd signed on for.* The thought of doing even *one* more gig got my stomach going gymnastic all over again.

"Listen, Slade," I said, "I didn't complain about the economy flight instead of the first class one you promised, and neither did I come running to you about the 'mix-up' with my accommodation—" Slade cut me off.

"Both of which wouldn't have been a problem if you hadn't taken so long to sign up for this rolling album release. Arrangements need to be made in advance, Pipsqueak. I would expect you to know that already, especially after a lifetime in showbiz. Though maybe as a roadie you've never had to deal with the economic realities of the *real* music business?"

"Like I said, Slade, I didn't complain about you not coming through with the things you said you would—but I *am* complaining now. I'm not doing any more gigs. One show was our deal."

"Then you won't get paid."

"What?" I said. Slade smiled. He had all the cards apparently. I scratched my head and let out a long sigh, wondering why I hadn't read the damn fine print. "Where are these shows? And when?" I asked, hating myself for not ever studying law—or karate. I felt like going all fifth dan on Slade's head. "And why are you only telling me now?"

"I didn't want to get your—or my—hopes up. Besides, my Nashville friends wanted to see you live before fully committing to what is another very special opportunity I'd like to tell you about." Slade waved to the cowboy-hat-wearing sleazeballs now snuggling up to the bimbos in the jacuzzi. "You, my friend are headed to the CMAs at the Grand Ole Opry."

"The Country Music Awards?" I said incredulously. "You want me to do this Hank Flynn Junior shit there?" Slade smiled again, immensely satisfied.

"As well as a couple of warm-up shows," he said with a tone of 'now you're getting it Dumbo'. "It's all about gearing up for the big Christmas push. You want this tribute album to sell, don't you?"

"I want my money—*our* money!"

"Then finish the job," said Slade. "Simple." At this point, Oli joined us. To distract myself from punching Slade I took off my glasses and gave them a clean. The numbing effects of my pre-performance alcohol had almost worn off and my growing frustration had steamed up my specs good.

"I love LA," said Oli, as enthusiastic as a waitress serving Steven Spielberg.

"You want to stay here?" I asked, pointing to the jacuzzi. "Or shall we get out of here?" A near-naked woman wearing a Catwoman mask—and not much more—walked by, purring.

"I'm stayin', partner," said Oli. "Forever."

"I'll see you back at the hotel then," I said. "I don't feel like drinking anymore." I put down my beer. For a moment it looked like Oli might change his mind and join me in leaving, but when the bunny girl returned without her tray, and with a couple more beers, Oli's eyes lit up.

"I've finished my shift," she said. "Fancy taking a late night dip?" Oli turned to me with a grin.

"Don't wait up," he said.

"No problem." I headed for a garden exit, happy to be alone rather than hang for one more minute at Slade's mansion. As far as I was concerned, Oli could have my share of what debauchery remained to be had. The Catwoman cut me off at the gate, seductively presenting a bowl of caviar. I was too tired from fighting with Slade to even voice my disinterest. As I walked around her, Catwoman clawed at me until I was free from her reach, alone in the street.

Outside Slade's property my first thought was to call Cherry. But with the news of my new commitments to the Hank Flynn Junior spectacular, I didn't see the point. It looked like Slade had me wrapped up for my foreseeable future. What's more, I knew Cherry was leaving early the next morning and I didn't want to wake her up by calling so late, just to say "Hi and Bye!" Instead I went back to my hotel and wrote a blues song about some poor sucker falling head over heals with a girl he was never going to see again. I was pretty sure this song had nothing to do with my childhood sweetheart Honey Rose—the first and last girl to inspire me to right a song—but didn't yet want to admit to myself it was probably all about Cherry.

How could I have such feelings for Cherry already?

*It takes a second to fall and all your life to forget*
*But what can you do but give it your all and your best*

96

*You're headed east and I am headed west*
*I could not love you more and I will never love you less*

I thought again about maybe calling Cherry. Knowing I'd never see her again upset me almost as much as knowing I was now Slade's puppet. If I didn't do the gigs he wanted me to, I'd go back with nothing, to nothing.

But I wasn't about to let that happen.

# Part II:
# Doin' As You Please

# QUICK

In the morning everything seemed better.

Outside hotel reception, and with my bags ready to go, I walked out from under the shadow of the drive-in carport to a patch of grass between the hotel and the pavement. Despite being so early in the day it was already warming up. Sunlight streamed down Sunset Boulevard casting long light-pole shadows down the famous strip.

Life in LA looked good.

With my notepad open, and a pen in hand, I intermittently looked around for my ride while jotting down more lyrics to yet another new song; the inspiration from the night before carrying over into the morning and bringing me another song.

*Picking up where we left off*
*The only number I still got*
*I called you to get a fix*
*Of a drug that don't exist*

I smiled to myself: these lyrics were good; I had a flow going. Ignoring Oli—lying on the grass, moaning and spluttering from the after-effects of his big night—I kept writing.

*I get nervous when I get close*
*So what? Ain't that just like most*
*It's true, love—it can make you sick*
*And oh, how my heart goes quick*

Excited about who was coming to pick me up, I realized the rhythm and meter of one line leant itself to a double meaning:

*'It's true, love, it can make you sick'* could also be:
*'It's true love, it can make you sick'*.

True love? I thought. What was all that about?

"My tongue feels like a dried turd," mumbled Oli. I may have been very happy with my current flurry of creativity but Oli wasn't happy at all. "Catwoman convinced me fish eggs are an aphrodisiac," he said. "I ate a cat-bowl-full." Between coming home and dragging himself out of bed to pack, Oli had already thrown up a couple of times. I watched him warily, ready to help him get to the closest clump of bushes should the need to empty his guts overwhelm him again. If he'd had the energy I think Oli would have killed me for springing the change in plans on him.

"Catwoman?" I said. "I thought you and the bunny had a thing going on?" Oli crawled off the grass and onto the concrete pavement, dragging his backpack around him to try and use as a pillow.

"What can I say, partner?" groaned Oli. "I love all of God's creatures." He opened one eye, the other closing tighter to compensate for the sunlight suddenly boring into his dull skull. "Why did you check us both out of this dump? I don't wanna go anywhere today." I think Oli thought he was facing me as he spoke, but putting his hand up to block the sun he realized he was facing the wrong way. Oli was talking to a brick wall.

"You don't have to go anywhere," I said. Oli, confused by the voice from nowhere, twisted around, seeking the source of the sound, falling off his 'pillow' in the process. "But you would have to change rooms anyway," I added. Oli bleated. He sounded like a beached humpback crying for water. *Roll me back in.*

"Check-out times suck orangutan balls," said Oli before burping, wiping drool from his bottom lip and clambering for the life-raft of his backpack. Maddeningly for him his spastic limbs only knocked his ballast further away.

"You hit it pretty hard last night, hey?" I said. Oli grunted.

"I feel like Wile E Coyote after Roadrunner tied him to a train track in the middle of the desert, stuffed dynamite in his ears and shoved cactus up his butt. Anus-suffocatus."

"That was a pretty violent cartoon," I said, laughing. "Wasn't it?"

"But funny. That Roadrunner was really a crazy clown." Still half-tanked from his big night drinking, somehow Oli had managed to right himself onto his backpack, which he was now using as a bed. Before he could nod off into hangover limbo-land though, a loud car horn frightened the remaining balance out of him. Oli fell on his back, landing on the concrete with a thump.

"Oh, shit!" he said, as I waved to the driver:

*Cherry.*

Immediately I felt like I would before going on stage. A similar sensation to what had almost overwhelmed me at the Elvis festival in Parkes—and then at the gig the previous night—took hold of me. My chest tightened, my breath shortened and a cyclone of butterflies exploded in my stomach before flying up my spine and down the back of my neck. Cherry was all over me.

"That's her!" I yelled. Oli's face screwed up in pain and he covered his ears.

"Too loud!" he said. "Give a cowboy a break, will ya?" Cherry pulled her Kombi into the hotel driveway and rolled her window down. Seeing Cherry put any depressing thoughts about Slade's double-crossing, and the bind I'd found myself in, completely out of my mind; Slade might have got me to America on false pretenses but now I had another reason to be there.

"I thought you had more work to do in LA?" said Cherry. She looked stunning. Her soft-pink T-shirt had a big red felt apple on the front. *Maybe she was going coast to coast after all?* I thought.

"Like I said on the phone, I've had a change in plans. Sure you don't mind?"

"It was my idea," said Cherry. "I asked you along, remember?" I gathered up my gear and gave Oli a gentle kick.

"And it's okay to go a little out of your way?"

"Like I said, my route's not fixed. Besides, it sounds like fun. I love Palm Springs."

"Cool," I said, grabbing the handle on the slide door. Ready to throw it open Cherry stopped me, putting her hand on mine.

"Only one problem," she said gravely.

"What's that?" I asked.

"What do we do with *him*?" Cherry pointed to Oli who'd just managed to get to his feet and was struggling to put his backpack on his front.

"I'll be alright," said Oli, drunk-dancing with his still-intoxicated self. "I got a kitty cat needs feeding anyway.

There's a bunny I could maybe shack up with for a while too…if I had her number…" Then, without any help from Cherry or me, the van door flew open. Inside, sitting on the floor with a pack of tobacco and some rolly papers in her hands, was Penelope.

"Hi there, handsome," she said, much friendlier than previously with Oli. "Guess what, sunshine? I called in sick." Penelope licked the cigarette paper and continued rolling up. "Sick, that is, of not being able to smoke on that goddamn plane." Oli was instantly resuscitated.

"Is there room in that stagecoach for a faithful sidekick?" he said. Penelope smiled, slipping a cigarette filter into her homemade smoke.

"Oli, isn't it?"

"It is! It is! Why, Miss, you've gone and breathed life into my ailing heart. Your unexpected—yet most welcome—arrival has filled me with glee."

"You always talk like a gunslinger?" asked Penelope.

"Yes, Maam," said Oli. "The way I figure, life's like Tom Cruise in a Western, too short to take seriously. But unlike the Top Gun munchkin man this fella standing before you—at five-feet and *ten* inches—is all about true romance, fantastic adventure and exploring the kind of wild frontiers movie-makers only dream of conquering in real life." Penelope giggled but, playfully, wanting to stay in the dominant role, stopped herself.

"Exploring wild frontiers, hey? The very reason I work a mile high." Penelope winked. "As well as all that romance and adventure. But especially the romance."

"Naughty," said Oli.

"Imagine what I'm like on holiday?" said Penelope suggestively.

Cherry and I shared a look as I finished loading my gear in the back. I moved to the passenger seat. Penelope tucked

105

a cigarette behind her ear and stared at Oli, sizing him up.

"You guys finished flirting?" said Cherry. "Can we maybe get going now?" Oli, still standing on the pavement, looked innocently at Penelope.

"A gentlemen waits for an invitation." Penelope was having too much fun though and so made Oli—and us—wait for a couple more seconds before announcing her decision.

"Climb aboard, cowboy." Oli gleefully tossed his backpack over Penelope's shoulder and jumped in.

We were on our way.

"So, where's this wagon headed?" asked Oli.

"Yeah, what wild destination have you guys got planned?" added Penelope.

"First stop is Palm Springs," I said. "After that— Vegas? If you're all up for it?" Cherry responded with a nod; Oli and Penelope likewise. "And who knows? Maybe we can drive all the way to New York?"

"Sure," said Cherry. "Why not? It's all East from here on in. Anyone got any music?" Instinctively I went to my knapsack before stopping myself, remembering the only thing I had was my demo CD.

"Angus might have something," said Oli, reaching forward and helping himself in my bag. Before I could stop him he'd found my CD, pulled it out of the case and was waving it Cherry's way.

"Perfect," said Oli. "In my hot hands is the latest hot import—all the way from Oz. This guy is going to be huge!"

"They don't want to listen to that," I said.

"Don't we?" said Cherry. I shook my head.

"It's just some rough demos I managed to get down at home, in between nursing Dad over the last few months."

"It's your music?" said Cherry. "Cool."

"Yeah," said Penelope. "Put it in!" Oli looked suggestively at Penelope, who slapped him on the thigh.

"Ow!" screamed Oli. "Here." Cherry took one hand off the steering wheel to take the CD and load it into the player. Nervously I waited for the sound of my voice. I went to press 'stop' but when Cherry grabbed my hand I lost my nerve to spoil the party.

*Besides*, I thought, *maybe it'll sound better than I think? Maybe they'll even like it?*

Anyway, what did I have to lose? I was on the road, in America, with my best friend and a couple of hot gals. Even Elvis would have been happy with that.

# ELVIS PRESLEY JUNIOR

When my demo recordings came to an end I ejected the CD and put it back in the case, which, for want of a better album name, I'd labeled with the working title of *Pipsqueak*. Resting it on the seat between Cherry and me I waited for a response.

Nobody said anything.

I hoped the lack of critiques was down to the excitement of starting our journey, and all the mesmerizing distractions of driving down the open highway with the windows down.

Like everyone else, while my CD was playing I'd lost myself in the unfamiliar views outside: service stations and burger joints, and a palm- tree-lined desert, the type of which we didn't have in Australia. And though I was nervous about what everyone would think of my CD I'd also realized something: my alternative country-blues suited the surroundings. My music felt right at home in America.

Cherry turned to me and smiled. For a second her gentle green eyes made me forget how vulnerable I was feeling for having played my demos to these virtual strangers. Oli seemed to read my mind.

"You fine ladies don't know what an honor that was," declared Oli. "Mr Angus Flynn has never played his home-recordings to anyone before."

"Really?" asked Cherry. "Why not? I don't know much about country—and to be honest, I'm not really a big fan—but that first song, 'The Orphan'? Sounds like a hit to me."

"I *hate* country," said Penelope. "But I'd definitely buy 'The Lonely Morning Light'." She smiled to Oli. "Or at least I'd download it for free." Oli frowned.

"I didn't figure you for a thief, Little Miss?" he said. "Or a pirate."

"It doesn't matter," I said. "I don't think I'll have to worry about that anytime soon." Cherry picked up my CD.

"So who's this 'Pipsqueak' then?" she asked. "Any relation to Angus *Pippin* Flynn?"

"I told you at the airport back in Melbourne. Pipsqueak was Mum's nickname for me."

"Is that going to be your stage name? You know, if you ever do decide to pursue your own career?"

"Probably not," I said. Cherry smirked, taking her eyes off the road long enough to show me what she was thinking: *of course you want a career in music.* "Maybe," I conceded. "Maybe I've been thinking about releasing my own stuff. One day." Oli slapped his hands in a single clap.

"You heard it here first, ladies!"

"But if I ever do finish enough songs—and come up with a recording I'm happy enough with—I won't be going out and playing live. I'm not cut out for it."

"Angus suffers from stage-fright," explained Oli. "Right peculiar for the son of a veteran professional performer, don't you ladies think?"

"Yeah," said Cherry. "I do think that's strange. I mean, it sounds like that gig last night went alright. Plus you'd think the King's long lost illegitimate offspring would love the stage."

*What the fuck?* I thought. *Why did she have to bring that up?* Besides Ginger I hadn't told anyone except Cherry what Hank had told me. Why start blabbing to the world about something that might turn out to be an old man's crazy imaginings?

"Don't you mean Hank Flynn's offspring?" Oli corrected. "I think you're getting your legends of rock confused with your legends of country." Despite wanting to keep Hank's revelation under wraps I didn't want to blame Cherry for *my* secretiveness either.

"She's not confused—I am," I said, turning to face Oli. "I haven't told you yet but Dad told me something which is…well, the reason for this detour." Oli looked confused; Penelope intrigued.

"What did he say?" Penelope said excitedly.

"Elvis might be Angus's real father!" said Cherry. Oli laughed in disbelief. Penelope punched Oli a firm 'how-about-that!' in his arm.

"Awesome!" said Penelope. "Guess who's paying for gas then?"

"Good one, partner" said Oli sarcastically. "Or should I say 'Elvis Presley *Junior*'? Seriously though, why would Hank tell you such a bunch of old bullshite?" Oli's Scottish accent always sounded stronger when he swore. "Has Hank finally lost his fuckin' marbles?"

"I don't think so," I said. "He's as switched on as ever. I think Hank thought he was going to die and he wanted me to know the truth—in case he didn't pull through. In case he doesn't."

"That's crazy," said Oli, warming up to the idea despite himself. "And anyway, how could you prove it?" Cherry pulled the Kombi out into the oncoming lane in order to overtake a slow-moving convertible. Two oldies flashed bright denture smiles at us all.

110

"Good question," said Cherry, "It might be hard to prove. The Elvis estate never gives out DNA samples. If they did there'd be how many thousands of crazy claims."

"And I don't think they take too kindly to folks spreading malicious rumors about their hound-dog cash cow," added Oli.

"I'm not trying to prove it to the world!" I shouted angrily. "I just want to know—for me! And even if it turns out to be true—even if Elvis is my biological father—Hank is still my real father. He's the one who raised me." My outburst took me by surprise. I hadn't realized how invested in finding out the truth I was.

"Family is the people who love you," said Cherry in a calming tone.

"Exactly," I said, taking a breath.

"And friends are the family we choose," said Penelope, leaning forward to hug Cherry.

"Careful sister," said Oli, pulling Penelope back into the seat. "One driver at a time." Cherry's phone started ringing with what sounded like an English boy-band cover version of Elvis's 'Suspicious Minds'. Without missing a beat Cherry took it out of her pocket and passed it back to Penelope, who frowned at the name flashing on the screen.

"You sure you want me to answer?" asked Penelope. Cherry nodded.

"He'll just keep calling until someone answers," said Cherry. Penelope shrugged.

"Hello, you are speaking with Miss Penelope, Cherry Ockham's personal secretary. How may I direct your call?" Penelope enjoyed pretending not to know who it was. "Oh, it's *you*," she said abruptly. "Why are you calling?"

"Who is it?" asked Cherry, joining in with the game. Penelope waved Cherry's attention back to the road. *I'll handle this.*

"Well, *she* doesn't want to speak to *you*. And, if you call again I'll have my associate—," Penelope squeezed Oli's leg,"—shoot your balls off. Okay?" Penelope hung up and swiftly handed the phone back to Cherry.

"That'll only make him try harder," said Cherry. "Brian doesn't know when to give up." *Brian?* I thought.

"Who's Brian?" I said. "Is he your boyfriend?" Cherry snorted. It was either a stupid question or one she didn't like the answer to.

"Was," said Cherry. "Brian *was* my boyfriend. Though I wouldn't really have ever called him that. But now he's just a pain in my ass." Penelope fired up her Zippo lighter and pulled a fresh-rolled cigarette from above her ear.

"He always was a pain in my ass," said Penelope. "How can such a cool chick get muddled up with such a dickless loser?" Penelope lit up.

"Dickless, hey? Does this Brian really have no penis?" asked Oli. "How does he wee wee?"

"Like a girl," said Penelope. "He sits down. I walked in on him once—yuk!" Their banter made me laugh but Cherry didn't crack a smirk. *This Brian guy must be bad news*, I thought. Cherry wound up her window; the air noticeably cooler outside now.

"If it's okay with you guys I don't want to talk about Brian anymore. Why spoil a beautiful drive?" I picked up the Pipsqueak CD and put it back in my knapsack.

"I agree," I said. "Let's focus on the road ahead. I mean, will you look at this view!" I pointed to the sun, low in the sky but just shy of sunset, looking more like an orange moon

"It is beautiful," said Cherry. "I told you the best way to see a country is by the road." She smiled. I smiled back, then raised my eyebrows as I let my eyes fall over her tanned legs.

"Yep," I added playfully, "there's a lot to enjoy on the road."

'Don't worry, Pipsqueak," said Cherry, "you'll get your turn behind the wheel. A little patience is all."

A short while later, after a lazy stroll around a shopping complex in the middle of the desert, we changed drivers and I took second turn. It was my first time driving in America though and being a passenger had left me drowsy. Everyone screamed.

"The other side!" Urgently, I veered back from the left side of the road onto the right—the wrong side for me.

"The other side," I repeated. *The other side. The other side.* I continued this mantra in my head, negotiating my way through a round-about and down the highway towards our destination. As the sun set the adrenalin rush of facing off with speeding oncoming traffic gave way to a gentle euphoria. I started to relax again.

We headed further into the sunburnt terrain and, for me at least, an eerie sense of otherworldliness. From the dark yellow-brown and deep cinnamon colors of the earth and hills around us I felt as though I was suddenly in the middle of a science-fiction movie; apart from the old wooden telephone poles, some abandoned road-side shacks and a couple of rusted out tractors it was easy to convince myself I was really driving an exploration crew through the rolling sands of Mars rather than a Volkswagen van along an old American highway.

But for sure it was another world. I pointed to a road-sign saying Palm Springs but Cherry had already seen it

"Twenty-six miles to go," she said. "Maybe we should stop off somewhere for a hot-tub freshen up before dinner? There's health spas everywhere around here, you know." In the rearview mirror I saw Penelope smile her approval, Oli too.

"One problem," said Oli. "I didn't pack any bathers."

Penelope squeezed his leg. I'd noticed already how much she liked doing that.

"No problem," said Penelope. "We can go Swedish." Turning to my left I saw a red convertible on the wrong side of the road. The elderly couple Cherry overtook were getting their own back on me. But their gleaming smile of false teeth had nothing on the smile I watched come across Oli's face.

"Swedish, hey?" he said. "Do you mean goin' bareback, like?"

"Yar," said Penelope in a sexy Nordic accent. "Exactly, partner." I glanced around at Oli, his smile threatening to stretch beyond his face, the backseat, and wider even than the expansive road we kept flying along.

It seemed everyone was enjoying the ride. I was happy too, especially now I was free of Slade for a while. But I didn't know how long my good vibe would last. How would I feel after I found out whatever Roy knew about just how serious Mum and Elvis had been?

And how much would Roy Watts really know?

# YOU KNEW ALL ALONG

L as Casuelas was jumping.

With the band playing a great mix of classic country hits, and after a long day in the hot car, the Mexican bar and restaurant Ginger had directed us to felt like an oasis.

I finished picking at our tortillas and rice, looking around at the packed house enjoying their meals and the live music. Wall-sized windows, opened vertically, provided an uninterrupted view outside of the hills surrounding Palm Springs. With the open roof of the wooden pergola and the moonlight and stars shining above it was mucho romantic. And very entertaining.

Roy Watts was making sure of it.

The star of the show had played guitar in Hank's band from before I was born until Hank and I left Memphis. Roy looked like an older version of the crusty muso Tom Waits, crossed with the *Easy Rider* actor Dennis Hopper— though Roy gave off an air of being more approachable than both. His diamond-studded suit jacket (real, he'd assured us) reflected colorful stage lights all around the room. The lapels on his original 'Nudie' suit jacket (designed by Nudie Cohn, the same guy who made Elvis's famous gold lamé suit) were adorned with two hand-stitched naked ladies but rather than come off creepy on an old man, they added to his eccentric charm. Roy was old-school showbiz: larger than life to fill the stage.

The old-timer all-rounder (Roy played piano, organ and steel-guitar almost as well as electric) wasn't just an awesome guitarist though—he had a set of lungs on him too. Man, he could sing! Hearing him live I understood why Hank was so happy to have picked up Roy after he'd finished playing with Elvis.

"For my next number," said Roy, "I'm going to do a song by a good friend of mine. I know him as Hank Flynn but you might remember him better as 'Killer'?" The audience cheered and applauded and Roy waved our way. "I'd like to dedicate it to Hank's boy, Angus Flynn, who has come all the way from Down Under to join us here at Las Casuelas tonight. How about we give him a big welcome?" The applause continued as Roy turned back to the band and began to play 'You Knew All Along', a lesser-known song of Hank's—but one of my favorites. To me it was one of the best examples of what I loved most about Hank's lyrics: they were intelligent. He didn't just write normal country lyrics about guys getting down 'cause they lost their woman. Hank wrote about staying centered in your own sense of self while being accepting of other's ways, as strange as those ways may seem to us sometimes.

Hank was a country philosopher.

*There's always some who'll be afraid,*
*Of what they don't know*
*There's always some who will be brave,*
*And now you know*
*The only thing that matters,*

*Is giving up your sadness*
*Make way for a new song,*
*One you knew all along*

"Pretty deep lyrics for a country song," said Cherry. "I'd never really listened to them before."

"Goes to show," I said. "Sometimes country music can be cool."

"I'm sure it can," she said, finishing her drink. "It's not all achey breaky heart." I laughed.

"I thought you'd be too young to know that one?" I said. Cherry smiled.

"It's called YouTube, Angus."

When Roy announced he was finishing the set with 'Killer', I smiled wryly as the lyrics returned to more common country themes of betrayal, self-pity and the threat of violence. I was quite impressed though when Cherry started singing along.

*When I came home and found you in*
*The arms of my best friend*
*I couldn't think how it began*
*But I knew how it would end*
*Now I am not a violent man,*
*I've never shot a gun*
*But I can no longer deny, what I have become*

"Is 'Killer' by your dad?" asked Cherry. "I know this song."
"Yeah, that was Hank," I said, joining in for the chorus.

*Killer, it ain't right*
*Killer, to take my life*

While Roy kept singing I looked around the room at

the rapt expressions on near everyone's face. Even the waitress—whom I knew must have seen all kinds of top-quality acts come through—was hovering at our table, ready to drop off our cocktails but mesmerized by Roy's voice, his sparkling matador-like jacket and a charisma impossible to define.

"This is fun, Angus," said Cherry, thanking the waitress with a smile when she eventually delivered our drinks. "And hopefully Roy will tell you everything you need to know?"

"We'll see," I said, raising my strawberry margarita to her lemon one. "But you're right—this is fun. Cheers!" We clinked glasses and turned to Oli and Penelope for the toast, discovering the two lovebirds kissing passionately, twisted together like horny swans. Cherry raised her eyebrows and took a sip of her drink.

"Get a room," she said. "Or at least a bed." They broke their kiss. Oli took a breath; Penelope looked stunned.

"Should we?" Oli asked her. "Is that a good idea?" Penelope grinned.

"Or we could find a corner in the garden somewhere? Do it under the stars." With a cheeky smile to each other, and a barely detectable 'catch you later' wave to us, they grabbed their drinks and dashed off into the shadows. Cherry and I laughed as she raised another toast.

"To inhibitions!" she said.

"And not having any," I said, removing my glasses with a stylized flurry, like Clarke Kent turning into Superman—but mainly so I wouldn't knock them off.

After Roy finished his set he came and joined us, as he had for our main courses. Even though I'd had plenty of opportunities I still hadn't asked him yet what I'd wanted to. I was nervous. I wanted to know but I didn't too. And then, just after I'd found the courage to ask Roy whether he knew if Mum ever had an affair with Elvis, the waitress returned and asked us if we'd like the bill.

"Put it on my tab," said Roy casually, winking at the waitress and turning his chair around to sit in it like a saddle. He waited for her to leave then faced me directly. "So, who told you?"

"Dad," I said. "*Hank*. He told me—well, he *implied* that—Elvis was my biological father." Roy nodded thoughtfully and stroked his short beard of grey stubble.

"Yes," said Roy. "Pretzel and April definitely had a physical relationship."

"My mum had sex with Elvis?" I said plainly, the absurdity of such a statement clear to my ears immediately.

"Yes. I always thought there was something pretty serious going on between your Mum and Pretzel actually. After Priscilla I'd never seen him look at another gal the same way—until April."

"It was serious?" I asked.

"Put it this way," said Roy, "you know that song of Hank's I just played? The song that gave Hank his name?"

"'Killer'," I said. "What about it?" Cherry leaned in, intrigued.

"Towards the end of his life," explained Roy, "your folks were right friendly with Pretzel. Your dad went from being an occasional opening act to a regular card-game partner for Elvis. They used to play bridge and poker all the time." Cherry nodded as though everything was making sense to her now. I was still playing catch-up.

"Is 'Killer' about Hank finding Elvis with April?" said Cherry, before reciting a telling lyric, "I've played cards with cheatin' men who look you in the eyes. They tell you 'my God's honest truth, I ain't gonna lie'?" After a brief pause, which I took to be Roy considering whether I was up for handling the news or not, he nodded.

"Exactly," said Roy. "Hank wrote 'Killer' after coming

home from a six week tour and finding your mum with Elvis at Graceland. At first April denied anything was going on but eventually the truth came out. I had a show with Hank that same night but before Hank could go on he had to get the whole thing off his chest. He made me promise not to tell anyone though. Ever. Hope he'll forgive me."

I was gobsmacked. I didn't know what to say. Strangely though, rather than thinking about the astonishing fact Elvis could be my father, all I could think about was Hank back in Oz, his health failing and our home still under threat of repossession.

"So, it's possible Elvis may have fathered an unknown son," said Cherry. "And that son could be Angus?"

"I'd say it's more than possible," said Roy. "I'd say it's likely." Roy noticed my silence and appeared to feel sorry for me. But he didn't seem the type of man to get all touchy-feely with his sympathy. I also got the feeling he'd seen more tragedy in his long life than the odd mixed-up paternity. Underneath an eclectic collection of chest jewellery Roy had at least one faded torn-heart tattoo and a string of names with arrows through. They reminded me of when Hank learned that Roy had lost his last wife to cancer a couple of years back; Hank not the only person alive to face growing old without a partner.

"I want to give you something," said Roy. "It was given to me by someone who wanted me to know I was part of something bigger than myself, bigger than any one man." Roy waved to his band who were taking the stage again, eager to finish their final set.

"I didn't come looking for hand-outs, Roy," I said, pointing to our dirty dishes and empty cocktail glasses, the remains of the feast he'd already treated us to. "I just want to know who my father is." Cherry and I watched Roy slowly remove a sparkling, diamond-encrusted ring from his gnarled old finger. He held the ring between finger and thumb, admiring it like it was a newly discovered gold nugget.

"It's a TCB ring," said Roy reverently. "A 'Taking Care of Business' ring. Ever seen one?"

"No, but I've heard of them," I said sulkily. Roy smiled, pointing out two lightning bolts.

"Elvis gave 'em to all of us in the inner circle." Roy handed the ring to me. "I reckon he'd a wanted you to have it. Besides, I've lived off that gig for long enough." Even in my hands, large compared to Roy's, the ring looked big. It lay on my palm unclaimed before Cherry took it and slid it on my middle finger.

"I can't accept this," I said. "It's too much."

"I got no children of my own to pass it on to," said Roy. "Might as well keep it in the family though, if you know what I mean?" Roy winked affectionately but I wasn't feeling the love, genuine as it was.

"That's an amazing gift," said Cherry. I knew I should have been more grateful than I was but I was still processing what Roy had told me about Mum and Elvis.

"Yeah," I said unconvincingly. "Amazing."

"So, where you headed next?" Roy asked as he got up.

"Eventually to New York," I said, "but the big gig is Nashville for the Country Music Awards. Plus there's a few more 'promo' shows before that. Tomorrow I'm due in Vegas."

"Perfect," said Roy. "Look up Doris White when you hit Vegas. Doris was real close with your Ma and I reckon she'd love to see you again."

"Again?" I asked. "I don't remember any Doris White."

"After your mother," said Roy, "Doris was the first person to hold you when you were born."

"Thanks for everything, Roy," said Cherry, getting up to kiss our friendly host on the cheek goodbye. "It's been a great night and you've been so kind." I pulled myself together to shake Roy's hand.

"Yeah, thanks Roy," I said. "So where exactly do you think I might find Doris?"

"Try the Golden Gate. It ain't what it used to be in the seventies but I heard on the ol' grapevine Doris's back working there again." Roy hesitated to go. It seemed he had something more to say.

"Hey Angus," he said enthusiastically, "how'd ya like to join me for a couple of songs?" Roy pointed to the stage. "We could do your pa's other big hit, 'My Best Present Ever'? Or maybe you've got one of your own songs you'd like to try out before Vegas?"

"No," I said, looking over to Roy's band. "I don't have any songs I'm ready to perform." Despite having already put in four big sets, the three black gentlemen (something very unusual for a country act) looked energized and ready to go.

"Come on, Angus," said Cherry. "You've got some great songs. What about 'The Orphan'? You've got plenty of others too?"

"No, I don't—okay?" I said angrily. "I appreciate the offer, Roy. I do. Sorry."

"What about an old Elvis hit?" asked Roy. "You probably know a few of the King's songs too?" I shook my head.

"No thanks. Some other time maybe?"

"No problem," said Roy. "I understand. You're not ready to step out of your father's shadow just yet. Whichever of those two fellas you think it might be." Roy winked at Cherry, who shrugged apologetically on my behalf. Roy turned to me with a searching look. I think he was checking to make sure he hadn't upset me more with his little joke about me having two dads now. "I know you're not askin' for my advice but since you're headed to the CMAs maybe I can offer you something from my experience?"

"Sure," I said. "What else have you got for me?"

"Whatever they've got lined up for you in Nashville, Angus, best thing you can do is remember, though your talents may be many, in Nashville *you gotta keep it country*. Give 'em what they want. And, as Hank and I found out many years ago, what they want in Nashville is country. Plain and simple."

"Got it," I said. "Simple country."

"Nashville rewards real men and virginal princesses," said Roy. "And of course the odd chick with really big tits." Cherry laughed. I cracked a hint of a smile.

"I'll try to remember all that, Roy."

"Good luck," said Roy, heading to the stage. "I'll look out for you in the funny papers, otherwise known as *Billboard* magazine!"

Cherry and I watched Roy go before Cherry turned to me and I watched the smile disappear from her face. I hated disappointing her by not performing with Roy but there was no way I felt like singing anyone's song. Not one of mine, not one of Hank's and not even one by the King of Rock n' Roll, the man Roy reckons could also easily be my real dad.

It seemed like Killer wasn't crazy after all.

# SLOW MOTION

After finding Oli and Penelope having a post-coital smoke outside the restaurant we decided to hit the road. Penelope had what Oli described as a 'hankering' for a night in the wild, and Cherry and I liked the sound of a sleep-out under the stars too. Fortunately, Cherry had packed the Kombi with tents and sleeping bags enough for four.

About an hour into Penelope's turn driving she pointed to a turn-off sign for Joshua Tree National Park. From the passenger seat, Oli gave her the thumbs up. In the backseat though, things were a lot cooler than I would have liked between Cherry and me.

"The least you could have done was sing one song with Roy," said Cherry, her arms crossed defensively across her chest. "The lovely old guy bought us dinner and answered all your questions. Clearly he would have loved it if you had."

"Maybe you're right," I said. "Maybe I should have. But I didn't want to make an idiot of myself. Performing doesn't come easy to me. The only way I've got past my nerves to do those two Hank Flynn Junior gigs so far has been by pretending I'm Keith Richards. Shameful as it is to admit— it's the booze gets me through." Up front, Oli smiled.

"Sounds like a right catchy line for a scotch commercial, partner" he said. "THE BOOZE GETS ME THROUGH! I can feel a celebrity endorsement comin' your way soon."

"Yeah, big celebrity," I said sarcastically, putting my arm around Cherry.

"You don't seem nervous to me?" said Cherry.

"Appearances can be deceptive," I said, pointing to her new Mexican hat, a recent purchase from the gift shop at Roy's gig. "Tell me—where's that authentic souvenir made?"

"America," she said, without checking. "Same place you were."

"Exactly," I said. "Something can look the real deal and in fact be a fake." Cherry took off the sombrero and put it on me as Oli's phone rang.

"Who in damnation could have tracked me down in this dark desert? I ain't gave my cell number to no man," said Oli before answering. "Hello? No, this is his partner, Oli. Whom may I say seeks aural audience with Angus the Kid?" Oli smiled at Penelope who took her eyes of the road in front just long enough to give him a quick wink. "Oh, sure," said Oli. "I'll put him on."

"Who is it?" I said.

"It's Slade," said Oli. "How did he get my number?" Penelope cast a knowing look into the rearview mirror back to Cherry. Cherry frowned. I assumed they were playing some girl game I, as a mere male, wasn't privy to.

"I gave Slade your number. You did say you were my road manager," I said. "Remember?"

"Oh yeah," said Oli, handing me the phone. "Glad to be of service."

"Hello, Slade—," I said,

"Where the fuck are you, Pipsqueak?" said Slade, cutting me off straight away and wasting no time paying out on me. "You were due in the studio here this morning. The producer only just got onto me to say you didn't show. What the fuck's going on?"

"There's been a change in plans," I explained. "I decided to take a bit of a sightseeing trip before the next gig. Seemed only fair, given the late notice you gave me and everything."

"You signed our contract months ago," said Slade. "You're bound to certain obligations. If you don't meet those obligations you'll be in breach and I'll have no option but to reclaim my losses in court."

"What are you talking about, Slade? You gonna sue me for taking a drive through the desert?"

"What desert? Where are you?"

"Look, Slade. I'll be in Las Vegas in time for the rehearsal tomorrow morning and in plenty of time for the gig tomorrow night. You've got nothing to worry about."

"You better be there," said Slade. "I'm this far away from cancelling the shows *and* the Christmas compilation. Then where will you, Hank and your mother's ashes be, hey? It'll be pretty cozy shacking up in a room above a pub with your poor, sick father. Is that how you want Hank to see out his final days?"

*Final days?* I had a strong urge to tell Slade to shove his promoter's fist up his tight promoter's ass.

"I'll see you in Vegas," I said. Slade hung up.

"Is everything alright?" asked Cherry. I took off the hat and handed it back.

"It was the promoter—or lawyer—or whatever the fuck he thinks he is. He's pissed off I disappeared and is threatening to pull the plug on the whole thing if I don't show up in Vegas."

""I love Vegas," said Penelope.

"I've never been," said Oli. "Will you show me around?"

"I'll show you everything," said Penelope suggestively. "Ever played the slots?"

"Ooh…ahh," groaned Oli.

"You guys!" said Cherry. "Is everything about sex?" They both shook their heads: *of course not.*

"Only the fun things," said Oli.

"And the naughty things," said Penelope. Cherry and I exchanged a knowing look, Oli and Penelope did the same.

"And the rest," they said in unison. We all laughed, leaving the mood set by Slade's call behind us somewhere in the dark desert night.

Our Kombi getaway capsule flew past cacti and rolling sand hills towards the camping ground Cherry had chosen for us. When we arrived at the site, sometime after midnight, we were thrilled to find we were the only ones there, thanks to it being a bit late in the season for tourists. The clearing was all ours. Whatever the reason for our privacy I was happy to be surrounded by nature again for the first time since leaving Flynn Station. I was already missing the solitude of standing outside my shack, gazing up at the stars and waiting for the local wildlife to bounce by.

"You won't see many kangaroos out here," joked Cherry, apparently reading my mind, "but don't be alarmed if you hear a few wild coyotes."

"What about Roadrunners?" asked Oli.

"Yeah, sure," said Penelope, dragging Oli off into the dark. "And you might get real lucky and spot a wild cat too."

After setting up tents by car-light I collected wood for a fire. Cherry warmed hot milk and cocoa on a portable gas-burner in the back of her Kombi; the opened back flap of her van making a pretty convenient kitchen area. While stacking logs with one hand I took a sip of a Bud Lite with the other, admiring my new TCB ring as I did. Thinking back to Roy's warm hospitality I wished I had accepted his offer to jam.

"So, when is Superman coming out?" asked Cherry.

"What?" I said. "Sorry, I don't understand?"

"Those glasses, *Clark*," she said, pointing to my specs. "Do you ever wear contacts?"

"Yeah, occasionally. But...I prefer my glasses. I'm quite happy being mild-mannered. Besides, that way my true powers remain hidden." Feeling the cold, and impatient for the fire, I gathered up some twigs and sticks for kindling.

"Mysterious," offered Cherry, adding another log to the stack.

"Exactly," I said. "Got any matches?"

"Sure." Cherry fetched the matches and I started the fire as she poured our drinks and brought them over.

"Cheers!" said Cherry.

"Cheers," I replied. We took a sip then looked around for Oli and Penelope.

"Hey guys!" yelled Cherry. "It's ready. Guys?" But they were nowhere to be seen, no doubt getting up to some mischief.

The growing warmth from the fire drew Cherry and I as we snuggled up on a rug next to it. Later, Oli and Penelope joined us and, after hearing about their joy at discovering a small lake—perfect for a moonlit skinny dip, apparently—all four of us relaxed around the campfire. Cherry was on her second mug of hot chocolate when she gestured with it for me to check out the others getting sexy again, this time under an opened-out sleeping bag.

"Get a tent," Cherry said dryly.

"Good idea," I agreed. Without a word, Oli and Penelope gathered their blankets and disappeared. Cherry and I were alone. I realized that since meeting at Melbourne airport we hadn't even kissed. In the crisp cool night, and especially with her face flushed by the glow of fire, I very much wanted to. But strangely for me, I also didn't feel the need to rush anything.

"What do you think?" I said. "Are you ready to hit the sack too?" I may not have wanted to rush but old horny habits die hard.

"I think I'll sleep in the van tonight," she said, standing. "The tent's all yours."

"Really?" I said. "All mine. I'm more than happy to share." A short, high-pitched scream came from the others' tent. Cherry and I exchanged a curious look: it sounded like Oli.

"Ow!" he yelled again. "I think I've got a cactus needle up my butt!"

"Kinky!" squealed Penelope. "I'll pull it out. With. My. Teeth!" They were going at it like animals in heat but it seemed my only warmth was going to be coming from the fire.

"See you in the morning," said Cherry.

"Yeah, okay," I said, disgruntled. Cherry smiled and pulled me to my feet to kiss me on the cheek. Taking a couple of steps towards the van she turned around and came back, taking me by the hands again. "I just want you to know I'm looking for something very special on this trip, Angus."

"Really?" I said. "Like what?"

"Like *someone* actually," said Cherry. "He's friendly, cuddly and makes me feel safe."

"Sounds like you're describing a giant koala?"

"Close. I'm talking about 'Smokey The Bear'," Cherry smiled. "I've been a fan of old Smokey since I was a little kid. If you happen to spot him on any of our roadside stops, make sure you point him out."

"You're talking about another stuffed souvenir?"

"I prefer to think of Smokey as the first great American icon of environmental awareness."

"I'll keep my eyes peeled." Cherry smiled and kissed me again, full on the lips this time. Her mouth tasted of marshmallow. It was a kiss worth waiting for. "Hey, you're shaking," I said. 'Are you cold?"

"No," said Cherry, rubbing the goosebumps on her arms. "You make me nervous."

"Really?" I said. "Why?"

"That's what I want to know," she said, playfully folding her arms in front. "We've only known each other for a few days and I can't stop thinking about you. What strange spell have you cast on me, Angus?"

"No witchcraft here. Just pure unadulterated machismo."

"That must be it," she said, laughing and letting her arms down by her side. "You're too much man for little ol' me." Cherry headed to the van.

"Doubt it," I said. "Not too much. But maybe just enough?" As Cherry settled in for the night I took out my guitar and lyric book and sat back down next to the fire, looking up just as a shooting star flashed across the sky. *The universe is naturally creative*, I thought, *naturally inspirational*. All I needed to do was pay attention; watch and listen.

On a fresh page I wrote a new song title: 'Slow Motion'. And with the frantic activity of the flight from Melbourne, the gig in Hollywood and the getaway drive from Los Angeles fading into the night behind me my thoughts settled on Cherry, sleeping in the van.

*You gotta make love in slow motion*
*All good things take some time*
*No good just wishin' and hopin'*
*Apply your heart and your mind*

The guitar riff sounded a bit Tex-Mex—something Johnny Cash, or that great modern alt-country band Calexico, might have recorded. For the first time, it occurred to me my country roots weren't anything to be ashamed of: my country was coming back.

*To live a good and fruitful life*
*You don't wanna be told twice*
*You gotta make love in slow motion*
*You gotta make love in slow motion*

Like a real cowboy out on the range I fell asleep that night under a blanket, next to the fire. Throughout a dreamy half-sleep I awoke at various intervals as the raging fire subsided slowly to embers, hot coals and finally sparkling dust.

But I never felt cold once.

# WAITIN' FOR MY SHIP TO COME IN

In Las Vegas there was steam coming out of Slade's ears. If Slade was a cartoon character that's what I would have imagined I could see. I'd arrived as the Stratosphere Casino Band Room perfectly on time that morning—well before the scheduled eleven o'clock rehearsal—but the guy was fuming. The band and I hadn't even started going through my set but even as the musicians were setting up mistakes were being made. Such was Slade's all pervading negative vibration.

A high-hat stand fell over, the bass player's rig rolled across the drummer's foot and the slide-guitar player couldn't for the life of him lock in the legs of his slide-guitar stand. The musos did their best to ignore the promoter's presence but it was impossible. The palpable tension engendered by Slade's screaming orders and general aura of autocracy infected everyone. I was glad I'd convinced Cherry and the others to go check out Vegas without me; I got the feeling Slade enjoyed making everything hard work for everybody.

"And make sure the posters outside the venue are in the main light boxes!" screamed Slade, pointing to a

Mexican cleaner. "I want every redneck in town knowing exactly where to find Hank Flynn Junior tonight." The befuddled cleaner pushed his plastic cleaning station towards Slade and me.

"How long is this going to take?" I asked. Slade ignored me. As the cleaner passed by I copped an intense whiff of ammonia and other undiluted chemicals. Instinctively I turned away, assuming whatever he was using to help rid the sticky carpet of stomped in bar-snacks, cocktail stains—and the other unimaginable solids and liquids drunken partygoers had left behind—was somewhat poisonous. It stank in there. But Slade's odorous emissions trumped all others.

"I know you're just the cleaner," he said condescendingly, pointing again to the blank-faced immigrant worker, "and it's 'not your job' but unless you want to be scrubbing piss and vomit for the rest of your life you might want to show some initiative. I'd appreciate it if you could check the fucking posters. *Please.*" Slade grinned his order to the cleaner who didn't seem to speak much, if any, English. The cleaner shrugged innocently.

"Isn't there a bar-manager or supervisor you could ask about that, Slade?" I said. "Surely it's the venue's responsibility to delegate jobs to their own staff? Not the promoter's?" Slade stared at me, incredulous at my meddling.

"Do you see anyone else 'delegating' this guy's responsibilities?"

"This 'guy' is right here in front of us, Slade. And I think he might prefer to at least be asked nicely rather than intimidated." The cleaner gave me a surreptitious smile and thumbs up. *Maybe he understands Slade perfectly?* I thought. The mild-mannered Mexican walked off, whistling quietly.

"Fuckin' wet backs," said Slade, turning to me. "Now, what about you? Am I going to have to lock you up between contractual engagements from now on?"

"I'm sorry you had to reschedule the recording session, Slade, but I told you it's not really my strength anyway. I also told you I'd be here for the rehearsal. Which I obviously am. You have nothing to worry about."

"Don't I?"

"No. I have every intention of honoring the revised contract and of doing all the new gigs you've got for me."

"That's good," said Slade, momentarily satisfied. "But I also want you to promote the promotional gigs. I need you doing radio slots and interviews ahead of the shows."

*Of course you do,* I thought.

"Anything you can fit into my road trip, I'll do," I said. Slade's smug expression dropped off his face. I could tell he didn't understand what I was casually informing him. "You gave *me* a new itinerary—so I'm giving you one." I handed Slade a copy of my travel plans, a single page I'd printed out that morning. "I've decided to make the most of my U.S.A. visit," I said. "Me and some friends are doing the tourist thing. But don't worry, I'll make sure to reach Albuquerque, Memphis and Nashville in time for each of the gigs." Slade shook his head, *no way.*

"I've already bought plane tickets," he said. "You're flying—not driving."

"I'm driving," I said plainly. "And another thing—I've got someone to see between this rehearsal and the show tonight so, if you don't mind, I'd like to get things started. Are you going to introduce me to my backing band?" Slade looked angry but I had a growing sense that a part of him actually enjoyed me standing up to him.

"Okay," he said. "Sure. And by the way it's a *dress* rehearsal." Slade pushed a plastic bag stuffed with red bandanas into my chest. "And—I'm filming it. We don't want to miss anything of Hank Flynn Junior's meteoric rise to fame. I'm gonna get a heap of footage in case I ever decide to release a DVD too."

"Fine," I said, bluffing confidence at the terrifying thought of performing without a drink.

"And before you run off for your 'meeting'," continued Slade, "I'm going to get a recording of you doing 'My Best Present Ever', here, straight from the live desk. So, whatever happens—if you dare fucking do a disappearing trick again—I'll already have everything I need."

"Whatever," I said, taking my guitar out.

"After today, Pipsqueak, even if you were to meet with an untimely fatal accident, I'll have enough stills, audio and video to market your image any way I like—for as long as I like. People love ghosts singing from the grave. And what a tragic story it would be: the son snuffed out in his prime while trying to keep his ailing father's music alive."

What could I say to that? The guy was turning out to be not only a crazy megalomaniac but a pure dick too.

"Covering all your bases, hey?"

"I always hit a home-run, whoever's pitching. Nothing sells like dead legends, Pipsqueak. Even those that didn't quite make it to the major leagues." It was lucky I didn't have a baseball bat myself right then. Otherwise I might have knocked Slade's block clear out of the state of Nevada.

A kick drum signaled the start of the band warming up. The other players jumped in and immediately they sounded as one—tight and punchy. Their music soothed my beast and I swapped my Buddy Holly glasses for Hank's trademark mirrors.

*Bring it on*, I thought. I pulled out the red bandanas, tying one around my neck, instead of head as the only protest I could offer. *At least Slade didn't make me wear Hank's flared denim jeans and 70s western shirt*, I thought. *That'd be too embarrassing.*

A roadie handed me my guitar and as I was still tuning up, the band starting jamming without me. It turned out they already knew all of Hank's stuff. But it surprised me further when I heard them fall into an old swamp-blues song of his, a rare B-side from the 'Killer' single (back when they pressed singles on vinyl instead of iTunes vouchers). Stepping up to the mic to begin our rehearsal, the simple lyrics came back to me and I happily joined in with the relaxed impro vibe.

*I'm waitin' for my ship to come in*
*I'm waitin' for my ship to come in*
*I can see steam on the horizon*
*I can hear the whistle blow*

Slade stopped what he was doing—chewing out the venue manager for failing to have all our posters up already—and shot me a strange look of disapproval. *Maybe my guitar was out of tune?* I thought. But it sounded alright to me so I kept going.

*I'm waitin' for my love to arrive*
*I'm waitin' for my love to arrive*
*I can see steam on the horizon*
*I can hear the whistle blow*

Turning to the slide-guitar player to indicate he should take a solo break, I almost crashed my guitar into Slade who'd stormed up onto the stage.

"No B-sides," he said, grabbing my guitar by the neck. "Just stick to the set list, Pipsqueak. No deviations."

"We were just warming up," I said. "Chill out."

"I'm not running a temperature—I'm running the show," he said menacingly. "Stick to the list." The guys in the band shrugged *whatever* and we moved onto the list Slade had made of 'Hank Flynn Tribute Tour Songs'.

Apart from that one interruption from Slade the rest of the rehearsal, recording and impromptu music video session went better than I'd imagined it would. When it was finished I was feeling pretty good, though I didn't know if my newfound confidence would last until the performance that night.

And, as I headed off to meet up with Cherry, I had other questions on my mind too. The main one being: what would Doris White have to tell me about April Devine?

Did she know more than Ginger and Roy about Mum and Elvis? Was I wasting my time trying to get to the truth about who my dad really was?  Or was I about to find out something I never would have dreamed before coming back to America?

# DORIS WHITE

A few hours after the rehearsal Cherry and I arrived on Fremont Street, the historical heart of Las Vegas, home to some of the smaller, less flashy, and older casinos. Even in the late afternoon it was buzzing with tourists. Following Roy's instructions, we ended up at the Golden Gate, a gambling and entertainment house no more or less run-down than those surrounding it. Standing outside, Cherry and I watched two disinterested go-go girls dancing on two small podiums at the entrance, their expressions neither happy nor miserable.

"What do you think they call that particular dance?" I whispered. Cherry smiled.

"The Lacklustre?" she said. "Guess it's a tough gig standing in skimpy bikinis out in the elements all day." I nodded and pointed to a stern looking black woman, maybe sixty, maybe seventy, emerging from inside the go-go girl's casino. She looked like Whoopi Goldberg with longer hair. Her eyes, heavy with pink eye shadow and false lashes focused on the clipboard in her hands, barely visible underneath a virtual mitten of sparkling rings. Looking up, and seeing the two girls loafing now, she shook her head wearily.

"Since when has this area been designated a zing-free zone, ladies?" said the spritely older woman. "At least try and *look* like you're having a good time up there. You gals have gotta find a way to fake it 'til ya make it. Put some go in your 'go-go'. Jeez!" Cherry nudged me and, armed with an old photo Roy had kindly given us, I agreed with what Cherry's expression indicated. Maybe that was her: Doris White.

"Excuse me," asked Cherry, "you look like you work here?"

"Unfortunately," said the Whoopi lookalike, and with as much sass. "Yes. On and off for the last thirty—shit—*forty* years. But I swear, if the almighty would just give me a sign, I'd pack up my leopard skin thong and my seventeen wigs and head home. Yes, Siree, all's I need's a sign." Noticing one of her dancers had taken off her bikini top, the woman let rip. "Darling, you put your money-makers away. They can't make you money out here. The street has a firm no-nipple policy, not to mention a no *firm-nipple* policy. What do you think this is? A giant brothel? Jeez!"

"Maybe you could help us, please?" I said. "We're looking for Doris White. I was told she works here."

"Who told ya?" blurted the go-go supervisor suspiciously, looking over both her shoulders almost simultaneously.

"Roy Watts," I said. "He's a friend of my family." Whoopi—or Doris—relaxed.

"Roy, hey? Well, Roy ain't got many friends left. Mostly they've all kicked the spittoon. There's only me, Ginger and an old crusty outlaw, long lost down under. That's all that's left of our old gang."

"Are you talking about Hank Flynn? Is that the 'old outlaw down under'? He's my father." She tossed her clipboard on the podium.

"Angus?" said Doris. "Is that you? Angus Flynn? You're a bit bigger than when I saw you last. You were only about six or seven. Jeez!"

"Seven," I said. "I remember you now. You saw us off at Memphis airport. There was a weird fog that day."

"Yes! Yes, there was," she said, turning to Cherry. "It was eerie. Almost like *someone* didn't want you boys to go." She pointed to the heavens, but instead of the moon or stars all we could see was a tacky movie playing on infinite loop across the curved ceiling. Every big-time entertainer ever to have performed in Vegas, from Frank Sinatra to Cher, flashed down at us like angels trapped in two dimensions.

"Well, we did leave," I said, "and, as it goes, this is my first time back."

"Come to trace your roots, hey?"

"Kind of," I said. "I'm doing some shows too. I've got a gig at The Stratosphere tonight." Doris shrugged, unimpressed.

"The Stratosphere, hey? It's not The Grand but it's okay. You a musician like your old man?"

"He's great," said Cherry. "Angus writes beautiful ballads—the best."

"But I'm not doing any of my own stuff here. They're paying me to play Hank's big hits," I explained. "We need the money or else we'll lose our home." Doris nodded.

"Whatever gets you through, kid. Look at me. I had to come back here after two decades living the respectable life in Memphis." One of the go-go-girls did a back bend, encouraging a sleazy-looking fella walking by to stop and tip her in the side of her bikini bottom. Doris spat it.

"This is not a public lap dance, girl! Both of you get down off there and inside, now. I am not paid enough to pimp." Doris pushed the girls into the casino. "Jeez!" Cherry and I followed them in. "Jeez!"

Having sorted out the dancers with a reprimand, and a reminder of house rules, Doris took Cherry and I into her small office. Surrounded by various casino surplus (broken slot-machines, stacked chairs in need of reupholstering) the three of us sat around Doris's old desk. While I decided how I was going to ask her about Mum and Elvis, Doris began busily packing her handbag with personals from her drawers.

"I asked for a sign—and I got it," declared Doris. "You, boy, are an angel, sent to remind me to get out of this hell-hole town once and for all. Hank is living proof you can start your life over again anytime, anywhere." One office wall was plastered with pictures of smiling punters holding beach-blanket sized checks, another wall seemed set aside exclusively for dancing girls, glamorous long-legged ladies in glittering outfits of sequins and faux peacock feathers—and not much more.

"Are any of these dancers friends of yours from the seventies?" I asked, pointing to a line of girls arm-in-arm kicking up their legs. Cherry pointed to another faded shot of a topless chorus girl.

"There's some very sexy ladies," said Cherry.

"Yeah, I knew most of them," answered Doris. "But, now, out of all those girls, I'm the last one left. I could never have imagined, all those years ago when I first met your mother—on this very street—I'd be the last one standing. Then again, some of those gals were wild, untameable things. I was timid back then. Compared to your mum, anyway."

"You met Mum in Vegas?" I asked, ignoring the rest—about her being wild. "I thought you two were friends from Memphis, from the elementary school she taught at?"

"We were both from Memphis, yes," said Doris. "But we met here, on the line. Your mother never taught at any school, not that I knew of."

141

"The chorus line?" asked Cherry. Doris laughed, getting up from her desk.

"Yeah, 'chorus'. You know, actually, we *could* sing—especially April—but nobody cared about that. Not when we had legs like we did." Doris pointed to a photo of two gorgeous dancers, one black, one white, and both naked except for a single vine leaf covering each of what Penelope would call their 'Pow Wows'. "And it wasn't just our legs that got us out of Memphis," said Doris. "They don't call boobies 'money makers' for nothing." Cherry pointed to a well-endowed, sexy black dancer in the photo.

"Is that you?"

"Uh huh," said Doris proudly. "Perky, wasn't I?"

"And who's this?" I asked, pointing to the other young woman, all smiles, legs and spectacular tits for the camera.

"It ain't the Colonel, kid," said Doris drolly. "Angus, that's April. The delectable young lady in this photo is—God rest her soul—your mother." Deaf to what Doris was trying to tell me, I stepped closer to the picture for a forensic inspection. Realizing what Doris had said I averted my eyes, but too late from having had an eyeful of my near-naked dear mother.

"I can't believe it!" I said. "I thought Mum was a teacher before becoming a singer. Are you telling me she was a Vegas showgirl?"

"You make it sound cheap," said Doris, offended.

"Sorry," I said. "I don't mean to. It's just not what I expected to find out."

"What did you expect?" said Doris.

"I came here to ask you if you think Elvis could be my dad?" Without missing a blink of her heavily made-up fake eyelashes Doris let me have it straight.

"He sure could. But there's no way you're gonna know for sure. They don't give out DNA at Graceland." I said nothing. Cherry squeezed my hand in support. Doris kept packing. Another bag for her stapler, pens and remaining desk knick-knacks. "Look I'm sorry," she said. "I knew this day might come and I promised myself I'd tell you the truth when it did. But I'm sorry I can't tell you anything more. All I know is what April told me. Elvis and her were a hot item, not long before he died." Doris picked a couple of favorite photos from the wall and stuffed them into the bag. "But," she continued, "if you're ever in Memphis I do have something back there for you. Something your Mum left with me to give to you if you ever came looking."

"Oh, yeah," I said. "What is it?" Doris looked like she was ready to set fire to what was left of her storeroom office. This woman was leaving town for good. Forever. Getting out of Vegas suddenly seemed all she could think about.

"Come to Memphis and find out," she said. "I'm gonna see out my working years back home. Maybe get my old tour-guide job at Graceland back." With a touch of sadness about her now, Doris took down the photo of her and Mum and handed it to me. She was offering it as a gift but I didn't feel like taking it. Doris looked disappointed, though, so I did.

"Thanks, Doris," I said. "This is very special." Doris smiled.

"No, thank *you* ,young man," she said. "Thank you."

"What do you mean?" I said.

"Angus, my time on this street is finally done. Don't you understand? *You* were my sign."

Doris turned off her desk-lamp and led us out of the office into the hall, where the bright light blinded me. Remembering the show I had to go and get ready to perform, Cherry and I headed back into the heart of Sin City while Doris made fast tracks out.

Whatever I'd just learned about Mum, though, and however confused I was feeling about it, the show had to go on. The thing was I didn't know if I had it in me. Right then I felt like forgetting all about the Hank Flynn Junior tribute show. I guess I was a long way from the seasoned Vegas stars it seemed my Mum and Dad were turning out to be.

# DOIN' AS YOU PLEASE

The gig rocked.

Rehearsal had been good but the guys I'd played with only once before (at Slade's mansion in LA) really turned it up a notch for the Stratosphere show that night. Maybe my anger at Slade helped spur me on past my nervousness. Maybe the shock of finding out my mother had been a showgirl—and not a teacher—had distracted me from my self-consciousness? Or maybe it was just the quarter-bottle of scotch I'd downed backstage that had fired me up enough to bring it on home for the two or three-hundred punters crammed into the 'Sports Bar'.

Whatever the reason, or reasons, my confidence was growing. I was almost having fun playing Hank Flynn Junior. But as I sang the last song, and the alcohol started to wear off, I started thinking how I'd never really known my mother at all. She wasn't who I thought she was.

Looking out to the audience, I saw Cherry was right up front.

Having filled my emergency contacts prescription that day I'd decided to give them a whirl underneath Hank's mirrors. Cherry was completely in focus now and the audience wasn't nearly as intimidating as I'd previously made any audience out to be. Cherry looked like she was having a lot of fun, singing along like everyone else.

After finishing 'My Best Present Ever' (the last song on our Slade specified set-list) the applause came loud and long. We'd played all the hits and it was more than enough to win over the Vegas crowd. Taking a top-up swig from a beer on stage, I noticed Slade was still busy up the back of the room bossing around the sound engineer and film crew. In the front, next to Cherry, Oli and Penelope cheered me on.

"Hank Flynn Junior for president!" screamed Oli, pointing to a banner overhead: 'HFJ and The All Whites'. When I'd first seen the name Slade had chosen for my backup band I'd questioned him about it but all he'd said was, "I know the market, Pipsqueak." From the looks of things, in the almost entirely white crowd, Slade was right.

"We want more!" screamed Penelope, turning to Oli. "I want more!" she screamed, before grabbing his arm and dragging him out of the crowd. Cherry waved to me to get my attention.

"Play one of your own songs, Angus!" she yelled. Cherry's request threw me.

"It seems I got a heckler," I said in a pretty good Nashvillian accent, a twang just like Hank's. "Or maybe a fan?" I added, opening the question up for the audience. "I can't be sure. What do you all think? Should I end the show with something new by yours truly?" Next to the sound desk up back I saw Slade frantically waving his arms, NO FUCKING WAY! His protest only urged me on though, my fear of failure overcome by my hatred of being told what to do. Besides, the audience seemed to like the idea of hearing something new. Something by me.

"Why not?" I said. "The guys are gonna sit this one out though. I think I'll go solo to finish up." Cherry smiled and clapped enthusiastically. "I'd like to dedicate this song to a special person in my life," I said. "It's about being true to yourself no matter what others want or expect of you. I didn't write it as advice, but feel free to take it anyway you like. It's called 'Doin' As You Please'. Tonight it goes exactly like this."

*There's no way out of here alive*
*If they tell you different then they lie*
*Can't take it with you when you leave*
*So get busy doin' as you please*

Cherry smiled. She seemed to like my indie folk/pop number a lot. So did the rest of the audience. Slade, however, had run up to the stage and was unsuccessfully trying to convince the fold-back engineer to pull *all* the plugs. But I kept singing.

*Some dreams will fade and some will pass*
*Some will come true and some will last*
*You can stay down on your knees*
*Or get busy doin' as you please*

When the lights went down, and the show was over, I waited in the green room for Cherry to come and tell me what she'd thought of my song. But she didn't show. Nor did Oli and Penelope drop in to share my little triumph of rock n' roll rebellion. Instead of congratulations all I got was an earful of Slade's wrath.

"What the fuck was all that about!" Slade really knew how to spoil the mood. "You weren't hired to play unknown songs by your unknown self, Pipsqueak." The musicians, who'd done such a great job on Hank's songs, took their complimentary drinks and disappeared, heading out to see what companionship their musicianship might have inspired for the evening.

"It was just one song," I said. "Keep your tie straight."

"I don't wear a tie, smart guy. But I do wear the pants." Slade held out an envelope and slapped it in my hand. "Let's see how you feel about messing with me when it starts costing you?"

"What's this?" I opened up the envelope.

"Per diems," Slade said smugly, "your touring allowance."

"But it's empty?" I said.

"Exactly. If you break our agreement you won't see any cash. If you want to do your own thing you can pay your own way."

"No problem, boss," I replied sarcastically.

"And if you try a stunt like that again you won't earn yourself a dime. Our contract is clear on that."

"Is it?"

"You play what I say or you walk away. Your choice."

"And if I do walk, what about the Christmas album? What about the gigs I've already done, in LA and tonight?" Slade looked mighty pleased with himself.

"Not. One. Dime." I grabbed another beer and turned my back to Slade. *Fuckin' bastard promoter.* Slade grabbed my shoulder and turned me around. "You want to save your dad's farm, Pipsqueak? Do what I say!" As I contemplated smashing a full beer bottle on Slade's skull he turned and left, making sure to get the last word on his way out of the green room. "Don't forget. Your ass is mine until we're finished in New York."

In a dirty dressing-room mirror I caught my reflection. I was still wearing Hank's red bandana but with my own glasses on now I looked like a nerdy gang member. Right then it wasn't clear who I was trying to be.

I waited an hour or so before begrudgingly accepting that none of my friends were coming to join me backstage. I headed upstairs to my and Cherry's room where, having given her both keys, I knocked, half-expecting no answer. When Cherry did come to the door she was already showered and snug in her Stratosphere-provided thick cotton dressing gown.

"Sorry I didn't stay around downstairs after your show," she said, opening the door and waving me in, "but I had to get out of there quick."

"Why?" I said, without moving. "I waited for you guys for ages."

"I don't know why I was surprised." said Cherry. "I mean I knew he would probably be there—here? I guess I didn't want to think about it before now."

"Think about what?" I said. "Who was here?"

"My ex, Brian," said Cherry. "He was downstairs at your show and I just didn't want to speak to him. That's why I left straight after you finished."

"Brian is here? What are the chances of that?" I said. "What's Brian doing in Vegas, and at a Hank Flynn Junior gig too?" Cherry looked nervous, as though she'd been a bad girl and knew it.

"Brian's your promoter, Angus. He's the one who booked you for this show, and all your shows." Clearly, Cherry was confused.

"No, he's not," I said confidently. "The fuckwit—as we say in Oz—who flew me out here economy after promising first class, the asshole piece of shit who stuffed up my hotel reservations, the loser lawyer-slash-promoter-slash-shifty-dealer who changed my contract to suit his own greedy plans—that guy is called Slade." Cherry nodded. Apparently she wasn't confused.

"Slade Gaitlin. Yeah, Brian doesn't see why only his acts can have stage names. He thinks 'Brian' sounds gay and 'Slade' sounds tough. So he uses Slade." Cherry was serious. I felt dizzy.

"How long have you known?" I said. "How long have you and Slade-slash-Brian been playing me both ways?"

"It's not like that, Angus," pleaded Cherry. "I haven't had anything to do with him for months. Not since I got back from Australia."

"Months? But he still calls you everyday?"

"I can't stop that. Please don't get upset. I wanted to tell you sooner but I didn't know how."

"Well, you found a way," I said, rubbing my forehead like crazy. "Now I know. And when it comes to what a manipulative prick Slade is it seems like you knew all along." I had about a hundred questions for Cherry but none I felt like asking right then. It'd been a long day and the night was not ending how I'd thought it might have, or how I'd hoped it would.

"Come in, Angus," said Cherry. "Please."

"I'll see you in the morning," I said, walking towards another room where I'd decided to shack up with the band for the night. Cherry stepped out into the hall.

"Are you sure?" she asked. She looked and sounded disappointed but nothing like as much as I felt. "Come in, Angus, and let me explain everything. I've got nothing to hide about anyone—or anything." I stopped and turned to look her in the eyes.

"I'll see you tomorrow," I said. "We've got an early start."

# FELT THIS WAY BEFORE

While Oli, Penelope and Cherry were busy taking tourist snaps and 'oohing' and 'ahhing' at the man-made wonder known as Hoover Dam, I scribbled down words in my lyric book.

Sure, the concrete mountain was an impressive structure, but I was still trying to make sense of Cherry's revelation the previous night that Slade was her ex-boyfriend. Slade was 'Brian'. And vice versa.

*Just when I thought, I seen it all*
*She comes along and shows me more*
*Well, I don't think I've felt this way before*

It was true. I never had felt the way I did about Cherry about anyone else before. We hadn't even slept together yet and I was falling deeper for her than any girl ever. She wasn't just the last thing on my mind at night and the first thing on my mind when I woke; Cherry was on my mind all the time. I was smitten bad, man.

"Water," said Penelope in the style of a nature documentary voice-over. She opened her arms regally, surveying the inland sea before her, "the great source of all life. Even our bodies are more H2O than anything else." Oli smiled suggestively.

"I'd say *your* body is something else again," said Oli, giving me a wink. Penelope wiggled her bum playfully. Since we'd left Vegas, Oli and Penelope had been doing their best to lighten the heavy mood in the van but neither Cherry nor I could be swayed out of our funk. As I failed to engage in Oli and Penelope's banter once again, Cherry wandered off down the bridge.

*Just when I thought she is the one*
*She gets up and moves right on*
*Well, I don't think I've felt this way before*

The song, like so many I'd written since coming to America, was writing itself. I finished off a couple more simple verses and pocketed my book, pretty sure there was almost a complete lyric waiting for when I got back to my guitar.

Coming back to earth from my writer's trance I noticed the other tourists were parading a variety of baseball caps, baggy shorts and mismatched travel wear. It seemed people had come from all over America (and the world) to visit this dam. I spotted one 'Sun Studios, Memphis, Tennessee' T-shirt and a couple 'New York Yankees' baseball caps as I weaved my way across the dam wall to catch up with the gang who'd already made their way to the other side. When I reached them, Oli and Penelope were still carrying on like high school kids going to camp, Penelope running off ahead of us again.

"Come on, Oli," yelled Penelope, "let's have some fun."

"You are my *siren* and I cannot resist your call," he said, chasing her. "I must do as you bid."

"Then follow me to the water's edge and swim in my

*lagoon*," cried Penelope. "Last one in's a rotten egg!" Oli stopped, then turned and ran back to Cherry and me.

"This could get ugly," he said. "I don't have my swimming trunks." Cherry smiled. "And I really should start wearing underwear," added Oli. He punched me in the arm and ran after Penelope again. Cherry stepped in front of me, raising her eyebrows to invite me out of Sulksville into Funland. But I wasn't sure I was quite ready to leave just yet.

"Look, Angus, I told you—I'm sorry," said Cherry. "I really am, alright? Anyway it's not like you and I are married or anything. You're making me feel like I cheated on you or something."

"Didn't you?" I asked sullenly.

"No. I haven't seen him for months. And when we *were* seeing each other it wasn't that serious anyway. It was basically a few dates and some sex, not a relationship."

"That makes me feel better," I said sarcastically. "Slade being just sex to you."

"It wasn't *serious* is what I mean. Not as far as I was concerned anyway. Somehow Brian—*Slade*—convinced himself it was way more than it was. As soon as I found out what a player he really was I told him I didn't want to see him anymore. I mean, I skipped the country to get away from that lunatic. But even Australia wasn't far enough away for him to get the hint."

"It just seems like a strange coincidence that you and I have hooked up. You sure you're not working for him now? Is he paying you to be my minder, to make sure I don't go off the rails again or something?" Cherry looked set to laugh—or slap me maybe. Feeling a bit foolish for voicing such a paranoid imagining, I climbed up onto the lip of the dam.

"Don't be stupid. Angus, I just liked you and wanted to hang out with you some more. And you called *me*—

remember?" Cherry reached to get me down to safety but was frightened back by the long sheer drop below.

"Yeah, I guess I did call you, didn't I?"

"Come down from there," said Cherry softly. "I want to show you something."

"What is it?" I asked. "A Hoover Dam snow-dome made in Ethiopia?" I jumped off the wall. Cherry pushed me back against it with her body. She kissed me.

"This," she said, taking a breath. "And this," she kissed me again.

"I'm glad you showed me that," I said.

"Yeah, well as it turns out you're a pretty good kisser. But I'm a bit worried. I'm not sure if I'm kissing Angus, Pipsqueak or Hank Flynn Junior?"

"Angus," I said confidently. "Those other guys can wait in line."

"Good," said Cherry. "Because Angus is the one I want."

"Cool," I said.

"Though you do look pretty sexy with Hank's mirrors on."

"Do I?"

"A bit."

"That reminds me," I said. "Hank Flynn Junior's got a radio interview in Flagstaff tomorrow. We better get the others and keep moving. I've never done a radio interview before and I don't want to miss it."

"Good practice for when you're selling your own album," said Cherry.

"Maybe?" I said. "Maybe one day." Cherry crossed the road to the full side of the dam and pointed over the edge, down to the rocky shore where Oli and Penelope had jumped a security barrier and run down to take a dip. I smiled at Cherry, both of us all better now.

"Good luck dragging them back into the van," she said. "They're like hippos in heat ready to cool off."

Gazing over the edge, I saw Oli and Penelope holding hands, contemplating the water. Oli had stripped down to his shorts and Penelope stood unashamedly nearly naked in her lacy bra and knickers. Unbeknownst to them a security guard was approaching from behind. With a word, unheard to us, he surprised them and proceeded to draw their attention to the 'No Swimming' sign he'd come to enforce. Forlornly, they picked up their clothes and followed the guard's orders, marching ahead of him back up to the road. Much to the delight of the many teenage boys now gathered by our side, but to the horror of most of the tourist mums, Penelope was in no hurry at all to get dressed. Oli treated the situation with similar contempt.

"This lady won't be happy 'til she's got me locked up in the town jail," he said, loud enough for the growing audience. "But, like I told this fine gentleman of the law, I ain't come to town lookin' for trouble, I just fancied cooling off my gonads a tad."

# FIRST SIGHT

By the time we reached the Grand Canyon it was pitch black outside. Even so, the deep gorge formed by the Colorado River looked awesome.

My first local view of the world famous tourist attraction was a painting, a large one hanging above the bed in our log-cabin-styled room. Looking at the artist's rendering of giant rock steps—formed from thousands of years of wind and water erosion—filled me with great anticipation of seeing the real thing come first light.

Perhaps the fact the real Grand Canyon was only meters away had something to do with my growing excitement; the fact Cherry was in her underwear laying back on the bed we were about to share probably contributed too. It was a very romantic setting and I was almost happy Cherry and I hadn't really had our chance until then.

But it seemed even Cherry was getting impatient now.

"Come on, cowboy," she said, "what's taking you so long?" Sitting on the bed, Cherry held out two empty champagne glasses as I squirmed on the floor, struggling to remove my boots.

"I thought you didn't mind waiting?" I said. "I'm just glad you haven't got me sleeping in a tent again."

"That was our first night together," said Cherry, leaning back on the bed. "Anyway, you're the one who walked away from a sure thing last night."

"Third time lucky," I said, prying free the second boot. I got up and took out one of the two bottles of beer chilling in an ice-bucket. Pouring Cherry's glass first, I went back to admiring the painting above her head.

"If the real thing is anywhere near as beautiful as that we're in for a real treat tomorrow."

"Now, aren't you glad we took a detour on our detour?" said Cherry. I poured a glass of beer for me too.

"I didn't mean to sound like a killjoy in the Kombi," I said, "but I just thought we should have driven straight through to Flagstaff so we would have been there bright and early tomorrow morning. I really don't want to miss that radio interview or do anything to give Slade an excuse not to pay up." Cherry turned down the jazz—Miles Davis—coming from a bedside clock radio.

"You won't miss anything," she said. "But you might have missed something if we hadn't stopped. How can you *not* visit the Grand Canyon when you're driving by so close?"

"You're right," I said. From a bedside table, Cherry picked up a complimentary Grand Canyon Cabin's pen, inspecting it briefly before putting it in her mouth and leaning back into her pillows, puffing on an imaginary long-filtered cigarette like some 1940s flapper.

*Smoking.*

"I wonder what time the souvenir shop opens?" I asked, enjoying her performance. "We might need to be on the road before you get a chance to extend your collection." Sitting on our queen-sized bed, Cherry flirtatiously pressed her foot into my leg.

"I don't think I'll have any trouble remembering this place," she said with a sexy smile.

"Neither will I," I said. Cherry's smile turned inviting. I put down my glass. This was the moment I'd been waiting for since we'd met. But I didn't want to rush it, our first kiss slow and gentle.

"Mmm," said Cherry, taking another puff on her pen before reading its side. "Maybe I don't need this pen made in China?"

"Just an Ozzie made in America?" I suggested. Cherry put down the pen and raised her eyebrows.

"Haven't got one of those," she said. We kissed again.

"They're a collector's item," I whispered. "Not your everyday trinket."

"Much more precious," mocked Cherry playfully. "Priceless."

"Exactly," I said, moving in for the kill, going for her neck.

"Rare," said Cherry, her breath quick.

"Maybe only one in the world?" I said.

"And he's all mine." Cherry grabbed both my arms and bit my neck, her animalistic play-fighting raising the stakes. We started tearing at each other's clothes, until suddenly Cherry put an abrupt halt to what I'd felt were very *very* pleasant proceedings.

"What's wrong?" I asked. "What did I do?"

"It's okay," said Cherry, her expression showing obvious concern about something very serious. "Though I don't know how to say this without upsetting you." Cherry looked really worried. I sat up, feeling the same. Sick.

"Just say it," I pleaded, feigning bravery. "Tell me what's wrong? What is it?" Cherry put a consoling hand on my thigh as she looked me in the eyes.

"Those socks," she said plainly. "They have got to go."

I followed her gaze to my bright pink socks. She was right: they were truly shocking. A circus clown would have been proud of how they illuminated the room. I pulled them off and threw them as far away from the bed as I could. Laughing and giggling, Cherry pulled me back onto the bed, back into action. Despite Cherry's vigorous and amorous affection, I managed to take a private moment to promise myself never to wash red with whites ever again. Ever.

The next morning, as we watched the dawn sky fill with pink, yellow and red streaks, and the shadows climbing down the canyon as the sun slowly rose, Cherry nestled into my arms; our close contact keeping out the cold as much as our coats. I looked over to Oli and Penelope, similarly embraced, but looking tired, no doubt from another night of Olympic lovemaking. A silence settled over us all, one filled with serenity and wonder. It was a true spectacle before us. Awesome.

After soaking up the majestic scene, the girls initiated photo opportunities of pairs, threesomes and foursomes with the ancient natural wonder an impressive pictorial backdrop. I was the only one to keep an eye on the time but didn't make a big deal about keeping to any schedule: how often would any of us experience a Grand Canyon sunrise?

After an hour or so of milling around with other tourists, the four of us walked as a group back to the Kombi. Penelope sneezed, and Oli handed her a tissue before using another one to blow his nose himself.

"You guys got a sniffle?" asked Cherry.

"Yeah," said Penelope. "We made love under the stars last night, by the edge of the canyon. I think we caught a bit of a chill. It was so cold—and dark. Scary." Oli nodded.

"That's nothing," he said. "You ever felt a wild moose's nose nudging your butt? I swear I nearly shat myself right in that curious varmint's face!" Penelope laughed.

"I don't know who was more terrified—you or the poor moose!" she said. I started laughing too.

"That's cruelty to animals," I said.

"I'm sure the moose will get over it," said Oli. "Me, on the other hand? I'll never look at a picture of the Grand Canyon without feeling the knob-shrinking, sinking sensation of a wet beast's noggin far too close to my ballsack. Too close for anyone's comfort. Mine or the moose's." Cherry snorted. Penelope was almost splitting her sides with laughter.

"It *was* pretty funny running to our room," she said between guffaws. "Some folk are so prudish. You'd think they'd never seen two naked people before."

"Funny?" said Oli. "You don't want to know where that moose tongue went!" Cherry was laughing hard too.

"Stop it!" she screamed. "You're right. We don't want to know." But Oli told her anyway.

"A moose's tongue is *long*. That's all I'm gonna say, partners. Moose. Has. Long. Tongue. Me feel it."

"Whose turn is it to drive?" I asked, opening up the sliding door.

"Stop it, Oli," said Cherry, about to wet herself laughing.

"It's *rough* too," said Oli. "A moose's tongue is rough and kind of spikey, like cactus." We all climbed into the van, Oli taking his turn in the driver's seat, Penelope next to him, and Cherry and I in the back. Cherry wanted to know more about our friends' wild encounter.

"You sure it was a moose?" she asked. "I only saw elk on the drive in?" Oli started the Kombi and adjusted the driving mirrors.

"Whatever it was," he said, "it was very friendly. And gentle. Affectionate even." The sound of our old Volkswagen engine accelerating wasn't exactly a roar, but we zoomed off together, each of us firing on all cylinders.

160

The romance, rest, sun, and historic scenic view charging us up for a fun day on the road.

I took out my lyric book, filling the page quickly with words to a new country love song.

*As I recall I saw her, by the light of the moon*
*What can I tell you? What could I do?*
*I fell in love*
*I fell in love*
*As I recall I heard her, calling my name*
*What can I tell you? What can I say?*
*I fell in love*
*I fell in love*
*It happened on one starry night*
*It happened on first sight*

Cherry looked over my shoulders to see what I was writing and I instinctively went to close my lyric book. With one hand on my leg she opened up the book with the other. At first I felt sick with vulnerability as to how she'd react to my scribbles about falling in love but then, when she smiled, I felt over the metaphoric moon.

"That's sweet," she whispered. "Don't stop." I kissed her on the cheek and turned on the bench seat, playfully using Cherry as my backrest. In a few minutes I'd finished the lyrics to 'First Sight' and was straight onto another song. At the rate I was going I'd have an album's worth before we reached our next destination: Flagstaff, Arizona—home to Flagstaff Magic, the radio station where I was headed to do my first radio interview ever.

But I didn't feel nervous at all.

# HANK FLYNN JUNIOR?

The plastic log bench in the reception area of Flagstaff Magic Radio was big enough for all four of us to sit on in a row. Cherry, Penelope, Oli and I twiddled our thumbs under a big banner promoting Top Two Country (the name of the double-act of DJs who'd be interviewing me) that was hanging from the ceiling. Silently contemplating my inexperience I went from bored to nervous in a shot, unsure how I was meant to play the promotion game. *Did I give it all Hank Flynn Junior? Or should I be more plain old Angus Flynn?* I wasn't sure.

Cherry's phone rang. She looked at it, rolled her eyes then shrugged to Penelope: *Slade*. Surprisingly, to Penelope—and me—Cherry decided to speak to him herself this time.

"I told you to stop calling," she said. Penelope shook her head in disbelief. "No!" said Cherry angrily. "I won't tell you where I am!" Hanging up the phone, Cherry stood up—then sat straight down again. She was edgier than me.

"Why won't he get the hint?" asked Penelope.

"Was that Slade—I mean Brian?" asked Oli casually, both girls either not hearing or choosing to ignore him.

"How many times do I have to tell him it's over?" said Cherry.

"Obviously Slade doesn't think it really *is* over." I said. "He must be getting the wrong signals." As lovely as our first night together had been, I realized I was still suspicious of Cherry's relationship with Slade and it probably showed in my tone. "Why do you think he won't give up?" I said, hoping she wouldn't notice.

"I have no fucking idea, Angus," said Cherry angrily, obviously noticing. "I'm not a man, am I? Who knows how you guys think?" Cherry got up and grabbed her handbag. Oli tried to make peace.

"We don't really think," he said. "That's the whole dang truth." Oli hunched over like a caveman, doing a pretty funny Neolithic Man impression. "Man want food and sex. That all." Penelope smiled.

"And a moose to call his own," she said. Oli and Penelope laughed but Cherry's anger only grew worse. She aimed right at me.

"I think I might just leave you to it, *Junior*," she said, pulling out a red bandana from my plastic costume bag and tossing it my way. "Don't forget your Hank Flynn glasses."

"Why are you getting so upset?" I said. "Please don't go, Cherry."

"It doesn't matter what I say, Angus, you won't believe I'm through with Slade." Though I didn't really understand why Cherry was mad at me, I still wanted to say the right thing.

"I thought you called him Brian?" I said jovially, but not close to the right thing.

"Forget it," spat Cherry, storming out of reception. Penelope watched, confused, and, with an apologetic shrug to Oli, followed Cherry out.

"I thought you two were gettin' ready to shack up together after your Grand Canyon love fest?" said Oli.

"What's happened?"

"No idea," I said. "I guess she's touchier about Slade than I thought." Just then the studio receptionist directed Oli and I into the studio proper. After a quick briefing from the producer, and as quickly as things can happen sometimes in show business, it was showtime.

Oli stood at the back of the studio, trying his hitherto-unplayed role of road manager on for size. He stayed out of the way though, understanding as well as I did who the real stars of this radio show were: the two local disc jockeys, The Top Two.

The Top Two were a classic fat and skinny act who looked as if they'd fallen off a country sideshow stage. Their big Stetson cowboy hats, jeans and sneakers were where the physical similarities began and ended. DJ One, as he introduced himself, was the leaner partner in the pair and, ironically, had the deeper voice. His bassy tone was perfectly suited to radio. DJ Two, on the other hand, spoke with a high-pitched, excitable voice, made more incongruous by his obese frame.

DJ One took his seat behind his mic as his big buddy signaled to me the commercial break was coming to an end. Their friendly—if insincere—manner had put me at ease and I was feeling surprisingly relaxed. Maybe not being able to see the blurry faces of hundreds of Hank Flynn fans helped—and maybe being in full costume did too. I was prepared and ready to take on the familiar persona of a cocky country outlaw; wearing mirror sunglasses in a radio station was so rock n' roll I was starting to believe my own reflection in the glass panels surrounding us.

"You're up, Junior," said Oli, with a prod from behind. "Don't forget to plug the gig in Albuquerque." DJ Two raised his chubby hand to signal for DJ One to take the lead off from the break, which he delivered in deep, down and delectable.

"Welcome back, listeners," said One. "For those just tuning in, DJ Two and yours truly are live today with Hank Flynn *Junior*." DJ Two squeaked in next.

"That's right, DJ One," he said, wobbling in his swivel chair. "Sitting in front of us today is the only offspring of country music legend, Hank Flynn." DJ Two turned my way. "So, what's it like followin' your daddy's big footprints?" he said, sounding like a down-south chipmunk. "Must be hard livin' up to a legend?" I shrugged and answered in no particular accent.

"Kind of," I said. DJ One smiled and piped up from his unfathomably sonic skinny chest. "Does it help wearin' your old man's trademark costume? Listeners will have to imagine a young looking Hank Flynn," he explained, before Two's nod indicated he'd cut in.

"That's right, folks," tweeted DJ Two. "The latest version is sitting right here wearing the *same* mirror sunglasses and the *same* red bandana so many country traditionalists got so upset about his daddy wearin' back in the 70s." Before I knew exactly why I dropped into Hank's accent.

"Ahh, actually I wear this gittup all the time," I said. Oli patted me on the back encouragingly. "I don't think of it as a costume so much as an inheritance. One I'm proud to call my own." Hank's spirit took stronger hold. I felt possessed.

"You're the real thing, hey?" asked DJ One.

"Try to be," I said. "God's honest truth," I added, plucking a lyric straight out of 'Killer'. DJ Two nodded, wiping sweat from his chins down his T-shirt.

"You just want to share your love of the best music there is? Right?" said DJ Two. "Country, right?"

"That's it," I said, stuck in the FM radio rhythm now, a frenetic pace forcing me to jump in anywhere I could.

"So what you're saying is this ain't no exercise in marketing and blatant audience manipulation?" asked DJ Two suspiciously.

"No, not at all," I said, digging myself deeper into my 'Nashville Cat' character. "I love my pa's music and grew up with it all my life. It comes natural to me." Oli looked confused, but smiled and nodded to the jockeys eagerly. The Top Two dropped their interrogation of my country authenticity. Apparently, I'd passed their test.

"Good," bellowed DJ One. "America needs genuine country music now more than ever, and nothin's more authentic than a Hank Flynn classic." DJ Two nodded.

"That's so right, my skinny little friend," he squealed. "What with all the faggoty pretenders spending more time on teeth whitenin' and fancy videos, the good people of this country want real men, God damn it."

"And dang," I said, "that's what I'm giving. Real country classics." Both DJ's smiled, showing their approval of me by simultaneously slamming their fists, like fleshy mallets or a judge's gavel, into the studio console desk. The judges had ruled.

"So where can we see you," asked DJ One, "ahead of the country awards, that is?"

"I just got finished in Vegas and our next show's in Albuquerque."

"That's not too far from here," said DJ Two, "not to anyone with a pick-up truck, a tankful of gas and a hankering for an old-fashioned good time. Even if you do have to drive a few miles outta town to see this fine young man—I for one think it'll be worth it."

"And I for two," boomed DJ One. "How often do you get a chance to enjoy the god-given talents of a bloodline legend?"

"Thank you," I said, sounding more southern than

ever. "Thank you very much." DJ One smirked, leaning into his mic.

"And one of the great fringe benefits of living the country music dream is you get followed around by sweet lookin' fillies," he said. The DJs exchanged knowing looks. "How 'bout those fine ladies keepin' Hank Flynn Junior here company?" DJ Two also clearly approved of the look of our female friends.

"No fear, DJ 'boney' One. I'm still a man—last time I looked. I saw those pretty specimens. That's some prime feminine company you got there, Junior." DJ Two turned to me. "One of those gals your wife?" he asked. "Or they both your girlfriends?" Both the DJs' jibes caught me off guard. And, besides the fact I didn't know what to call Cherry yet, I was pretty sure they didn't want a sincere answer anyway, just more radio talk.

"Umm…well, it's early days yet," I said, keeping in my Junior accent. "I'm not really sure what to call her—*them*—yet?"

"We got a name for 'em," said DJ One.

"Groupies," said DJ Two. Hearing Slade's voice in my head, about how I was only employed to promote the Hank Flynn image, I decided to play along.

"Yeah, that's right," I said, keeping rhythm. "They're my groupies. Got bunches of 'em—coast to coast." The two DJs shared a look of mutual approval.

"I knew it," said DJ One. "You *are* a bad boy."

"A ladies man just like your daddy," exclaimed DJ Two gleefully. Then DJ One took the lead on wrapping things up.

"And it's been an absolute pleasure talkin' with you, Hank Flynn Junior. I am DJ One…"

"And I am DJ Two. Together, we're Flagstaff's own Top Two! And this week's Top Two country classic is 'My Best Present Ever' from Hank Flynn's smash hit album of 1977, *Killer*. Look out for it on re-release this Christmas."

The DJs saluted each other as they signed off, in unison, with what I took to be their signature FM adios.

"See you all in church!"

As 'My Best Present Ever' played, the Top Two interviewers removed their headphones, high-fived each other, then shook mine and Oli's hands. Oli patted me on the back for a job well done. Inside the studio it was smiles all around, but all I could think about was where Cherry was and, if she'd listened, what she'd made of my first radio interview ever.

I'd thought it went pretty well.

# PIPSQUEAK

Excited to finally be getting his turn behind the Kombi's wheel, Oli drove the next leg of our cross-country adventure, on a journey now loosely following Route 66.

Heading out of Flagstaff towards Albuquerque I was riding shotgun, satisfied with what I felt had been a pretty good radio interview. Penelope was in the backseat, as bubbly as ever, and Cherry was sitting next to her, staring out the window.

When Oli and I had got back to the van, Cherry and Penelope were already waiting in the back seat. I'd got the feeling Cherry hadn't wanted me to sit next to her. It seemed my feelings were spot-on.

"Groupies!?" blurted Cherry, sounding pretty pissed off. Obviously she *had* listened to my radio interview but hadn't thought it went as well as I did. "That's what you think we are—what I am? A *groupie*?" Caught off guard by the attack, I didn't know what to say. Oli tried to diffuse the tension for me.

"Groupie? It's not the best word for a committed music lover, is it?" he said. Cherry's unimpressed expression proved Oli's attempt at peacemaker had failed.

"I thought the interview went pretty well?" I said. "Apart from the 'groupie' comment then. Don't you think?" Cherry said nothing. Oli tried again, this time to rescue me from the silent treatment.

"Yeah, partner. It did go well," he said. "You remembered to mention Hank Flynn Junior's next gig in Albuquerque—and the awards show in Nashville. Slade would have to be happy with that." Cherry and Penelope swapped the same look, contempt boarding on disgust.

"Why are you trying to make someone you *hate* happy, Angus? Who cares what Slade thinks?" said Cherry. "And why have you given up on doing your own music—before you've even tried?"

"I haven't given up on anything. I'm trying to pay off my father's debts to save our home," I said. "And maybe to save Hank's life too! What's got up your skirt?"

"She didn't like you calling us groupies," explained Penelope. "Personally, I quite liked it." Cherry frowned. Penelope smiled awkwardly back. "But Cherry didn't. Cherry didn't like being referred to as some kind of cheap slut." Penelope winked at Oli, who was checking her out in the rearview mirror.

"You like being treated like an *object*, do you, Pen?" said Cherry, appalled. Penelope considered her answer carefully before nodding affirmatively.

"Sometimes," she said. "Yes."

"It was just part of the act, Cherry," I said.

"What about 'fuck-fan'?" suggested Oli. "That's a better name for a groupie, don't you think?" Penelope mouthed *yeah!* and blew Oli a kiss. I nervously waited for Cherry's response, not sure how she'd take Oli and Penelope's determined effort not to take her upset at all seriously.

"Well, it just made me feel a bit stupid, that's all," said Cherry, her face breaking into a smile. But in her voice I could still hear how I'd hurt her. I didn't like how that made me feel.

"I'm sorry," I said quietly. "I really didn't mean anything."

"It's okay," said Cherry. "I'm probably over-reacting." Penelope leant forward, whispering to Oli loud enough for everyone to hear.

"Hey, driving man, next chance you get—pull over. This little 'fuck-fan' fancies a pit-stop." Oli sat up sprightly.

"Just check the water? Or full service?" he said. Just then his phone rang and, with Oli otherwise occupied by looking out for the next safe pull-off point, I picked it up. Cherry and Penelope kept chatting softly in the backseat.

"Didn't you guys learn your lesson at the Grand Canyon?" asked Cherry. 'You know? With your alfresco love making?"

"Moose only come out at night," said Penelope.

"Hello?" I said chirpily, before repeating myself minus all enthusiasm. "Oh, hello." Hearing Slade on the other end, I covered the phone and waved a hand to shush the girls.

"This is a courtesy call to let you know I've cancelled the gig in Albuquerque," said Slade. "You should drive straight on through to Memphis and meet me there for the next showcase."

"Sorry? What?" I said. "Albuquerque's cancelled?" Slade sighed, bored, ignoring me. I asked again. "Why? What happened? I've just got through plugging the hell out of that damn show on the radio?"

"My schedule's full with other business in LA," said Slade. "Since I can't be there to make sure you behave yourself, I've decided to pull the gig. It's small-time anyway.

Besides, I've already got plenty of footage of Hank Flynn Junior in Vegas. Maybe I'll get some more in Nashville? But whatever I decide, I won't need any from that shit-hole in Albuquerque."

"It sounds like you knew you were going to pull the show *before* I fronted up to the station. Why would you let me promote a gig that wasn't even going to happen?"

"It's part of the game, Pipsqueak," said Slade condescendingly. "All publicity is good publicity. But don't you worry about those basics of marketing like supply and demand—leave the business to me. Just get your ass to Memphis."

"Right," I said. "See you there." I hung up, childishly happy to at least have been the one ending this call.

"What's going on?" asked Cherry.

"The gig in Albuquerque is off. Slade's pulled it. Basically because he can't be there to film it, or watch over me to make sure I don't stray from the approved set-list."

"That's stupid," said Cherry. "He's just throwing his weight around to remind you who's boss. Dickhead."

"I'm sorry, guys," I said. "Now I'm dragging you all the way to Albuquerque for—for what?" Oli slapped his thigh, then clicked his fingers as though he'd just come up with the best idea of his life.

"For a gig," said Oli confidently. "But not as Hank Flynn Junior. Tonight a new star is born." Penelope, Cherry and Oli exchanged looks, a smile growing on each of their faces as whatever plan Oli had in mind apparently jumped into the girls' minds too. I was the only one who didn't immediately get it.

A few hours later, standing outside the High Noon Bar and Restaurant, I watched Oli take down a Hank Flynn Junior bill poster and stick up a freshly-printed new one:

*TONIGHT: ONE NIGHT ONLY—ANGUS FLYNN*

IS *PIPSQUEAK*!

Oli had taken a photo of me with his phone, sent it to Penelope's laptop (which, she'd explained, never left her side since a onetime room-mate had found some private videos and uploaded them to a German porn site) and Penelope had added a retro-style font to the design for an instant image update. My new Angus Flynn poster looked more professional than the one Slade's people had come up with for Vegas.

Cherry had jumped online at an internet café and spread the word about the 'Australian singer-songwriter's debut' by contacting a few entertainment blogs she'd done stories with before. As Oli had promised, the gig was going ahead after all.

"I could get into this management caper," said Oli proudly. "Only need follow one motto…"

"The show must go on," said Penelope.

"Yeah," said Oli. "Or, to put it another way—fuck the promoters and do it yourself."

"You sure the venue is cool?" I asked again.

"I told you," said Oli, "the manager is happy to have you sing any songs you want. You don't have to do any of your dad's stuff if you don't want to. Slade's last-minute cancellation took her off guard as much as you, and the way she sees it you're doing *her* a favor debuting Pipsqueak tonight."

"Nobody's coming to hear me sing my own songs, though?" I said.

"Of course they are," said Cherry. "They just don't know it yet."

# CALL IT A DAY

Cherry was right. The audience loved Pipsqueak.

Closing in on midnight, and as I started thinking about finishing up, The High Noon was still packed with punters. Some were still seated at the small tables scattered throughout the bar and restaurant, but most were standing. A few were even dancing.

Wearing my own glasses instead of Hank's mirrors allowed me to see a slightly more cosmopolitan crowd than I'd played to in Vegas. By the bar up the back, the very attractive female venue manager was keeping Oli and Penelope entertained with flirty cocktail making and, from the looks of things, some pretty funny jokes. From the stage, I watched Cherry make her way from the bar to her position up front.

Center stage, in a venue not much bigger than the Green Onion, I grabbed my trusty scotch bottle and took another mouthful. Wiping my lips with the back of my hand when I was done, I raised the bottle to the crowd, most of whom responded by doing the same and raising their drinks to me. Though I hadn't been quite as manic with nerves as I was before a Hank Flynn Junior performance, I'd still needed a drink or five ahead of my original debut.

"What song you want to finish with?" asked the bass player, and The All Whites band leader. "We've played all of your own stuff except for that love song, 'Treasure'." Since Slade had also failed to inform the band about him cancelling the gig in Albuquerque until after they'd arrived in town, they'd been happy to go on with the show. Amazingly, they'd learned two sets of my stuff in two hours. And with the help of a few cheat sheets of chords and changes I'd written out while everyone else was having dinner, anyone would have thought we'd been playing together for years.

"I might do one I didn't teach you guys in rehearsal," I said. "Why don't you all sit this one out?" The guys happily downed their instruments and drum sticks, and waited side-stage for me to play a song I'd written in the van after the Grand Canyon visit. It was about a couple who'd broken up but couldn't let each other go. Cherry had gotten upset again, thinking I'd written it about Slade and her, but I didn't think I had. I'd just thought it was a good melody.

And I loved the lyrics:

*She's got a bad heart, it's such a shame*
*She can't forget the boy with no name*
*She never speaks yet always keeps with her*
*He's got a sadness, in his eyes*
*No kind of smile can ever disguise*
*The pain that he feels is still real and alive*
*And no one wants to say*
*Let's call it a day*

While I played out the last chorus of 'Call It A Day', I noticed Cherry had been forced back from her position at

175

the front of the stage to now being a few rows deep. Between Cherry and me, a moshpit of mostly female fans pawed and clawed at the stage. It was all Cherry could do not to spill her glass of wine.

I finished the song and the crowd erupted into applause. I gave them a thumbs up, adjusted my Buddy Holly glasses, and took another swig of scotch before looking at my hand-written set on the floor. Deliberating over what song to finish with, I remembered Roy's words of advice about 'giving them what they want'.

"Thank you," I said, acknowledging the applause still going. "Thank you very much. And again, sorry you're not getting the full Hank Flynn Junior experience, as you were expecting—but I really appreciate you hanging around to hear my songs." From the middle of the shoulder-to-shoulder crowd two gorgeous girls pushed themselves to the front.

"We love you, Angus!" screamed one of the girls, a tall blond reminding me of Cameron Diaz in *Something About Mary*.

"I love you most!!" screamed a voluptuous redhead, the spitting image of my favorite of Elvis's leading ladies, Ann Margret.

"Ahhh…I love you too," I said, falling into a convincing (at least to me) Southern twang. "I love you so much I'm gonna give you my version of my pa's classic Christmas hit, 'My Best Present Ever'. It's being re-issued for Christmas this year, so make sure to look out for it." Channeling old Hank and making mention of his country classic sent the crowd wild again. It was like that's what they'd really been waiting for. Cries of "Yeah!" and "Woo hoo!" and the sound of yet more applause filled up the High Noon.

As I got the band back up on stage the Cameron Diaz

lookalike handed me a shot of tequila. I smiled, took it, and quickly skulled it down. It was hot on my throat. I coughed, but managed to smile, hold it down and gestured *thanks.* Not to be outdone, Ann Margret's double pushed past her friend, presenting me with her own offering: the whole bottle of tequila. I took it and downed a couple of slugs before handing it back.

"Keep it," said Ms Margret. "It's all yours!"

'My Best Present Ever' went over great. I could hardly hear my vocals above the sound of everyone singing. Everyone, that was, except Cherry. I wondered what was wrong?

"There's time for just one more song," I said. "But I'll leave it up to you. Do you want to hear a new number by me called 'Treasure' or an old Hank Flynn classic called…'Killer'?"

"Play 'Killer'!" yelled Ms Margret.

"Yeah, Angus!" agreed Diaz loudly. "Play 'Killer'!"

"Killer! Killer! Killer!" Ms Margret led the chant, which spread instantly through the venue. And, though it wasn't really the answer I'd been hoping for, I nodded to the drummer and signed off my first original show giving the audience want they really wanted: a cover, 'Killer'.

*I've played cards with cheatin' men*
*Who look you in the eyes*
*Tell you my God's honest truth*
*I ain't gonna lie*

Everyone loved it. Almost.

After the show, I waited for Cherry in the band room. At my feet, sitting on the floor (after sneaking in with the rest of the band), the girls from the front of the stage—the blond, Diaz and the redhead, Margret—were sharing a joint. They still hadn't introduced themselves and I was feeling too exhausted (maybe drunk?) to ask their real names. While they smoked, I drank from the tequila bottle, in between making small talk with the band members, who were congratulating me on a good show.

I was fast approaching wasted.

"I didn't know your dad shared the stage with Elvis?" said Diaz. "That's amazing." Ms Margret put a hand on my knee, slowly running it up my thigh.

"To think my hands are only three degrees of separation from the King? It's enough to make a girl lose all her inhibitions." Diaz looked jealous.

"Well," she said competitively, "I've got no inhibitions to lose."

Done with the bottle of tequila I straightened up and rubbed my now watery eyes. For a second I thought I'd spotted Cherry at the door, but when I looked again she wasn't there. Ms Margret climbed up to sit in my lap. Diaz took the empty bottle from my hands and put herself in my grip.

"Hey!" I said, pushing them away playfully. "I'm a taken man. You girls can hang around and finish up the rider if you like but I'm gonna go back to my hotel room."

"Is someone *special* waiting for you?" asked Ms Margret seductively.

"I hope so," I said, moving to the door.

"Is she *really* special?" asked Diaz, pouting.

"Yeah," I said. "She's really special."

In the main room I was surprised to see the whole place already empty of all punters. *Maybe I'd been clapped out longer than I thought?* There was no sign of Oli, Penelope or Cherry either. Remembering how I'd been all alone after the Vegas show too, I wondered whether my friends would ever join me in my after-show celebrations? Then, unable to find the manageress to thank her for everything, I gave up and headed back to our accommodation, a Mexican-style adobe cabin only a short walk from the High Noon.

Outside the room Cherry and I were staying in, I struggled with a foot-long plastic chili attached to our room key. Eventually I got the chili out of my way and quietly let myself into the room. It was dark and silent and as I sat on the floor to take off my cowboy boots I listened out for any sign that Cherry was awake. Hearing nothing I climbed into bed as quietly as I could. Cherry's feet felt icy cold.

"Hey, you're freezing," I whispered. "How long have you been in bed?" Cherry moved her shoulders so slightly I couldn't tell if she was asleep and fidgeting, or awake and not interested in a late-night chat. Feeling completely slammed by now I rolled onto my back and waited for the room to stop spinning. "Cherry? Are you awake?" I whispered again. "What did you think of the show?"

Letting out a big exhalation I closed my eyes, unsure if I'd actually vocalized my last question or only asked it in my mind. Since Cherry failed to respond, I tried to stop worrying. Maybe in the morning she'd tell me what had upset her enough to leave another gig without saying anything?

It was becoming a habit of hers.

# Part III:
# The King

# THE LAND OF ENCHANTMENT

The next morning I felt like shit.

I was sure I felt worse than Oli had after his big night in Hollywood, when he'd drunk a swimming pool's worth of beer, champagne and scotch (and eaten a jacuzzi full of caviar). My tongue tasted like plaster—with a dash of bile. I was thirsty and hungry and desperate to rid my mouth of the effects of a mysterious shit-biscuit I had no recollection of munching on the night before. But as keen as I was to find out why Cherry had cleared out so quickly after my Pipsqueak debut, I was quietly glad she wasn't around to watch my hungover self peel his tongue from the starchy bed sheet. It wasn't pretty.

So, after a quick—*slow*—shower I slumped through the garden of our bed and breakfast until I spotted Oli and Penelope, inside a communal dining room. Just sitting down at a table, behind a large window looking out onto the lush garden, they failed to notice me.

Entering the dining room, I pulled out a chair and sat down with my friends just as the last of the more punctual diners was up and leaving. Oli, Penelope and someone I hadn't spotted from the garden, the sexy High Noon manageress, were all waiting for the waiter to finish clearing another table before serving them.

"Casa De Seunos means 'house of dreams'," said Oli, explaining the name of our accommodation. "But if you fine ladies asked me, I'd say last night was more of a *fantasy* than a mere dream." The three of them shared smiles and giggles and I wondered if I'd suddenly turned invisible.

"And Albuquerque means 'land of enchantment'," cooed High Noon as the threesome briefly acknowledged my presence, with a unison glance, then continuing as before.

"Morning!" the three of them said, without a single eye on me.

"It was fun doing it in the garden," said Penelope, gently brushing the manager's long wavy hair off her shoulder with a flirty hand.

"Do you want me to send you the photos?" said sexy High Noon. Oli and Penelope shared a look: *definitely*. Oli reached for a jug of orange juice on our table but was too slow. The waiter snatched it up out of his grasp.

"Sorry, Sir," said the waiter, his Mexican accent straight out of an old Clint Eastwood flick. The waiter looked like Zorro without the sword; dark circles around his eyes creating the illusion of a mask. "Breakfast is no longer being served." On a wall decorated with framed photos of colorful hot-air balloons, he pointed to a sign: *BREAKFAST SERVED 7 am to 10 am.*

"You're kidding?" said Oli, following Zorro's gaze as it transferred to a large wall clock: *10:05 am.* Oli smiled and changed his tone, doing his best to grease the wagon-wheels. "Hey, partner, we three here spent up a lot of energy last night. If ya catch my drifter's drift? Can't you-all at least rustle up a little muesli or something?"

"We don't have muesli," said the waiter. *En garde.* "Maybe you can have some eggs—if there are any left?"

184

"Thank you," said Penelope sweetly. "We're very sorry we're late for breakfast."

"No problem, Miss," said Zorro, responding much better to Penelope. "Would you ladies like some New Mexican sausage?" Sexy High Noon smiled back *thank you*, but waved her hand *no*.

"Not for me," she said. Oli looked peeved. I guessed he didn't like being out-flirted by the waiter.

"I'll have hers," said Oli, snatching back the jug of orange juice. As the waiter headed off, I wondered whether he'd return with muesli, eggs or a serve of his special sausage for me too. Suddenly a wave of nausea washed over me. *Maybe I'll wait for lunch*, I thought.

"Thanks for last night," I said, trying to distract myself from my gurgling gut and self-pity by showing my appreciation to High Noon. "All of you," I added, with a nod to the others. "I couldn't have done it without a push and without a venue to be pushed into. By the way, have any of you guys seen Cherry?" Oli and Penelope shared another look. Something was up.

"She asked me to give you this," said Penelope, handing me an envelope. "Sorry."

"What are you sorry for?" I asked.

"Cherry was pretty upset," explained Oli. "She even offered to take a plane and leave the van with us, but we decided to fly instead." I took out the letter inside the envelope, and whether because I was still drunk or sleepy, or just not thinking it might be a private communication, I read it aloud.

"Dear Angus. Congratulations on a great 'Angus-Pipsqueak-Flynn' debut. Sorry, but I had to head back to LA unexpectedly. Will call you sometime." I looked to Oli and Penelope for more information. *What's going on?*

"She didn't want to wake you," said Penelope. "She said you looked wrecked."

"Looks like she was right," said Oli.

"I wish she had woken me," I said. "What's going on? What do you mean you guys are going to fly. Where to?"

"Penelope and I are gonna fly straight to Nashville, partner," explained Oli. "We've had enough of the road for now and feel like spending a few days in one spot."

"There's some great bars in Nashville," said Penelope. "And I want to see Oli ride a bull."

"Mechanical, I hope," said Oli worriedly.

"No, I'm going to buy me some horns, partner," said Penelope with a wink.

"What about Memphis?" I asked, dumbfounded by my imminent abandonment. Penelope put a consolatory hand on my shoulder.

"We're not crazy Elvis fans like Cherry and you," said Penelope apologetically. "Oli and I aren't bothered about seeing Graceland. A *city* full of *cowboys* on the other hand?" Before I could ask any more about Cherry, the waiter returned with four plates fully loaded with scrambled eggs, toast and piles of tiny sausages.

"They may be *small*," said Zorro defensively, "but they are tasty. So very tasty," he added passionately. "The flavor they release in your mouth! My God! It's like a pork piñata party on your tongue." The three lovers, so happy in their bubble before I came along, smiled and rubbed their hands together in anticipation of a hearty breakfast. I didn't feel like smiling though, and, even more than before getting the letter from Cherry, I didn't feel like eating.

It wasn't just my appetite I'd lost. The girl I'd fallen hard for had disappeared too. And soon, when Oli and Penelope went on their merry way, I'd be all alone again, stranded in The Land of Enchantment at The House of Dreams.

I though I felt bad when I'd woken up but now I *really* felt like shit.

# WHEN YOU LEFT ME IN ALBUQUERQUE

Slade was madder than a feather-tickled rattlesnake.

The High Noon show I'd thought had gone so well hadn't only resulted in Cherry leaving me, it was also the reason Mr. Promoter From Hell was now giving me an earful. I was still getting a brow beating from Slade on Oli's phone as our taxi pulled up in front of Albuquerque's *'Enchanted Car-Hire'*.

"I don't care, Slade," I yelled. "Fire me then!" I was sick of listening to him tell me about the fucking fine-print of his fucking contract, a contract he'd used to get me doing a bunch of shows and appearances I'd never knowingly agreed to.

"You had no right to re-negotiate with the venue," screamed Slade. "I'm the fucking promoter, *Pipsqueak*, and I did not authorize any sideshows. You're pushing it, fella. Don't push it too far."

"Look, the audience wanted something so I gave them…me. Just because you weren't there to direct everything shouldn't have to mean everyone should have to miss out." Slade grunted a few more threats down the line before finishing up with a reminder of my next showcase in

Memphis. "Yeah, Memphis," I said. "I'll see *you* there too."

Climbing out of the taxi, I noticed the car yard jammed with a variety of old and new cars of every shape and size. Oli and Penelope looked out of the taxi they were to continue to Albuquerque airport in.

"Slade pissed off about you doing your own show last night?" asked Oli. I shrugged.

"He threatened to call the whole thing off. Again."

"What a fucker," said Oli.

"Dickless asshole," agreed Penelope.

"You sure you don't mind leaving me with the phone, Oli?" I said, offering his mobile back to him in case he'd changed his mind. Oli pushed the phone back my way.

"No one needs to get hold of me, partner," explained Oli. "None but she who is always within my reach. Such delicate hands you have too, Miss Penelope." Oli smiled and squeezed her hand. Penelope reached for Oli's thigh, veering at the last second to grab him by the balls.

"Is this 'delicate'?" said Penelope, squeezing his nut-sack tight. Oli's eyes watered. They both liked it.

"I'm putty in your hands," cooed Oli. "Clay for you to shape into any form."

"Wait 'til I fire you in my *kiln*," threatened Penelope sexily. "I'll make you hard as volcanic rock!"

Before unwittingly bearing witness to any kind of eruption, I closed the door and sent the young lovers on their lovemaking way. Watching them go, I wondered if the taxi-driver would know what a 'fuck-stop' was, and whether he'd keep the meter running.

Inside the reception of the car-hire joint I opened up my wallet. Things looked bleaker than when I'd opened up the letter from Cherry. Now I had no woman *and* hardly any cash. Since my safe and secure life as a gainfully employed roadie, I'd transformed into a walking country song: a down-on-his-luck dude adrift in a strange land without a wagon or a horse to pull it. I grabbed one of my two credit cards, unable to remember which one was maxed-out and which one was *almost* maxed-out. With Slade withholding my per diems, the fifteen-hundred bucks High Noon paid would have to keep me going until New York.

"I really don't want to run up anymore debt on this trip." I said, airing my thoughts out loud for the benefit of the lanky, pot-bellied fella behind the counter. The receptionist-cum-mechanic's overalls were covered in grease. An ironic 'joke' badge hanging off a buttonless chest pocket reminded me how people are the same the world over: I remembered the mechanic who did my truck back in Australia having the same badge:

*Mechanics are good with their tools.*

"It's the cheapest car I've got," said the overalled one, pointing to a picture of a small four-door rental car in a faded photocopied brochure; the vehicle he suggested coming under the heading 'SUPER Economy Class'. I turned away, pondering how to escape my predicament of being broke and on the road to nowhere. In the yard outside I spotted an old side-car motorbike. The beat-up rust-bucket was being loaded onto a trailer by what looked to be a clone of the scruffy fella serving me.

"What about that?" I said, half-joking. "You got something else with only three wheels? Maybe I could get another twenty-five percent off?" Car Hire Guy put his hands on his hips proudly.

"Just done my first eBay sale," he said. "Sold that as a 'vintage classic' to some poor sucker in Nashville," he added, scratching his chin and frowning, as the pride quickly vanished from his grease-streaked face. "Costing me more to deliver it than he paid for it, but."

"Does it run?" I asked hopefully.

"Maybe," he said, folding his arms and clicking his tongue. "Probably not."

A short while later I was standing in a dirty men's room next to the car yard, peeling of the last single paper towel from a plastic roll dispenser. I cleaned a little area next to the basin, took off my glasses and placed them down carefully. From my pocket I pulled out my emergency contacts. It was time for Superman to make his first appearance.

The old-style motorcycle goggles, thrown in as a sweetener to make sure I safely delivered the three-wheeled mean machine to its new Nashvillian owner, wouldn't allow for my prescription specs. I needed to wear the contacts, or I couldn't have told a stop sign from a bus-stop. And I knew I'd need all my perceptive abilities for the road ahead, a road I now had to navigate alone.

Looking in the grease-smeared broken mirror, I thought I resembled a bi-plane pilot from World War I. *Red Baron, look out.* I loaded my guitar-case into the side-car and, after confirming the delivery details, bid farewell to the hire-car joker and his enchanted Albuquerque.

On the way out of town I drove through a burger-joint and picked up a root beer. Cherry had given me the taste for American flavors, and I was hooked on something we didn't get back home. An hour or so later I bent over from my driving position to retrieve the container to finish my drink. When I came upright, I found myself—and my three-wheeler—face to face with a Kenworth truck and its eighteen wheels. My contacts almost popped out of my eyes as I just managed to swerve back onto my side of the road, narrowly escaping a head-on I doubt the truck-driver would have even noticed, but one that would have smashed me to smithereens.

Heart racing, I gripped the handle bars with two shaky hands, telling myself to never fucking drink and ride again.

Riding on, car after car and truck after truck overtook me, speeding passed me and my old jalopy as though we were stationary. It wasn't just the eighteen-wheelers that made me feel small. Even the big late-model pick-up trucks dwarfed my bike. I felt like a kid on a tricycle alongside giant coal-mining earth-movers. But I wouldn't be scared off the road or distracted from my destination; I had a bear to buy.

Arriving in Capitan, a tiny town with about half-a-dozen shops and barely one made road, I found the 'Smokey Bear Museum' was right where Google said it would be. Pulling up next to a 'Souvenirs For Sale' sign I turned off the bike and, on Oli's phone again, called Cherry. Getting her message bank, I hung up without saying a word.

*Maybe she just needs some space?*

Inside the museum dedicated to a very famous (if in a previous generation) fire-protection mascot, the drop-dead gorgeous redhead behind the counter immediately started giving me the eye. 'Daisy', as her name tag announced to the world wandering through, battered her eyelashes and puffed her chest as though she was getting over-filled with air from an invisible pump. With bee-stung lips, and a revealing tied-off denim halter-top, Daisy was next to impossible to ignore. But I wasn't interested.

"You happy browsing, or can I take you out the back and show you our special items?" said Daisy.

"I am looking for something special," I said, careful not to sound interested in Daisy's 'special items'. "But I think I can find it out here." Despite my neutral tone Daisy's eyes lit up. She moved from behind the counter as I pointed to the shelf. "That's it," I said. "That's exactly what I want."

Daisy's smile dropped as she watched me pick out a koala sized 'Smokey The Bear' soft toy. "Perfect," I said. "How much?"

"Twenty-five dollars," said Daisy, with a sorry air of resignation I wouldn't be taking any special storeroom tour. "For an extra five you can have the shovel." She held up a pen-sized shovel.

"Great," I said. "I'll take them both."

Back on the road, the sun was already starting to set when I decided to take a pit-stop at a derelict gas station to stretch my legs. The rusted out pick-up out front—a bombed-out car that had caught my imagination from the road—looked like an old Chevy. I took out my guitar and, perching myself on the rusty bonnet of an American classic, strummed a few chords. Nearby, cars zoomed passed sporadically, but I noticed them less and less the more I concentrated on writing my latest country ditty. In the middle of the day's journey to my next destination, part of me was still stuck in the past. Part of me was back in Albuquerque trying to figure out what went wrong with Cherry.

*When you left me in Albuquerque*
*I went on alone*
*Not knowing where the road would take me*
*Or where my heart would roam*
*It was heavy with the weight*
*Of all that I'd done wrong*
*I knew you could not take*
*One more wrong turn on—the road*

Just as I was deep in lyrical contemplation about what I might have done to piss Cherry off, a car pulled up and broke that moment with a new one. A kind-looking mother jumped out from the driver's seat and opened the door for her young son. The boy ran behind an abandoned building—I thought perhaps once a roadside deli?—turning back to make sure his mother was watching, to make sure it was safe for him to go where he was going. The mother glanced over at me, the three-wheeled biker making music in the middle of nowhere. She smiled: clearly I was no threat to her or her boy.

Satisfied my impromptu writing session was finished, I packed up my guitar and piled it and me into and on Bob, as I'd decided to call my motorcycle of much character. As I kick-started my ride (Bob was even older than I'd thought!) the boy ran back to his mother, who gave him a big kiss and a pat on the back into their car.

*Happy families,* I thought.

Not long after the ghost-gas-station scene, I was driving through the town of Roswell—home to alien abductions, UFO thrift stores, and other unexplained phenomenon, when I spotted a father and son walking out of an *Alien Costume Shoppe.* The boy appeared upset—maybe having been scared by one of the one-eyed hairy monsters in the shop window—and his father was hurriedly leading him back to their car. Before the boy climbed in he reached to his father for a hug, the boy getting the reassurance he so badly needed that everything would be okay, that the aliens and monsters weren't following them.

Pulling up at a red light my mind drifted back over these two vignettes of parents watching over their children. I thought about Hank back home in Australia. I thought about his heart problems, both physical and emotional; I thought about calling him when I checked into wherever I was going to check into for the night. Suddenly a loud car horn startled me from behind. A bunch of urban cowgirls honked and hollered, alerting me to the now-green light in front of me. I raised my hand to acknowledge them, then put it back on the throttle. But even giving it everything Bob had, there was something slightly pathetic about how slowly I left the impatient local girls of Roswell behind.

A Harley Davidson Bob was not.

Eventually I made it to the last stop for the day in Amarillo, where, lying on the bed of my cheap hotel room, I thought about maybe calling Cherry or Hank—or both— before deciding I was too tired to make much sense for either of them.

Not wanting to fall asleep in my clothes, I forced myself up to unpack some of my stuff, as I did, briefly pausing to look at my photo of Mum.

To my little Pipsqueak, with all my love, your guiding star, Ma xxx.

And then, even though I fell asleep thinking about Cherry, and how much I realized she meant to me, that night I dreamt of Pipsqueak riding in the front carriage of an old wooden roller-coaster, alone except for the presence of an unmistakable silhouette.

Elvis was on the roller-coaster too, right there up front, both of us pointing to the big dip quickly approaching.

It looked like a doozy.

# CADILLAC RANCH

A row of randomly-painted Cadillacs stood upright, half-buried in the Texas soil. The Amarillo art installation, dog-eared and highlighted in a tour-guide Cherry had left behind in Albuquerque, comprised of ten classic American cars covered in colorful graffiti so layered I could hardly make out a single word.

'Love'? 'Peace'?

Apart from a few lovers' names enclosed in odd-shaped love hearts (which I got the feeling had been sprayed by drunken locals—rather than tourists on the road like me) nothing clear stood out from the otherwise haphazard bright splashes of yellow, red and orange covering each rusty relic. The Amarillo Cadillac Ranch was a mess of paint and rust, all the more striking for being in the middle of a wide, open field, a field I had all to myself.

Starting at the first car, I walked slowly down the line, bending over to pick up a complimentary can of red spray paint, one of many scattered on the ground by the keepers of Cadillac Ranch. Contemplating where to leave my mark, I realized I had two more pressing questions on my mind: *Was Elvis really my father? Why had Cherry left me?*

I hoped to have at least one answer after making a phone call.

"Hello, Cherry? It's me, Angus." With one hand on the phone, I shook the can of red paint, the ball-bearing inside making a clickety-click rhythm. "Are you okay to talk right now?" I said.

"Sure," said Cherry. "Sorry I haven't returned your message yet. I was going to."

"Oh good," I said, with a tinge of sarcasm. "I was starting to worry maybe you clearing out of Albuquerque without explaining why was a bad sign," I added. "I mean I thought we had some something…kind of…I don't know? Special?"

"I thought that too," said Cherry sweetly, before trailing off. "I thought…"

"What is it? What was so urgent you had to go without saying goodbye?"

"I had to come back to LA, Angus. But maybe it's good I did. I think I thought you were more serious about me than you obviously are, Angus," said Cherry. "I mean, until I saw you with those girls," she added. Her tone turning aggressive. "I *saw* you with those girls, Angus!"

"What girls?" I said. "What are you talking about?"

"Anyway," said Cherry, ignoring my questions, "I left you a note."

"Yeah, thanks," I said. "I got that. But why didn't you talk to me before you left?"

"I guess I was more upset than I realized," said Cherry, "watching you flirting like some lizard king with those *groupies*."

"Flirting? Me? No, I wasn't."

"Yes, you were. After your Pipsqueak show. I came to meet you backstage and you were already very busy."

"Was I?"

"Yes. Very."

"I didn't think I was flirting, Cherry. It wasn't intentional if I was. I'd just put on the best show of my life, and I was actually just looking forward to sharing some of the glory with you." Cherry didn't respond. I hoped she was still listening. I softened my approach. "I'm really sorry if I upset you—by anything I did. I'd just been so worked up and nervous about performing my own stuff." Testing my graffiti talent, I sprayed a big 'X' on the hood of a vertical Cadillac. "Plus, I don't know, I was probably acting out after being fucked around by Slade."

"Let's try not to talk about Slade for one day, okay?" Cherry said angrily.

"Are you sure you don't have feelings for him anymore? I mean you get pretty upset talking about him."

"Seriously. Slade is a *dick*. I didn't come back here to see him—if that's what you're worried about—or even to get away from you, Angus. I came back here for my grandmother."

"Really? What's wrong?"

"She had a bad turn. I'm at an elderly nursing home in Pasadena. I visit with a few of the other oldies here too, coming in and reading and sharing stories about my adventures on the outside. That's why I buy so many souvenirs. It makes those who can't get out anymore feel like they're seeing the world with me."

*Cherry's grandmother is sick and she's volunteering at an old person's home?* How stupid did I feel? I didn't really think she'd gone running back to Slade, but having not known what had sent her away, in the last couple of days I'd more than once imagined the worst.

"You're a very special person, Cherry," I said. "Is your grandmother alright? Was there an emergency or something?"

"Every day there's an emergency when you're as old as she is. But she's a strong one."

"Well, I guess you won't be meeting us all in Nashville," I said. "As much as I'd love it if you could, obviously I understand you have to be with your grandmother right now."

"Yeah. I think it's best if I stay here. Mum hasn't been able to make it yet and I'm the only family she has here right now."

"Fair enough."

"Anyway, what about Memphis?" asked Cherry, more chirpily. "Aren't you going to Memphis before Nashville?"

"Yeah, another Hank Flynn Junior spectacular," I said sarcastically, adding a red sprayed 'X' to my chosen Caddy. "I can't wait to play for more record executives."

"Have you been writing some more too?"

"Yeah, I have. *When You Left Me In Albuquerque* is the name of my latest heartbreaker hit."

"Glad me leaving is working out so well for you," said Cherry, the smile in her voice reassuring me we were on much better terms now. "Is it another ballad?"

"Yeah. Mid-tempo country."

"You're speeding up, hey?"

"What do you mean?"

"Most of the songs you've played me have been slow. Have you ever written something a little, I don't know, rockier? Might be a good contrast with the rest of your stuff."

"Up-tempo's not really my thing. But, yeah, maybe you're right? Maybe I need one pop-rock bundle of catchy riffs to catch the ear of the world."

"That's a big ear!"

"Should see the cotton bud goes in it." We laughed as I shook the spray can and finished my last graffitied letter.

"Good luck with your gigs," said Cherry. "I better go now, Angus. I'll speak to you soon. Okay?"

"Okay." Cherry hung up before me and I realized I wasn't ready to let her go. Not from the phone call or my life.

Standing back from the Cadillac I'd chosen to leave my unique mark on, I took a picture with Oli's phone of my spray-can handiwork. No doubt, soon enough, someone else would be along to paint over my romantic marker, but for that brief moment in time at least, I'd made the surreal Texan art installation all mine. And Cherry's.

Walking back to my scrappy side-car motorbike, parked by the side of the highway, I checked Oli's phone to make sure the photo I'd taken had my tag in focus.

'ANGUS LOVES CHERRY XXX'

*Perfect.*

# DEAD MAN WALKING

Driving on a rusty side-car motorbike, wearing an open-faced helmet and old-school goggles, isn't how I'd ever imagined I'd one day cross the great Mississippi river, headed for my birthplace. But that's how I did it. And I was glad Bob—my old three-wheeled bucket—didn't fall to bits. Though it sounded as if he may have at any moment.

The rack-rack, clank-clank noise Bob made crossing the bridge had me thinking the side-car part of my junk jalopy was going to detach, take a detour off the bridge into the drink, and drown my guitar in the same river that claimed one of my favorite singer-songwriters, Jeff Buckley. Luckily, bargain vehicle Bob miraculously held together long enough to carry me from Louisiana over the border, and further still into Mississippi, as I continued following the blues trail north, en route to, firstly, Tupelo, the birthplace of Elvis Presley, and then Memphis, his spiritual home, and the town where I was born.

But would I make it? I may have been closer than ever before to returning to my childhood hometown, but without a working fuel gauge on old Bob I could have run out of gas at any moment. Not knowing how many more miles I had before I needed to refill, and to avoid the possibility of being stranded in Texas, Louisiana, or any of the other sprawling states of the United America, I'd gotten into the habit of pulling into a gas station about every hundred miles or so, or every couple of hours. Maybe it was overkill, but better to be safe than stranded. And besides, I liked checking out the locals and eavesdropping on the sing-song of the southern dialects.

On my way in to pay at my latest fuel stop, I noticed an old black man sitting outside on a rickety bench. The perfect image he presented to me of all I'd imagined about the home of the Delta Blues made me smile; his slide-blues acoustic-guitar playing the perfect background music for such a setting. After paying, and as I made my way down the stairs of the service area back to Bob, I heard a deep and resonant voice address me from behind.

"You not from around here?" I stopped and turned, making sure the old man was talking to me. "Riding on that old jalopy ,you can't be a local, boy," he said with a grin. I noticed, as his sentences got longer, the sonic boom of his voice got louder, heavier—big. "Youngsters 'round here'd eat you alive if you turned up to a gig on board such a...modest...mode of...trans...por...tation."

The old man was pretty much bald except for a patch of grey on the back of his head, a patch I watched him slowly run his hand over. It was warm outside—not hot, but the old guy had been cookin' up a storm and he threw off the sweat with a flick of his wrist. He raised his head and greeted me with his eyes closed tight.

"It's getting me where I'm going," I said, pointing to Bob. "But you're right—I'm not from around here. Well, I sort of am. I was born in Memphis but I grew up in Australia. Did my noisy three-wheeler really give me away, though?" The old guy smiled.

"Yes, it did. Plus I heard you chattin' inside when y'all was payin' for your gas. You sound like that Hank Flynn cat's son. The boy who's headed to Nashville to play his daddy's hit song. I heard you on the radio, didn't I?"

"If you're talking about the Top Two country classic DJs' show then yeah, I guess you did hear me. Didn't think they'd broadcast out this far?"

"There ain't too many hills 'round these parts. Radio waves travel pretty far on the open plains. Far enough for me to hear you braggin' 'bout your groupies n' all anyway, weren't ya?"

"Something like that."

"Those fellas are a coupla rednecks," he said, shaking his head and rubbing his closed eyes, "but now and then they play alright stuff. I still listen to the radio, you see. Not much for the computer, or surfing on the interweb, me. Still like my music AM'n scratchy." He put his ear to his fretboard and I watched him tune a few strings. It was then I realized why the old guy could hear so much, so well: he was blind.

*The Blind Blues Man of Mississippi?* I'd walked into a book—maybe a movie—featuring a character every muso dreams of meeting. I was intrigued to find out what my mentor's gift would be; what pearl of wisdom I would now discover at this roadside gas station surrounded by cotton fields, and with the raging Mississippi river and her many muses so close by.

"So, it's true," I said. The old man put his guitar back into playing position but strummed nothing. "It's true what they say?"

"What do they say, boy?"

"You know, how when you lose one sense your others get stronger."

"And what did I *lose*, boy?"

"You know—your sight. You're blind, aren't you?" Old man river nodded.

"I *am* blind but I did not *lose* my sight. You can-not lose what you nev-er had, boy."

"I'm sorry," I said. "I shouldn't have presumed."

"That's right—you shouldn't have. But no harm. Maybe y'all learn something though?" Here it comes—the reason for my broken fuel gauge, the reason I was destined to be alone on the road.

"Maybe I will," I said. "I *would* love to learn that tuning you've got going on there. Sounds wild."

"And it will not be tamed. But I will happily share my hard-earned knowledge—when it comes to coaxing steel strings into singing sweet sounds—of what works and why. Pull up a crate."

Sitting down on a wooden box with faded apples painted on the side, I wasn't sure if I'd fallen under a spell or was willing one upon myself. Did I simply wish this amazing character to be a shaman or crossroad magician—or was he the real thing? Was my head getting in the way of a true revelation coming my way? Or was my heart opening to a change?

"So, you've heard of my father, hey?" I said, showing I was listening. "I didn't think Hank's brand of country was so popular around these parts?"

"I have, and it's not. But we hear it, boy. Like I said, I still listen to the radio and, as such, I can't control everything they throw at me—only what I refuse to catch. See sometimes I can't be bothered to get up and turn off the wireless, so I end up discovering something I might not have otherwise. A lot of what you hear in life, you ain't gonna like. But you hear it. Life is funny like that."

"I guess. But you can't unhear it either, can you? What happens when you don't like what you hear? If you don't get up to change the station, sometimes you end up with a terrible song stuck in your head. And life's too short for bad music?"

"You're right," he chuckled. "Life is short—for some.

That's why you've got to keep your compassion—for everyone, even people who make bad music and stick it in your head. They don't know any better. Bad music-makers is just people who don't trust themselves, they don't sing and play from here." The old man touched his heart. "And they worry too much what other folk think. You can hear it when someone is tryin' too hard to please another or imitate another. Sounds God-awful—no spirit, see. They think doin' what everyone famous has done before 'em is gonna get *them* famous too. But they're just scared. Too scared to stand up for anything, they *follow* everything—from the latest trend to the latest religion." I nodded, not completely sure I was getting it.

"What do you mean? I'm not sure I understand."

"The only thing kids worship these days is fame. And the desperate need for fame always comes from the same place. All comes from fear. But I ain't got no time for fear. Always lived my life like a dead man walking and I will 'til I meet my maker. Came into this world with nothin' and I'll leave with nothin'. Only way to live while I'm here is to remember I'm gonna die one day and I don't know when. Might as well sing my own song 'til then."

"I think I know what you mean," I said. "Material things don't matter as much as being true to yourself. Is that what you mean?"

"Stuff don't matter at all!" he said loudly, like a preacher in full flight. "Some folk get angry for what they ain't got or what they think they lost—or for what they think got stolen from 'em." I shrugged and nodded, forgetting I was *showing* I understood to a blind man. "It's like how lots of my kin got no time for your daddy's friend Elvis cause they think he stole all our music and mosta' our moves."

"Don't black people like Elvis?" I asked.

"Some do. Most don't. Guess it's easier to play the

victim than to get busy taking care of yourself."

"I guess," I said, though again not sure I got his drift.

"Anyway, don't matter. Elvis is long gone now. On top of that, who wants to be famous for havin' sung to a hound-dog—on national television too!" I laughed as the old man slipped a brass slide onto his ring finger. "Show business is a fool's game."

"You're tellin' me," I said. The old man stopped smiling.

"Yeah, but are you listening?" He began to play again. I was sure my next encounter would be with the Devil himself, some shapeshifter waiting for me at the next crossroads with a question for my soul:

*Which way you headed, boy? 'Fame and Fortune' or 'Infamy and Pauperdom'?* But now, I was pretty sure I had my answer ready. I knew where I was going and what I was going to do; if I was Doris White's sign in Vegas, then this old guy in Mississippi was mine.

I thanked the old man and happily bought him a beer before I left, thinking how you never know how one person can change the course of your whole life.

By the time I made it to Tupelo, and to the rebuilt shotgun shack birthplace of the Elvis tourist attraction, it was dark and well past visiting hours. The replica of the house Elvis was born in, and grew up in until his family moved to Memphis, was aglow with warm light in the cool night.

*This was where the King was born.*

Though I was still many miles from my own birthplace of the Memphis Hospital I felt like I was finally home too. Thinking how I was likely looking at my birth father's home, I was sure I was exactly where I belonged.

When I was satisfied the security car had done the final run around the shack, church and museum which made up the whole attraction, I emerged from the shadows, climbing off Bob and heading first to a garden area where a life-size bronze statue of Elvis as a young teenager was the dramatically lit centerpiece. Lights from all around the circumference aimed in giving Elvis an otherworldly luminescence. I was glad I'd come at night. There wasn't another soul except me there.

Before going to check out the shack, I headed back to Bob and pulled out my guitar. Since it looked like nobody was going to bother me, and nobody could hear, I headed over to sit on the porch and see what might happen.

*Would the muse come?*

For a while I tried playing my guitar on the swing chair, doing a version of *The Lonely Morning Light*. But I soon found out it was kind of hard to play *and* swing. Next, I found another spot sitting at the top of the wooden stairs where I could lean against a banister, and catch a glimpse of the full moon. It was more comfortable there, with plenty of natural light on the blank page in front of me. At the top of the page I wrote the name of a new song, the lyrics I'd been forming in my head and a melody I'd been humming since last filling up with gas:

'Dead Man Walking'

The old man had inspired me.

*Crossed the path of a bluesman*
*Sat down on his own*
*Said son, you can choose*
*But one of these roads*
*At your final call*
*Will each word ring true*
*You might have it all*
*Without love, what's the use?*
*So live each day like a dead man walking*
*And life won't be a prison for you*

Ten minutes later I had a whole song down and another one coming. At the rate I was going by sunrise I thought I'd have a hundred. As it turned out though, I only wrote one more song that night. A song about someone I'd always loved but was only really just getting to know on this trip. A song called: 'The King'.

And I was pretty sure it was the best song I'd ever written. Though I wasn't sure I'd come up with it all by myself.

Maybe I'd had some help?

# GRACELAND

The morning after visiting Elvis's birthplace shrine I continued on my pilgrimage to his final home: *Graceland.*

Not wanting to leave my guitar in the open side-car while taking the tour of Memphis's most famous mansion, I carried it with me. With my old-fashioned pilot goggles hanging around my neck, and my black cowboy boots dusty from the open road, no doubt I appeared like either a homeless fan or maybe some crazy crop-duster eager to jam with the ghost of Elvis. Possibly even both.

Standing on the bottom of the stairs of the surprisingly modest-sized stately home, lyrics from my latest song, 'The King', about how Elvis loved going out in public and pretending he was someone else, came into my mind.

> *He walked the streets of Memphis*
> *With just this here guitar in his hand*
> *People stopped him said, "I know your face."*
> *"No Sir, that is some other man."*

I couldn't believe it had taken me so long to get to Graceland. I was so giddy there was no denying it to myself anymore: I'd loved Elvis long before knowing anything about our possible blood connection; whatever else I may have been to Elvis, I was first and foremost a fan.

*He made his name by singing*
*Love and pain, rock and roll*
*And they took all of his possessions*
*Thank God they could not take his soul*

I'd grown up watching his movies on television almost every weekend, and enjoying his music on CD, vinyl and cassette (in private mostly; Hank often got jealous when I played Elvis records more than his).

*He met some pretty ladies*
*He would give them all the time*
*Oh, man he got so busy*
*Oh, man he surely did not mind*

What's more, I'd long admired Elvis for one of the same reasons I looked up to Hank: they'd both made music their lives: something I'd only ever dreamed of doing.

*What have I done with my life?* I thought.

And what had taken me so long to make this journey to my roots, a trip filling me with inspiration at every turn? I could have come to America years ago instead of schlepping around from one tropical backpacker's to the next Eurotrash pub in search of a quick good time. The only thing I'd taken away from all my bacheloring around was my friendship with Oli. And, as close as I was to him, I doubted we'd ever get married!

And why was I suddenly thinking about getting married?

As someone who'd never committed to anything more than a head guitar-tech position on a three-month tour, how could I even begin to think of settling down? What did I have to offer anyone? Unlike Elvis and Hank, my two main male role models, I'd never put my heart into anything or anyone. And it showed. I had virtually no money, maybe soon no home, and no idea what was happening with Cherry.

As the rest of my small tour group disappeared inside ahead of me, I was momentarily left by myself outside. For a second or two I enjoyed the solitude, imagining what Graceland was like when Elvis first moved in. A tap on my shoulder startled me out of my reverential trance.

"Didn't think I'd let you beat me to it, did you?" An unseen female planted a kiss on my cheek and ran up the stairs ahead of me. "No way!" At the doorway she turned, pointing to her eyes then mine. "I like the new look, Superman. Clark Kent couldn't make it, hey?" It's the first time she'd seen me without my prescription glasses but my contacts were working fine: Cherry looked beautiful.

"I thought you were in LA?" I said, bounding up the stairs after her.

"They're called planes, Angus. I took one after finding out from Oli where you'd be today."

"How did he know?"

"He's got a copy of your itinerary and told me your gig here in Memphis is tonight. I figured if you didn't come here to Graceland today you'd have missed it. And I knew you wouldn't miss this. Not for anything." Face to face in the doorway, I gave her a quick kiss and we shuffled in together.

"I'm so glad you're here," I said, gesturing around the hall and open living rooms. "Isn't this *fantastic*?" From behind a security rope, cordoning off the lounge room, a uniformed tour-guide—a black woman with her hair pinned back—stepped forward. It was none other than former Las Vegas show-girl, Doris White.

"It's a living," said Doris, her go-go-girl wrangler persona's sass transplanted perfectly to her new role. "Welcome to the home of the King," she said with feigned regality. "Memphis's own Elvis Aaron Presley." A few tourists applauded. Most were already too enraptured by Pretzel memorabilia—a state-of-the-art 1950s television; a six-foot tall '60s table lamp—to bother listening to Doris's official tour script.

"Doris!" I said. "What are you doing here?"

"Told you, boy. You were my sign to get back home. I'm all done with Vegas. I'm gonna see out my working years sittin' on that comfy chair right there." Doris pointed to an exotic looking recliner with an 'Elvis sat here' sign on it. "Hey listen, you guys fancy a private tour?" Cherry put her arm around my waist and squeezed, indicating her excited approval.

"Sure," I said, side-hugging Cherry right back. "Who wouldn't?"

Minutes later, the three of us were looking at the Graceland mansion from the furthest corner of the property. Doris had brought us to where the horses roamed free on a few green acres normally off limits to the general public. The Graceland mansion looked even smaller from so far away; from where we were it looked like a dollhouse.

"The last time I saw your mother, Angus, I dropped her off here at Graceland, at the front gate. April had something belonging to Elvis and wanted to give it back." It seemed our isolation was no accident; Doris had wanted the extra privacy for what she had to tell me.

"What was it?" asked Cherry, immediately fascinated with Doris's story. "What was it Angus's mum had that belonged to Elvis?"

"The night before," Doris continued, relishing in her ability to build the suspense, "on his last 'public' appearance, Elvis hired a local fun park called Libertyland, for him and some friends to have…well, fun at."

"That was his favorite amusement park, wasn't it?" said Cherry.

"Yes, it was. And while he was riding his favorite roller-coaster his belt buckle came loose and fell off."

"The 'Zippin Pippin'?" I said. "That was his favorite ride, right?" Doris nodded. Cherry raised her eyebrows, a detective with a clue.

"*Pippin* hey?" said Cherry knowingly. "Just like your middle name, Angus?"

"Look at this," said Doris, pulling out a photo from an envelope in her purse. Without a frame protecting it the colors had faded, and it was weathered and torn, but the happy couple standing in the front of the old wooden roller-coaster were instantly recognizable.

"That's Mum and—Elvis?" I said. "That is Mum cuddled up to Elvis, isn't it?"

"The one and only," said Doris. "You can have this. I've got others." As Doris handed me the picture, Cherry took it for a closer look.

"Was this taken on Elvis's last night out?"

"It surely was," said Doris. "And on his last ride on that roller-coaster—on the last ride of his *life*—somehow Elvis, as I said, lost his best big old buckle. But later, without telling him, your mother went back and found it. When I picked her up, April told me she'd hunted for about two hours after everyone else had gone home."

"What a great story," said Cherry. Doris nodded and smiled mysteriously. *There's more.*

"After Angus asked me about his Mum and Elvis and whether Elvis could be his real father or not, I remembered

212

it. You see, Angus, April didn't ask me to wait to take her home the night I dropped her off. Your Mum stayed that night here at Graceland—alone with Elvis."

"It doesn't prove anything," I said. "Does it?" Doris seemed to think it did.

"Angus, your mother was almost nine months pregnant. Elvis died ten days later. And what's more, the night April gave Elvis his buckle back wasn't the only one she'd spent at Graceland. When you were born your Mum was basically living with him!" It felt like something in my gut kicked my heart. My eyes popped wide open. For the first time I didn't have any doubt. It was true.

*Elvis was my father.*

But what could I say? I had nothing. Doris had more.

"April told me if you ever came back digging around for the truth, I should give you this." Doris took a diamond-encrusted sparkling buckle from her purse and handed it to me. "Elvis gave it back to her. It's the buckle Elvis lost and your mum found." Three letters, TCB—the same as on the 'Taking Care of Business' ring Roy had given me—were flanked by two gold lightning bolts. It was heavy too. And not just with physical weight; I felt like I'd been struck by both those bolts of lightning.

"Did Dad know?" I said. "I mean, did *Hank* know? And if he did why didn't he tell me?"

"It's not so cut and dry," said Doris. "April may have shacked up with Pretzel for a while but she really loved Hank. He'd been away on tour and…well, I guess your Mum just got lonely."

Slowly I drifted off, away from my hardline questioning, imagining what it would have been like to grow up at Graceland. Bizarrely, an image of me as a kid, playing with Lisa Marie on the shag-pile carpet in the Jungle Room, seemed as vivid as a memory. I don't know if Hank ever brought me to Graceland before we moved to Australia but in that moment I swear I'd been there before. Home.

My phone rang. I jumped. Jolted out of my fantasy land, I shook my head and answered. It was Slade telling me to get my ass over to the hotel where I was due to rehearse. I told him I was busy and hung up. Then, when it was clear Doris had nothing more to say, I called a taxi for Cherry and explained to her that, since I would have to ride there on Bob, I'd meet her at our next destination. Despite the bombshell Doris had just dropped, and before heading to rehearsal, I had one other must-see on my Memphis list of attractions.

An hour later Cherry and I were collecting our tickets for the official tour of Sun Studios: where rock n' roll was born.

"So what are you going to do, Angus?" asked Cherry. "Are you going to call up Lisa Marie with the good news? I'm sure she'd love to know she has a half-brother. She seems lovely from everything I've read."

"I don't think so. It's not something I'm going to burden anyone else with. How many wackos must she have had to put up with in her strange life already?"

"Michael Jackson wasn't that weird," said Cherry with an ironic smile. "Now, Nicolas Cage on the other hand…"

"Exactly. That girl has had enough life drama already." Cherry looked surprised.

"Really?" she said. I shrugged and stepped forward to join our next tour group.

"It wouldn't change anything," I said.

Walking into the main studio, I was immediately overwhelmed by the same sense of belonging I'd felt at the Tupelo shack, and then at Graceland. The guide told us to look around a bit while we waited for any latecomers. Cherry stood behind a '50s microphone and I took a pic of her with it on her phone. She pulled an Elvis pose under a picture of Elvis recording in the very same studio.

"I don't know why Dad never told me any of this though," I said.

"Are you kidding?" said Cherry. "How hard must it be for him? How hard must it be to raise a child that you know isn't yours? Well, genetically at least."

"Yeah, but whatever happened—however I got here—nothing changes the fact Hank brought me up. And he never tried to cash in on me either. Imagine what I'd be worth—how Hank could have benefitted financially if he'd made a song and dance about it by making my paternity public." A rockabilly engineer brought in a vintage Fender amp and started setting it up. Cherry gave me a nudge. She pointed to his name badge, *Sun Studio: BILLY.*

"Do they still do recordings here?" asked Cherry.

"Yep," Billy answered, a little reluctantly. Cherry and I shared a look, *maybe he wasn't supposed to talk to the tourists?* "We're setting up for Gil Teaman." Billy added, rolling his eyes and taking a seriously sarcastic tone. "Can't wait. I love working with egomaniac soft-cock country 'superstars'." We nodded as he unwound a guitar lead. "We're a fuckin' *rock n' roll* studio for God's sake. Damn Nashville cats think they own the world."

"Wow!" said Cherry, turning to me. "This studio still does recordings! Imagine recording Pipsqueak's debut album here, in the same studio Elvis made *his* first records?"

"Don't know how that's going to happen," I said. "I'll just be happy if Slade keeps his end of the deal and pays me enough to save Flynn Station. I think it's gonna be a long time before I can afford to launch my own music."

"Once you're finished doing this tour you can do whatever you want," said Cherry. "Maybe you could get a record company interested in your demos and they can pay for you to record here?"

"Do record companies sign up thirty-something debutantes? I don't think so. Not unless you've been on a reality show or won American Idol. Besides those demos still need a lot of work," I added, shaking my head. "Look, I don't even want to think about recording my own stuff right now."

Cherry gave me a comforting hug and a gentle kiss on the cheek. I felt the tension in my body relax a little, but was still pretty wired up. She took her phone from me and handed me the retro microphone, indicating it was my turn for a photo op.

"Well, one day maybe you will record your stuff—somewhere," she said. "I'm sure it would make BOTH your dads proud if you had your own album." Billy the engineer gave us a strange look then headed off for more gear. The tour guide gathered the group and began his well-practiced patter.

"Welcome to Sun Studios, the legendary home of Elvis Presley's first ever recordings." Cherry leaned in to whisper in my ear.

"One day he'll have to add 'and the place where Angus Flynn recorded his chart-topping debut!'"

I nodded and forced a smile. But I didn't think the tour-guide would ever have to revise his script. At least not for me.

# SO

**M**emphis seemed blacker than I'd remembered. Perhaps because I'd lived in a predominately white suburb before I'd left, and at such an impressionable age.

But although it was true I hadn't seen one white person working as a tour guide or sales assistant at Graceland, not all of the black Memphians Cherry and I encountered were working class. Riding the lift in the famous Peabody Hotel, a bejewelled black woman stood very proudly, happily admiring her mink coat in the lift's mirror; like many western cities around the globe, Memphis was one of contrast: rich and poor, happy and sad, black and white.

Back at our room, and after our showers, I stood in front of a full-length mirror checking my Hank Flynn Junior reflection. Cherry, still wrapped in a towel, was in the middle of putting her make-up on for that night's warm-up showcase, when she took a break and came up behind me.

"You're in the home straight now," said Cherry buoyantly. "Only three more Hank Flynn tribute gigs and you'll be all done with Junior and can get busy launching Pipsqueak." I adjusted my mirror glasses and loosened the tight knot holding the red bandana around my neck.

"I can't wait to finish," I said. "This thing gives me a headache. And as much as I love Hank's songs…well, they're not mine. And this look ain't mine either." Cherry moved in front of me and took off my prop glasses.

"You've got your contacts on?" she said, surprised. "I thought you liked it blurry? So you're not so intimidated by the audience?"

"I guess I'm getting more comfortable on stage. Maybe, in an odd way, wearing this get-up has helped me…it's a costume, isn't it? A mask between the real Angus and the rest of the world." Cherry nodded.

"Try this," she said. Cherry took the red bandana off, opened it out, and folded it into a wrist-tie she wrapped around my wrist. I put my hands underneath Cherry's dressing gown and on her hips.

"What's that?" I said "Is that how the kids wear 'em these days?"

"Some of them."

"It's better than around my head, at least." Cherry put her hands on my hips too.

"Just be patient, Angus. A few more shows in daddy dress-up and you'll have all the money you need to save your home."

"You sure you're ready for this?" I asked Cherry, changing the subject.

"Had to happen sooner or later," she said.

"Maybe it'll be fun?" I said. But Cherry's look suggested what we'd decided to do together before the show would be anything but. Still, it had to be done.

Minutes later, emerging from the lift, Cherry and I arrived on the top floor of the Peabody Hotel where the ballroom was in full swing. The back-patting, slapping and power-hand shakes of a roomful of musicians rubbing shoulders with music executives reminded me of all I detested about the music industry; if great music required sincerity and simplicity it seemed the business side thrived on falseness and pretensions.

I wanted to get out of there straight away. But I couldn't. The night before the Country Music Awards in Nashville, local and out-of-state record companies had come from everywhere to showcase new acts and new recordings in Memphis. And I was Slade's number one act.

Looking for a break from the stiff air already, Cherry and I took a brief walk outside onto a rooftop balcony where the famous Peabody ducks lived—in between their hotel lobby red-carpet appearances. After checking out the great view over the Mississippi river, we wandered back inside where we prepared to face the dragon.

From the other side of the room, as if sensing our presence, Slade emerged from a pack of sycophantic suits, his face dropping any trace of the smug top dog when he saw Cherry on my arm.

"Are you ready?" I asked her.

"Bring it on," she said. "Maybe he'll finally stop calling me." As Slade marched directly to us, we held our ground, even finding time for a quick kiss; I realized I was kind of enjoying the fact that until then Slade had had no idea about Cherry and me.

"You're fucking kidding?" barked Slade. "You two? Together? I don't believe it." He looked madder than a freshly castrated bull, and just as likely to charge.

"You don't have to *believe* it, Slade," said Cherry. "But it's true. It was Angus's idea to tell you but I told him there was no need. We don't owe you any explanation."

"You couldn't *explain* it," said Slade angrily. "You and…*that!*" He pointed to me, I assumed in an attempt to draw attention to how ridiculous I looked, resplendent in my outlaw costume.

"I thought it best you know, Slade," I said with a smile. "Cherry doesn't want you calling her anymore. Okay?" Slade turned to face—or maybe punch—me. Cherry stepped forward between us.

"We didn't have to tell you anything, Brian—*Slade*," she said. "You and I were over a long time ago." Slade turned to Cherry.

"Is that so?"

"Yes."

"So, when I asked you to video Angus's performance at the Elvis festival we were 'over', is that right?"

"Yes it is. I went to Australia to get away from you," said Cherry. "I couldn't believe you followed me out there either, but when you called and said you couldn't get to Parkes in time to see the act, I agreed to go because it sounded like something fun for me to do in Australia. I didn't even know about the Elvis festival until you told me about it. But I'm glad I went. It *was* fun."

"What are you talking about?" I asked Cherry. "You were at Parkes—and working for Slade—before we met?"

"Yes, I was at Parkes, but no, I wasn't working for Slade, Angus." Cherry looked upset with me but I was sure it was my right to be upset with her.

"How come you never told me that?" I said.

"Told you what?"

"That you watched me perform that day."

"I didn't know it was you, Angus. When I met you at the airport you didn't look anything like Hank Flynn Junior. You weren't dressed like you are now, then."

"But afterwards you must have figured out," offered Slade. Cherry and I both turned to him.

"We can sort this out without you," said Cherry.

"Yes, we can," I added.

"And not here," said Cherry, still eyeballing Slade. "I don't want any more of your bullshit." Cherry turned to me. "Angus—I'm sorry but I can't stay in this room for one second longer, not with him." Slade opened his palms to his sides like a pickpocket claiming innocence. "I'll tell you anything you want to know about what I was doing when we met, Angus, after your show." She kissed me on the cheek and stormed off. Slade and I watched Cherry leave, him stepping into my line of sight just before she disappeared into the lift.

"You're takin' this outlaw country shit too seriously, Angus," said Slade menacingly. "Just because you think you look bad doesn't mean you scare me. Mirror sunglasses or not. Remember, I'm the one who can make you or *break* you."

"And I'm the one who can keep this 'outlaw country shit' alive—or kill it," I said. "Now, I may not be the original 'Killer' but don't push me too far, Slade. You may know the law but you don't seem to know people at all." Slade laughed.

"Unlike you? You really know people, hey? He who had no idea his little Cherry—his little groupie from California—has been working for me all this time. You think you know people so well but you didn't even know Cherry was in the audience at your very first gig in Parkes. That's a pretty juicy piece of information she obviously hasn't bothered to let you in on."

"I'm not listening to you, Slade. You're just trying to make trouble between Cherry and me. I'm going to do my song tonight then I'll see you in Nashville. After that it's just one gig in New York and we're done, right?"

"Just tonight, Nashville and New York. Then you're finished."

"And then you can find someone else to play dress-up for you."

"There's plenty will," said Slade. "You're not the only offspring of a 'legend' I've got feeding in my stable."

"Well, enjoy the ride. For now. It's not going to last forever." Walking to the stage to tune my guitar, I heard Slade behind me, forever with the last word.

"Oh, I know, *Junior*. I know it won't last forever."

After checking my guitar, and making a little small talk with my band, I tried to join in with the party, schmoozing with the executives as best I could. Maybe Cherry was right? Maybe I needed to be making my own contacts, finding someone who'd listen to my demos?

But I couldn't do it. I couldn't make any inroads at all, not with my mind buzzing with everything Doris had told me, and not with the situation with Cherry now too. I wanted this showcase done so I could go talk to her and sort it all out.

Just before I was due to do my number, I bumped into the number one country artist in the country himself, Gil Teaman. Gil may have been a country superstar, but he looked like one of the most popular Hollywood comic actors in the country, Will Ferrell. Gil had a big blue cowboy hat on his head, a plastic looking blond on one arm and a botoxed brunette on the other. The party of three was having a grand old time, seemingly as drunk as Spring-breaking high-schoolers.

"Hey, Angus—innit?" said Gil. "You're the son of old Hank Flynn?"

"That's me," I said, pulling off my mirrors so I could look into Gil's bloodshot eyes. "Think I'm up next. Good show by the way."

"I only did one number," slurred Gil. "That's the kind of set I wish I did more often!" He laughed like a wild coyote trying to cough up a fur-ball. It was an at once hilarious and frightening sound. Then he came over all defensive, frowning like a paranoid acid-tripper. "You know I never drink before a show?" Then Gil smiled. "But after? Fuckin' whiskey lips, bourbon breath, Kahlua-kiss me to oh-fuckin-blivion! Woo hoo!! Champagne?"

Gil offered me a straight-to-my-mouth top up from his bottle of French bubbly, which I politely declined with a wave of my hand. Gil wasn't fazed, his pogoing spirits bouncing back up again.

"You know I can't wait to get to New York," he said passionately, as though it was the one and only destination he'd ever dreamed of reaching. "I shouldn't tell anyone this but this Christmas compilation shit came along just in time for me. I ain't writ a song in five years. Five fuckin' years in the muse-less desert." Gil went silent. He seemed to have lost his train of drunken thought. "Did I say muse or *mule*?" Gil turned to the girls. "Do I mean a mule-less desert? Is my subconscious telling me I don't have an ass to sit on?"

Pondering his own question for a moment, Gil looked back to the girls for an answer. The blond, who was tall enough to be a basketball center, looked puzzled. The brunette, whose bosom reminded me of two blow-up exercise balls stuffed into a shoebox, smiled nervously. Suddenly Gil burst out with wild animal howls of laughter again.

"Course I got an ass! I got a donkey and a whole heap a' horses back in Dallas too." Gil gleefully addressed his escorts. "I love my ranch." Then to me, deadly serious. "I simply love it."

"Well," I said, "it'll be an honor to be on the same CD as your good self, not to mention to share the stage in New York together. Guess they couldn't have a country music Christmas album without your biggest hit on it, could they?" Gil smiled proudly at his lady friends.

"You girls know what Junior here is talking about. Don't you?" *Maybe they're too young to know*, I thought. That song of Gil's I was referring to probably having been most popular years before they were born. "Don't you?" Gil looked worried until the girls nodded and excitedly announced Gil's famous tune in unison.

"'Santa Claus Is Coming When The Sun Goes Down'!!"

Gil smiled proudly again before frowning (again) and scratching his chin.

"Hey, I just realized me something. There's a double meaning in that. 'Santa' is 'coming' when the 'son' goes 'down'. When his 'son goes down!'" Gil looked serious, like he'd discovered the formula to clean atomic power. A second passed and again he was howling at his own joke.

*This guy is really a crazy clown*, I thought. *I like him already.*

After my performance of the Hank Flynn song I'd been brought to promote above all others ('My Best Present Ever'), I looked around to hook up with Gil again (he was about the only one there any fun). Gil had disappeared, but Slade made *me* hang around all night. I was still eager to check in with Cherry—mostly, to make sure she was alright—but Slade was determined to have me meet every music executive (and their 'escort') in Memphis that night.

Patiently I played along with Slade knowing that if I could make it through that night and the Country Music Awards the next I'd only have one final show in New York to do. Then I'd be able to pay off Hank's debt and take off his red bandana. For good.

*My time will come*, I thought. *But not tonight. Tonight I gotta play along to somebody else's tune.*

By the time I headed downstairs to see if I could have a chat with Cherry, it was well after midnight. When I got into our room she was already asleep. Not wanting to wake her up simply for the sake of sorting out the emotional mess Slade seemed always able to sling us into, I quietly retreated into the hallway. Maybe this time I could give Cherry the benefit of my doubt?

224

Coming over itchy with song-writing inspiration, I headed back upstairs to the now empty ballroom and the piano Gil Teaman's player had tinkled so sweetly. When the last of the cleaners had cleared out, and I was pretty sure I was the only one in the entire ballroom, I dusted off my basic keyboard chops and started to write a new song, one about Cherry and what I felt I could give her. I didn't have much but I had music. And my reluctance to write love songs was quickly being overcome by my desire to tell Cherry how deeply I already felt for her.

*So now I've got nothing to offer*
*Except this heart on my sleeve*
*So now I've got nothing to say*
*Except I hope you don't leave*
*But I won't make guarantees or promises I won't keep*
*Or say anything that's untrue, at least not often or to you*
*What I will do is my best, to be the one you can't forget*
*And the only one you know who loves you…so*

When I was satisfied with the new lyrics to a country ballad (reminiscent of Willy Nelson's 'Blue Eyes Crying in The Rain') I decided to call 'So', I tested out a few of my other recent compositions to see what they sounded like on the piano instead of guitar. With the new accompaniment, 'Not Another Country Song' felt even more old school classic country, as did 'Slow Motion', the Tex-Mex-Soul song I wrote in the Joshua Tree National Park. But it was the last song I tried that night which really sparked with a new arrangement, sounding more honky-tonk and bluesy on the piano than it had on my acoustic; I got goosebumps hearing 'The King' coming alive in that Memphis hotel ballroom.

On a songwriter's high I finished the night with a walk down the famous Beale Street. I spent a couple hours listening to The Beale Street Girls, an all-black, all-girl and all-rockin' blues band in a jumpin' joint like none I'd ever seen. There was not one other white person in the bar but I wasn't threatened at all, in fact I embraced the feeling of being an outsider.

*Maybe this was how Elvis felt when he first moved to Memphis from Tupelo?* I thought. *A kid with a dream nobody but he could understand. A dream to make music his life.*

And on his own terms.

When one of the waiters told the band who I was (Hank Flynn's son headed to the CMAs) they invited me up for a jam. Feeling brave in my otherwise anonymity I accepted the offer, deciding to rock up 'The King', the only song I had with an easy to follow, true blues pattern. Once again the American musicians amazed me with their ability to pick up a new song.

These girls rocked.

And as the girls and I played the blues into the early hours of the morning, I started wondering if the band Slade had chosen for Hank's music (the guys who'd done such a great job on my songs in Albuquerque) was the best band for my music too—as eclectic as it was becoming. As good as The All Whites were, jamming that night with the The Beale Street Girls made me think how cool it would be to one day have my own band, one not chosen by Slade.

Or anyone else but me.

# MUSIC CITY

Cruising on Bob into Nashville I found another world again.

As I sought out the street of my hotel I checked out the people, stores and cars. 'Music City' was a land of many cowboy boots, flags outside shops (I even spotted one Confederate flag) and an abundance of oversized pick-up trucks. But as different as Nashville was to Memphis, it shared at least one thing in common: both cities were all about the music. Almost as soon as I'd arrived in Nashville I understood how the place had got its nickname. Music was everywhere in 'Music City'.

Before my awards ceremony sound-check, I had a quick poke around some of the bars on the Boulevard. Bands were already playing, even this side of lunch. Every bar I went into there were guitars being strummed, fiddles being plucked and drums being thwacked, whacked and shuffled upon.

And the talent poured out of every performer.

Touring with Hank over the years I'd heard some mighty fine players but none with the same spark as those Nashville cats. Even the unknown, undiscovered players gigging down the Boulevard were in a class above most musicians I'd ever heard. This town *owned* country.

Maybe I should have been intimidated by so much amazing musical competition but as it turned out, I wasn't. It looked like I was about to get my chance of being heard too, and not just in Nashville. Backstage at the Grand Ole Opry House, where the Country Music Awards were about to go out live on national television that night, the country's biggest country star, Gil Teaman, told me again how he was going to make sure of it.

"I'm going to make sure of it," said Gil, responding to my question about how he could be so confident of turning my song into yet another number one release for him. "The music business ain't as complicated as you think, boy. Find the best song you can, make a great titty-ass video and then tour your own ass off. Great song plus hard work equals chart toppin' good times." Gil smiled widely, sitting back into his reclining make-up chair in the dressing room he'd summoned me to.

"That's fantastic news," I said. Gil smiled again and puckered his freshly glossed lips. I knew I was standing before real country royalty, and if Gil Teaman did even half the business with my song he'd been doing every year for the last thirty or more, it would mean an end to all my financial worries. And Hank's. "That's just fantastic news," I gushed again.

"It is, isn't it?" said Gil. "This is your time in the sun, Angus. Looks like you're gonna finally come out of your old man's shadow and shine on your own, hey?"

Unbeknownst to me, when I'd done my impromptu late night performance the night before at the Peabody, Gil had been clapped out in a booth up the back of the ballroom. He'd heard my latest song come to life and it seemed Gil had very much liked what he'd heard.

"A lot of folk offer *me* songs but I turn 'em all down. 'Cept with you, boy—I'm askin' you. I'd like to record 'So' as my next lead single. You got a way with a ballad I ain't heard since Dolly gave the Colonel the finger and kept 'I Will Always Love You' for herself."

"That's a great song," I said.

"Yep," agreed Gil. "And *so* is yours. 'So' is my next big hit. You—well 'we'—can bank on it."

"When do you think you'd like to record it?" I asked, well aware of the looming deadline for paying off biker Max and his Growling Harleys.

"I got studio time booked for Memphis right after these awards," said Gil. "Then, I'll mix and master the track at my Dallas ranch next week." He smiled at his reflection in the make-up mirror. "I *love* my ranch."

"You move quick, hey?"

"Lightnin! Quick as lightning, boy—and smart."

"As smart as lightning?" I joked.

"No," said Gil. He stopped his busy make-up lady to show me he got my facetious humor. "Funny. That's funny. No, I mean my instinct tells me 'do it now', Gil Teaman. Do that 'So' song now. The audience is ready."

"You think so?"

"I *know* so. I don't *think* so. 'So' it is. See?"

"I think I do. I mean—I know."

Gil smiled broadly. I'm not sure if his pleasure came from my joining in with his playful banter or from his joyful anticipation at the sight of his personal private nurse (well, she had the uniform) readying her remedial hands with massage oil. Probably the nurse.

"Good," said Gil. "Now if you'll excuse me, I've got me some…private preparations." Gil turned to his long-legged masseuse and I got the hint: it was time for me to go. "Some pre-performance tension requires special release!"

"I've got to get ready too," I said, leaving them to it. In the hallway outside I bumped into Cherry. We still hadn't talked out the latest Slade thing, since she'd had to get up early to hitch a ride on Gil's tour-bus into Nashville. We hadn't even been in our hotel room at the same time yet.

"Yes, you do have to get ready," said Cherry, pointing to my glasses. "You're up soon, Angus. You need to change from Clark Kent into Hank Flynn Junior." Though we still hadn't had a proper chance to talk about Slade's claim Cherry was working for him when we met, I didn't want to bring it up then either, not right before my performance.

"It's just sunglasses and a bandana, Cherry," I said, my tone more dismissive than I'd intended. Perhaps I was more upset than I'd thought. "There's no mystical transformation." Cherry looked puzzled.

"Are you still angry about yesterday?" asked Cherry. "I told you—Slade is an idiot. He's trying to rile you up, that's all. Don't listen to him."

"You must have figured out who I was when I told you why I was going to Los Angeles—on the plane."

"I did. But by then we were already getting to know each other on our own terms," she said, smiling. "I didn't want to bring Slade into it at all."

"Well, Slade seems to think you were working for him all along."

"I wasn't working for him," said Cherry firmly. "And I'm not. So drop it alright!" Cherry wasn't angry but she definitely meant business. She closed the dressing room door and locked it. Before I could say another word she pushed me back with a kiss until we were up against the wall.

"What are you doing?" I said, between kisses.

"You." Cherry unzipped my jeans.

"Fuck."

"Exactly. You spend too much time in your head, Mister. Time to get down here." Cherry stepped back and unzipped. She kicked off her Converse sneakers and, without taking her eyes off me, slowly wriggled out of her jeans. "On the floor, cowboy." Instinctively I dropped, as though I was back in the airport where we first met and being strip-searched in public again. I started to pull at my cowboy boots until Cherry stopped me with a foot on my chest. "Don't bother." Cherry bent over to pull my jeans down around my knees and lowered herself—none too delicately—onto me. Any thoughts I had about going over my set-list before the show went out of my mind. All I could think about was what a fucking idiot I'd been for not trusting Cherry completely before.

"Are you sure you locked it?" I said, gesturing to the door.

"No," said Cherry casually. "But that's what us 'groupies' are like. Don't you know? We're reckless." She bit my neck.

"Ahh! Not to mention wanton sex-maniacs," I said. Cherry stopped and smiled.

"Not to mention." She kissed me again. Luckily for us nobody knocked on the door for the next twenty minutes. By the time someone did come by, Cherry had finished putting her clothes back on, and I was beginning to get dressed for my performance.

"You could have just wished me 'break-a-leg'," I said, ignoring the first few knocks on my dressing room door.

"Actions speak louder than words," said Cherry. "And sometimes sex says it best."

"Sounds like a Hallmark card," I joked, making sure Cherry was composed and ready for me to open the door. "Sex says it best."

"You heard it here first," said Cherry. As close as we'd cut it, we should have guessed who was, by now, thumping on the dressing room door like a starving zombie in search of fresh meat: Slade.

"Hey, Cherry," said Slade coolly, as I opened the door. "How you doing?" Cherry kissed me on the cheek, smacked me on the bum then turned to Slade as she left.

"Give up, will you, Slade? Just give up." Slade watched her go then turned, smiling smugly at me.

"She seems a bit upset," he said. 'Her cheeks were all flushed."

"She's fine," I said. "But thanks for your concern."

"Don't mention it. I want you to be at your very best tonight," he said. "Channeling outlaw attitude is all I want you thinking about." Slade stood with his hands on his hips as I tied on my bandana. *At least I didn't have to wear a grey ponytail wig as well*, I thought.

"After this there's only New York—right?" I said. "You haven't got any more 'reasonable promotional obligations' lined up for me, have you?" Slade nodded.

"Just New York," he said innocently. "You're two shows away from having all the money you and your old man need. You'll be back down under growing beans and brussel sprouts before you know it."

"Good," I said, snatching up Hank's mirror glasses from the bench in front of me and putting them on.

"Soon you'll be back where you belong," said Slade. "Back where you were when I first sent Cherry to fetch you." I took off my mirrors and stared at Slade curiously.

"What? Sorry? Where you *sent* Cherry to *fetch* me? Cherry told me she wasn't working for you." Slade smiled.

"And I told you yesterday, Cherry was my scout."

"You're lying. I don't believe you. You're just mad about me and Cherry being together."

"I don't get mad," said Slade. "I make money. That's why you're here. I'm the only person who can help you and old Hank." Slade checked his watch and tossed me a suit-bag he'd hung on the doorknob. "Now, you better get a move on, Junior. The show's about to begin. You don't want to mess these CMA crew around. Not if you ever want to work in this country again."

Slade winked and walked off, leaving my dressing room door open and me staring at a gold star above my name on the door. I swiveled back in my chair to check my outlaw reflection then suddenly jumped up and pushed the door all the way open. After ripping out the narrow card with 'Hank Flynn Junior' printed in black ink on it, I slammed the door. Back in my seat, I turned the card over and took a pen, ready to write a new name.

But I didn't know what to write. And I didn't know who really belonged under that gold star stuck on my door; Hank, Hank, Junior or maybe someone else? Opening up the suit-bag Slade had left I found a pair of flared denim jeans and a 70s western shirt, complete with tassels, just like Hank used to wear. It was very clear to me: Slade didn't care what sort of dickhead I looked like out there. He had an image to sell; and I was his fucking dress-up doll.

# THE KING

Standing on stage behind a thick velvet curtain, I felt surprisingly calm. Unlike the awards-show stage manager in the wings—the flustered chap who'd almost managed to spoil my plan to change my back-up band from the one I sound-checked with—I felt good, confident. Even though I'd only had a couple of beers before the show, awaiting the big reveal of Hank Flynn Junior and The All Whites, I had no stage fright at all.

But the stage manager looked like he was in fear of his life.

The man whose job it was to make sure things ran exactly to schedule—exactly as rehearsed—stood side-stage with his hands on his skinny hips, shaking his head in disapproval at the all-female, all-black musicians behind me. Having accepted my request to join me for a very special performance, The Beale Street Girls—the musos I'd jammed with into the early hours of the morning back in Memphis—were ready, waiting and eager to go in Nashville, Tennessee.

As one of the girls had said when I'd bigged up the exposure element such an opportunity presented all of us,

234

you can't get much more rock n' roll than a black blues band playing a country gig. And this was the biggest country gig of all, the Country Music Awards.

The All Whites had been surprisingly cool about my last minute change too, happily giving their security passes to the girls and hanging back at our hotel after the sound-check. It probably helped they felt about the same as me towards Slade: he'd won no favors by delaying their payment (until after the whole tour had finished), nor by giving them hardly any notice at all when he'd tried to cancel our Albuquerque show.

And though I was pretty sure I wouldn't get any of the same helpful understanding the band had shown me from Slade, however my untrusty promoter ended up reacting, I knew this was my big chance. As Gil had said, it was my 'time in the sun' and I wanted to do something I felt I'd been destined to do my whole life, something I was born to do.

After being spiritually guided by the Blind Blues Man of Mississippi, filled with emotion visiting Elvis's old shotgun shack in Tupelo, and inspired by my visit to Sun Studios, it was clear to me what I'd come to America to do. There was only one song the Universe had delivered me to sing, and it wasn't Hank's country classic or even any of my slow country ballads, it was a rockin' blues number called…

'The King'.

The lights came up as the curtain rose, and the looks of shock, bewilderment and confusion spread throughout the theatre like random pockets of falling dominos. Music superstars scratched their heads; executives turned to each other for a goddamn clue to what was going on; somewhere, I was pretty sure, Slade was shitting in his suit. *What the fuck's going on*, I imagined him thinking.

There was no trademark Hank Flynn mirror sunglasses

and no red bandana around my head (or wrist). Instead of Hank's gold Fender Telecaster I had my acoustic strapped around my neck. Without hesitating or acknowledging the confusion spreading throughout the Ole Opry House I stepped up to the mic.

"Good evening, Nashville. My name is Angus Flynn and these fine ladies are The All Blacks." Immediately I felt the audience split in two. Some seemed horrified (by my scantily clad blues bad-girls, maybe?); many applauded despite the obvious confusion caused by the electric banner overhead introducing Hank Flynn Junior. "Tonight we'll be performing a rockin' tribute to the country kid who refused to be put in a box. They called him a hillbilly for playing up-tempo country blues, and though country music may have been the beginning for Elvis, it definitely wasn't the end. This is my tribute to a country boy who left Tennessee and went out and done good. Real good." The drummer, a gorgeous girl with the biggest afro in the band, counted the other girls and me in, throwing me a wink on 'four'. And before the vision switcher upstairs could turn off a single television camera we were into it. Nobody could stop us now.

> *He made his name by singing love and pain,*
> *Rock and roll,*
> *He made his name by singing love and pain,*
> *Rock and roll,*
> *And they took all of his possessions,*
> *Thank God they could not take his soul.*

I stepped back from the mic to rub shoulders with the long-haired bass player babe on my right and the crew-cutted guitar girl on my left. Then back to center stage for the second verse.

*He walked the streets of Memphis*
*With just this here guitar in his hand*
*He walked the streets of Memphis*
*With just this here guitar in his hand*
*People stopped him said "I know your face"*
*"No, Sir that is some other man"*

It was poetic license to quote a make-believe conversation between a giddy fan and a reluctant to be recognized long-gone Elvis, but surely his only living son had the right to tell any story about his father he liked? Even if nobody knew I was his son.

*They called him the King*
*And good lord could he sing*
*They called him the King*
*And good lord could he sing*
*He drove 'em wild by God he did*
*A white boy movin' like a black man did*

At the end of our performance the audience was still split. Some applauded enthusiastically, perhaps gambling on the thought it might have been a set-up stunt orchestrated by the CMA producers; others shook their heads disapprovingly, no doubt bewildered further by the big screen video of Hank Flynn's best ever country performances (from the seventies) which had run all throughout our blues rock number.

But I was happy. I'd done the song I wanted.

Back in my dressing room, I was also thrilled to see Oli and Penelope had arrived in town just in time to catch my performance. In my make-up seat I smiled and waved to

237

them standing behind Cherry, who was waiting for Slade to finish paying out on me.

"You just buried yourself!" screamed Slade. "You'll never play Nashville again. What the fuck do you think this is? And who the fuck were those bitches?"

"Don't speak about them that way. Calm down! Those girls rocked it."

"And *you* fucked it. You fucked it all—all by yourself. Why the fuck didn't you play the song I flew you here—from the ass-hole end of the world—to play? You were meant to sing 'My Best Present Ever'? That's what you rehearsed! Jesus! Our backers have all pulled out now. Nobody who witnessed *that* display of unprofessionalism is willing to put another cent into you. You can forget New York. You're done."

"What are you talking about? It'll be good publicity," I said. "I was just playing the role you wanted me too, the 'Offspring Outlaw', remember?"

"If you wanted to fuck yourself over, Junior, you could have just stayed on your farm and waited for Max and his gang. What do you think that stunt out there is going to achieve? Nothing, that's what."

"It felt right," I said plainly. "I wanted to sing my song."

"That's not what I was paying you for! That's not what my Nashville contacts invited you here for! They're even talking about re-pressing the Christmas album—with a month to go before release—just so they can take Hank's song off! You'll get nothing now."

"You're serious? You're pulling the plug?" I was starting to feel about as stupid as Slade's look indicated he thought I was.

"This is business. And you just put yourself out of it."

"Well, fuck it then," I said, picking up Hank's mirrors and bandana sitting on the bench in front of me. "I'm sick of wearing this stupid costume anyway. I want to do my own thing." I tossed the glasses down.

"You can do whatever you want now," said Slade. "But you better come up with my money soon or you'll have more trouble than an unpaid mortgage and some mad Ozzie bikers on your tail."

"What money?" I said. "*You* owe *me!*" For the first time since barging into my dressing room Slade smiled.

"No, I don't. You owe *me*. By playing 'The King' you broke our contract. And on top of the airfare and accommodation costs I've already paid for, you'll need to cough up the wages for the band at that Albuquerque gig— and the gig they didn't play tonight, too."

"I don't think that's very fair."

"I don't care." Slade punctuated his last sentence with a finger jab to my chest. He turned and left, barging past Cherry without acknowledging her. "You'll be getting my bill!"

"Well, I haven't heard that one before," said Cherry, taking Slade's place next to me. "And I don't mean Slade losing his temper—I mean your song. 'The King' was great, Angus."

"Did you like it?" I said, trying to forget about the shit Slade had just dumped on me. "I only just finished it in time for tonight."

"Good thing you did. I loved it," said Cherry. "Caught it all too," she added, holding up her handheld digital video camera. "More up-tempo than your other stuff— rockier. Your *dad* would be proud." Cherry gave a cheeky, knowing grin.

"I'm glad you liked it," I said, "but maybe I should have waited. You heard what Slade said, he's going to pull the New York show and my place on the CD."

"No time like the present," said Oli, coming in with Penelope to join Cherry and I. "You took the bull by the horns…and fucked it in the nose!"

"So you must expect the old bull, Slade, to make a charge," said Penelope. "But don't give up the fight just 'cause it's getting a bit bloody."

"I appreciate the encouragement," I said. "But maybe I did go too far?"

"Hard to say, partner" said Oli. "Unfortunately, we missed your performance," he added apologetically. "Penelope and I got arrested for conducting sexual relations in the ladies room at the Country Music Museum."

"Maybe they'll show your part of the show on the news," offered Penelope, by way of compensation. "Bit of controversy."

"Hopefully they won't show ours," joked Oli. Penelope faked a shocked expression then turned to me.

"From what the other artists and backstage crew were saying, your performance was both 'unbelievable' *and* 'outrageous'," said Penelope. "Sounds like whichever way it went you made a big impression."

"It was a fantastic performance," said Cherry defensively. "I'll bet there are record company reps on their way to this dressing room right now, ready to sign you up tonight. Fuck Slade, he doesn't know anything."

"Yeah," agreed Penelope. "Fuck Slade."

"Like they both said," said Oli. "Fuck Slade."

I nodded, feeling my pride at going out on a limb quickly vanishing. In its place was the horrible feeling the only person I'd fucked was myself.

## WHAT IT TAKES

The next morning Cherry tried to cheer me up by taking me shopping. I knew she meant well offering to buy me a genuine, Nashville-made cowboy hat, but I would not be cheered. Having woken up with none of the confidence I'd had the night before, I was still second-guessing my choice to perform 'The King' and double-doubting my by-default decision to prematurely put an end to the Hank Flynn Junior tour.

At a gift shop on Broadway—full of Taiwanese-made Hank Williams T-shirts and made-in-China wooden guns—Cherry finished paying for a desk clock in the shape of a horse while I tried to share some of my mixed-up feelings.

"What I did last night was stupid," I said, shaking my head in frustration. "I thought it was my big chance to get my music out there but now I'm not so sure. I was a bloody fool."

"It wasn't stupid, Angus," said Cherry, leading us out of the shop. "Like I said, you never know who might have seen you last night. If you ask me you've got nothing to worry about at all. You'll see. Something will come up to help you pay off those bikers. Don't worry," she added encouragingly. "You've got it what it takes, Angus. Otherwise I wouldn't be hanging around. I believe in you."

"I'm glad you're confident," I said, baulking at the next shop Cherry had us aimed for, a cowboy boot emporium the size of a barn. "But I'm starting to think I made a big mistake."

"You didn't make any mistake. You did what you wanted. You were brave. It took guts to give Nashville the finger."

"I didn't mean to give anyone the finger," I said. "I just wanted to sing my own song."

"Well, you did. And I'm proud of you. You should be proud too. Maybe you will be when I show you the video footage I took? It was an awesome performance." Cherry kissed me, but I was in no mood for lovey dovey.

"I'll have to call Hank," I said, "sometime soon, I guess. We're going to need to come up with an alternate plan now that we won't be getting the money from Slade. Maybe we can sell off some of our stuff and keep Max at bay for a while longer? I know Hank's got a couple original '57 Strats. They're worth a few grand each, at least." Cherry grabbed my hand, stopping me, and held it still in both of hers.

"You don't have to sell any of your guitars," she said. "There is one other option you have—*we* have," said Cherry timidly.

"What's that?" I said, noticing a bar across the road. The Full Moon Saloon was just opening for business.

"I'd be happy to ask my Mum for a loan of the money you need."

"What are you talking about? Your *mother*? Is she loaded?"

"Uh huh," said Cherry matter-of-factly. "In fact, Dad left Mum straight after she first appeared on the cover of Time Magazine. Apparently being married to the 'Business

Woman of The Year' was too much for his male ego. I haven't seen him for about seven years. And Mum I see exactly twice a year, at Christmas and—no, I lie. I see Mum *once* a year."

"That's a shame," I said. Cherry shrugged.

"And this Christmas she's busy. Opening a chain of jewellery stores in China."

"Sounds like she must do alright."

"She does. And I'm not proud. That's how I get to play the constant tourist. Blogging doesn't always pay the bills. It's Mum's way of taking care of the family, not with an emotional relationship but with money."

"So does she travel a lot?" I asked. "Your Mum?

"Yep," said Cherry. "And always for business, never for pleasure. So what do you say? Would you let me ask her for the money you need?"

"That's very kind of you to offer," I said, "but it isn't her problem. No, it's my and Hank's debt, and I'm not going to offload it on anyone else. I'll think of something." Cherry smiled and pointed through the window of the enormous shoe shop to row after row of cowboy boots behind the glass.

"Well, can I at least buy you some new boots then, cowboy? Those other ones you've got seem to be a bit small for you. You're always wriggling around on the floor trying to get them on or off."

"I think I've had enough shopping for today," I said. "But I wouldn't mind getting a beer or two."

"It's hardly even lunch time," said Cherry.

"You won't join me, then?" I said, pointing to the bar on the other side of the Boulevard.

"I don't think so," said Cherry. "You go though. I'll see you later at the hotel."

"Thanks," I said. "Sorry I'm not much fun today."

"That's okay," said Cherry. "It gives me an excuse to do some more shopping. Maybe Grandma needs a travel-sized banjo with a Tennessee flag painted on it?"

We kissed and parted happy, agreeing to meet later for dinner. Minutes later I was drowning my sorrows in a quiet stall at the back of the Full Moon Saloon. The band up front was just starting the early afternoon shift and I was hoping the booze and music would be enough to momentarily distract me from the mess I'd got myself—and Hank—deeper into.

Just as the despair had almost overwhelmed me, I spotted Gil Teaman coming into the bar. Remembering his plan, and our agreement for him to record one of my songs, my mood immediately improved. Gil was, after all, one of the most successful country artists ever and I realized maybe Cherry was right?

*Maybe I didn't have anything to worry about at all.*

"Hey Gil!" I yelled. "You looking for company?" Gil wandered over, a little sheepishly. I thought maybe he didn't want to be recognized and hassled by fans or autograph hounds.

"Cherry was right," said Gil. "Drowning your post 'no-award-for-you' country blues I see."

"Something like that," I said.

"So," said Gil tentatively. I waited for him to break into his praising of my Memphis-penned song again. But he didn't. There was no clowning around today. "So," he said, "about that song—'So'."

"You done a recording already?" I joked. "You do move quick."

"Afraid not," said Gil. "I did have some studio time all booked up and ready to go in Memphis—but we pulled it. Shoot, got nothin' new to record now. Don't know what I'm going to do?"

"What do you mean? What about my song? What about 'So'? I thought you loved it?"

"I *did* love it—I do. But unfortunately with your little 'lordy lordy movin' like a black man' punkin' of old Nashville last night, I'm putting my precious image in danger simply by being seen with you today." Gil looked around for any prying eyes. I realized he wasn't worried about autograph hunters; he didn't want to be photographed with *me*.

"Why don't people understand, I wasn't trying to be disrespectful of anyone?" I pleaded. "I love country music and I love Elvis. He started out country after all—he's in the Country Music Hall of Fame for Christ's sake! I was just trying to give a good show!"

"You did," said Gil with a wry smile. "It was high drama alright. Some of the TV cutaways of the shocked country establishment were hilarious. I thought Garth Brooks was gonna spit out his spleen. You certainly surprised the big guns with that blacking—I mean 'backing'—band. The Beale Street Girls? My God! You got some nerve, boy, not to mention some bowling-ball-sized nuts. I'll hand you that." Gil got up ready to leave.

"Actually, it was the first time I didn't have any nerves," I said forlornly. "How wrong have my instincts turned out to be?"

"I'm sorry, kid," said Gil. "You hang in there. One day you might even get your own tour bus like me—maybe even your own ranch. I love my ranch." As Gil disappeared down Broadway, the band struck up on the very song I was supposed to do the previous night. They played it a bit too fast for my liking but their version of 'My Best Present Ever' sounded pretty damn good. Listening to the lyrics I understood again why it was such a popular Christmas song: Dad had written his love for Mum into a gift that kept on giving.

*All my Christmases have come at once*
*Now I have you in my arms*
*All my loneliness has disappeared*
*Now I have you right here*

Alone in the middle of the afternoon, under a painted full moon on a wall surrounded by country-music band posters, I finished what was left of my warm beer to the lyrics made famous by Hank Flynn, Senior:

*Oh, I thank the heavens*
*For my best present ever*

Moving to the bar, I placed my empty glass on the counter, positive I could never write a song as simple and good as Hank's.

"Another beer, thanks," I said. "And a double shot of your cheapest whiskey." I laid out my change on the bar as a friendly Dolly Parton lookalike behind the counter fetched my drinks and returned to watch me counting pennies like a kid who's busted open his piggy bank. "Not sure I've got enough, actually," I said. Dolly pursed her lips then started counting for me.

"You've got the money, honey," she said, smiling. "Cheer up sunshine. Look, even a dime for my tip." She took the last of my money and gave me a wink. "Long as you got enough for that you got everything you need."

The band finished their set and the guitarist came to the bar, ordering a beer too. Suddenly feeling the muse on my shoulder, and with it a compulsion to play guitar right then, I asked the guitarist if I might be able to borrow his for a few minutes. Recognizing me from the CMAs ("Pretty good Elvis tribute, that song you did!") he agreed—as long as I didn't take his cherished ax out of sight. I climbed up on the stage, and there, in the near empty bar, opened up my lyric book, rested it on the bass amp and started writing. I tried not to think about comparing myself to Hank—or anyone else—and just did my best to let out whatever it was I had. And what I had sounded a lot like the blues.

*You've got the money honey, you've got the looks*
*You've got something you don't get from readin' books*
*You've got style, you're lookin' cool*
*You're gonna be nobody's fool, no more*
*It was well worth the wait*
*To find you've got just what it takes*

For a moment I stopped playing, thinking about Cherry and how much more of my future was now on the line than just saving the house I shared with Hank.

*You've made mistakes like we all do*
*That gives you the power to choose*
*You've got no room for regret*
*There's so many things that you have not done yet*
*It was well worth the wait*
*To find you've got just what it takes*

When the band break was over, and they came back on stage, I thanked the guitarist before heading out into the street and the blinding daylight. I knew what I needed to do next and I was pretty sure I'd had enough of drinking.
Plenty enough.

# THE WHEEL OF DEATH

Back at our Nashville hotel, I told Cherry my plan.

The following morning, I was going to fly to New York and do whatever it took to convince Slade, who'd already left town, to let me back on the final showcase. The big country Christmas gig was still a week or so away and with that much time I hoped maybe Slade would cool off and see reason. If not, maybe I could spend the last days of my stay shopping my Pipsqueak demos to record companies. Both ideas sounded slightly less brilliant when I shared them with Cherry than when I'd had them at the Full Moon Saloon, but Cherry thought it was worth a shot.

"And you're not going alone," she said, as she set about helping me book two plane tickets—on *her* credit card. "I love New York in November. It's so cold, and so romantic."

I told Cherry I'd pay her back for the flights; she told me not to worry about it. We found Oli and Penelope and filled them in on the developments. They decided they wanted to hire a car and see out the coast-to-coast trip on the road, making plans to visit Niagara Falls and the Amish country on the way. Quickly it was agreed: we'd all meet up in the Big Apple in a few days.

The four of us were about to head out down the Boulevard, for one final dinner together before heading our separate ways, when I remembered Bob. With all the build-up to the Country Music Awards I'd almost forgotten about the other job I'd taken on in Albuquerque, namely, 'motorcycle delivery guy'.

With a quick apology to Oli and Penelope, and a promise to Cherry to drive carefully, I left the others to dine without me and fetched Bob from the hotel car park. I strapped on my helmet, gave his fuel tank a pat, and congratulated Bob on getting me halfway across America. I was probably still a little inebriated from my earlier drinking session but I wasn't going far. From my delivery instructions, I knew Bob's new home was only a few miles away.

As the evening fell, and I got closer to my destination, the moon grew brighter and big in the sky. By the time I reached the street address I had for Bob's rightful owner, the night had an eerie, almost daylight glow. It was kind of surreal.

I slowed down to check the street numbers and was surprised when they led me to a weed-infested car park. The delivery address I'd been given was nothing more than a broken slab of concrete stained with oil and grease. I pulled up outside an old shop-front and turned Bob off.

Looking inside the window, I could see someone had been living in the disused shop but was nowhere to be seen now. From the looks of all the fresh rubbish—beer cans, take-away food scraps, and empty bottles of Jack Daniels strewn around the place, I gathered someone had made a quick, or at least messy, getaway. And they'd left without waiting for Bob.

I double checked my delivery instructions and even asked a neighbor—a grumpy old guy peering over the fence—to make sure I was in the right place. Apparently I was. The nosey old neighbor informed me "that troublemaker done left without returning my Phillips head screwdriver. Damn him to hell." It seemed like a bit of an overreaction to me but I felt less guilty knowing I hadn't stolen Bob; instead, I'd simply swapped him for a screwdriver.

Listening to Bob's coughs and splutters when I started the old fella back up, it had probably proved a fair swap too.

Back on the road to downtown Nashville, the moon glowed even brighter than before. I was overcome with a peculiar sense of calm. But when I spotted a sign for the turn-off to Memphis and heard a voice in my head say "Go for it!", I thought maybe I was still drunk.

Before I knew what I was doing, at the last possible moment, my foot kicked down a gear, my hand opened up the throttle and I leaned with all my might, swerving across the road and dragging Bob down the unplanned route. Honks and high-beam flashes of traffic all around me jolted me into gripping the handle bars tighter as my instincts sent me off on a new course.

It seemed Bob and I weren't quite finished our journey together. Not yet.

Back on the road, I was getting close to Memphis when a gang of bikers engulfed me. For what was probably only a matter of thirty or forty seconds—but with how sick with dread it made me feel, seemed a lot longer—I was surrounded by a wild bunch of bearded, leather-jacket-wearing scoundrels. From their snarls and grins they were obviously enjoying the fear their stealth attack instilled on an unsuspecting lone rider, but I tried not to let it show. As they sped up ahead of me I adjusted my goggles, blinking my eyes with confusion after the lead biker turned to me as he passed, pointing his finger-as-a-gun at me and firing off a 'friendly' shot to indicate his great pleasure at having a faster machine between his legs.

*It's not him*, I thought. *It can't be. Max is in Australia.*

The possibility that Max and the Growling Harleys had somehow transported themselves to America, and were hunting me down for their money, caused me to unwittingly hold my breath for long enough to feel dizzy. Rounding a long bend, a flash of bright orange light—*fire!*—startled me out of my paranoid hallucination and I gasped for air as I shielded my eyes from the glow. A couple of road workers were waving fire-extinguishers and pointing to flames leaping out of the grass on the other side of the fence, and distracted by the fire and commotion all around, I let Bob drift out of our lane. When I looked up, the headlights of an oncoming car totally blinded me.

"You fucking idiot!" I screamed, before realizing *I* was the one in the wrong lane.

Swerving back I overcompensated, hitting the gravel, which gripped my front wheel like quicksand, making it impossible for me to steer. I was headed directly for the road-worker's truck until I hit a large mound of earth and Bob and I launched into the air, over the fence and towards the flaming field.

Miraculously, Bob and I landed as one, crashing down into the burning field with a thump; my holding-on-for-life grip on the handle bars causing my body to bounce off the seat and come down chest first onto the fuel tank. Bob sliced a path through the burning field until hitting a rock and bursting a back tire, sending me flying one way and Bob the other. When I woke up, I was sure I was dead.

The first thing I noticed was the sound of unfamiliar voices; concerned good Samaritans surrounded me.

"Is his arm broke?" said one, his accent making me think I might have been rescued by hillbillies. "It look like he done busted it in half."

"It's not broken," said a female, with the impatience of

an experienced nurse, "it's just bent. See." I felt her move my arm and was relieved when it only hurt a bit, not quite enough to make me scream.

"Make sure that bandage is wrapped tight around his head," said another voice. "Don't want the poor fella bleedin' to death." My eyeballs flickered under their lids. I wasn't sure if what I saw was through tiny open slits or if I was dreaming: it looked like the circus had come to town. A clown with full white make-up, red nose and an expression of childlike wonder held my wrist, I realized, taking my pulse.

"He's alright," said the clown. "A little sad maybe but alright!" A Strong Man with bulging, tanned, oily muscles pulled me into an upright sitting position, holding me there with his Samson-like grip.

"He's strong," said the Strong Man. "If he survived what I witnessed—he must be." A Trapeze Girl, dressed in a skimpy bikini and a flesh-colored full-body stocking underneath, put her hand on her heart and the other on my thigh.

"He flew over a fence," she said, amazed, "and through a fire! It's a miracle he's alive."

"What happened?" I said, feeling the bandage around my head.

"Those dumb road workers started a fire," explained Trapeze Girl. "One of them was smoking and flicked his butt into the field. Civvies are such losers."

"They didn't even call an ambulance," said Strong Man, shaking his head in disbelief at the inhumanity of it all. "I think they were worried about getting fired for messin' up or something." Clown honked his horn.

"Since those workers had spotted us earlier, setting up in the next field," explained Clown, "they thought we'd have a medical officer on staff…"

"Which we do," said the Trapeze Girl, proudly holding

up a shoebox-sized medical kit.

"…so they drove you over here and dumped you."

"What about Bob?" I asked. "Is my motorbike alright?" Clown shook his head sadly and stuck out his oversized bottom lip.

"Afraid not," he said, before holding up a miniature cycle and breaking into a manic smile, "but maybe you'd like to borrow mine?" Strong Man grabbed my chin and turned my face towards his.

"You're very lucky, kid," he said. "You must be made of steel." Trapeze girl squeezed my thigh, moving the hand on her heart to test my other leg.

"Just like Superman," she said sexily. "Maybe you should stay and join us? We always have room for a brave stunt man like yourself," she added with a wink. Strong Man helped me to my feet. For the first time since waking up under the circle of circus faces, I saw I was in the middle of a Big Top. Standing in the main ring, on freshly thrown sawdust, I was surrounded by elephants on chains, tigers in cages and a woman strapped to a spinning wheel. Her partner tossed a knife and the thwack of a sharp blade piercing old wood alerted me to action.

"I must have lost my contacts in the crash," I said, blinking sawdust and ash from my eyes. "Has anyone got my bag?" Clown handed me my knapsack and I opened it to retrieve my glasses from their case. Amazingly, they weren't broken.

"So what do you say?" asked Clown. "Wanna join the circus? It's every kid's dream? We've even got an opening in 'The Wheel of Death'." Clown pointed to a giant round cage with a motorbike lying on the metal grill floor next to a broken helmet I didn't think was a prop.

"The last guy lost his balance," explained Strong Man. "Poor fella."

"Thanks for the offer," I said, dusting myself off and making room under the bandage around my head for my glasses to fit, "and thanks for patching me up too. But I've got to get moving now. I'm running out of time and there's somewhere I need to be."

"Really?" said Trapeze Girl. "Where?"

## TODAY, TONIGHT

S un Studios.

Two hours after the crash which saw Bob totaled and me badly bruised and battered, I was standing in front of the very first dream factory ever. Having hitched a ride with a Memphis-bound truck driver (who'd enthusiastically related the entire history of his employers, The Precision Tool company) I was back again in the place that gave birth to rock and roll. The neon light sign of, perhaps, America's most famous recording studio seemed to glow brighter than the full moon. Or maybe I was still a bit dizzy from the crash? (I certainly had a sore head) But this time, being there at night, it felt different from when I'd first visited with Cherry, and not just because I had a bruised ribcage.

Without hoards of other tourists around, it was easier to imagine what it was like when Elvis first walked through Sun's doors and jammed with Scotty Moore and Bill Black all those years ago. On a still Memphis night, one like almost any other, they'd come up with something brand new—and that's what I wanted to do too.

I wanted to make my record in Memphis. Right here at Sun.

But I was broke. Flat broke. And with maybe only a couple of hundred bucks left on my credit cards, I didn't know how I was going to make it happen. Plus, I was short on time. What could I do?

"Nice sound, guys," I said, approaching two teenagers pounding out a rhythm on a couple of plastic buckets and a three-stringed bass guitar (plugged into a car-battery powered amp). The young and astoundingly talented musicians had set up right outside the doors to Sun, I assumed in an effort to get the attention of a music producer more so than that of any of the straggling tourists and local drunks walking by. The drummer stood up smiling, nodding at my compliment as he and his bass-player buddy started to pack up their gear and collect their earnings. I walked around the building to the side door where I found Billy, the jaded young sound engineer Cherry and I had met briefly on our group tour.

Wearing his jeans turned up about six-inches at the hem and his hair slicked back with some greasy product, the cigarette pack in Billy's T-shirt sleeve completed the picture of the authentic blend of rock and roll and hillbilly known as *rockabilly*. He lit up and flashed me a furtive grin. I noticed that on one arm he had a Carl Perkins tattoo, on the other, The Cramps.

"G'day," I said, leaning casually against the wall and wondering how Billy might feel about country ballads by an Australian roadie. "Taking a break, hey?" Rockabilly Billy took a drag.

"Nothin' to take a break from. The session's been cancelled. But, since it's paid for they make me hang around here all night in case the almighty Gil Teaman changes his fuckin' mind." Billy took another drag. "Fuckin' Nashville."

"Yeah," I said. "Fuckin' Nashville."

256

Billy turned from staring off into the dark Memphis night to look straight at me.

"Hey, ain't you Hank Flynn Junior? I saw that tribute to Elvis song you did at the awards. Pretty cool punkin' of the establishment, man."

"Glad someone thinks so. My name's Angus, actually. But yeah, that was me." Billy nodded, impressed. *Cool,* I thought.

"Nice one," said Billy. "Those chicks played hot."

"Hey," I said, "since you're not doing anything else, how would you like to make some music with yours truly?"

"And who else? We don't have a house-band standing by, Mr. Junior." I stood straight and smiled.

"Maybe we can come up with something?" I said. Billy took another drag, a closer look at me (my torn jeans showing off a bloodied knee; my face scratched and bruised), and flung his cigarette onto the concrete. Billy walked over to extinguish the butt with a single swivel of his leather lace-ups.

"Maybe we can," he said. "Let's see what else you got besides one helluva rockin' blues number."

Before I got into the session, I called Cherry and filled her in on everything that had happened. I played the accident down so as not to concern her but she was still pretty worried and very glad I was okay.

"You sure you don't need to go to hospital?" she said. "You might have been concussed."

"Maybe, but I don't think so. I feel pretty good, considering."

"So you're about to start a recording session now? At Sun? I thought you were just going to drop off that old motorbike."

"I thought so too. But something happened on the road and I got the idea to head here. It looks like I might have made the right decision."

"But what about tomorrow morning? Will you make it back in time for our plane to New York?"

"Probably not. But don't worry. You go ahead and I'll meet you there. This is too good an opportunity to miss. I just want to see where the night takes me."

"No problem," said Cherry. "Enjoy yourself. I'll see you in New York." We made a plan to meet at the hotel Slade had already booked me into and Cherry wished me luck one more time.

"You're going to make the best record to come out of Sun since Elvis," said Cherry. "Music's in your blood."

Inside the studio proper, as Billy plugged in microphones, aimed amplifiers and got everything ready, I realized I didn't even have the most basic tool of my trade.

"Shit!" I said. "I haven't got my guitar. I left it back in Nashville." Not missing a beat, Billy disappeared into the control room, returning with a vintage Gibson acoustic, a big J-200 with a natural finish.

"Since you're obviously a fan of ol' Pretzel's, maybe you'd like to try a few songs on this?" Billy handed me the guitar, which instantly felt familiar, always a good sign for any guitar player; a recognition of compatibility, like the kind I felt when I first saw Cherry.

"Thanks. It's awesome," I said, playing a few licks. "It feels…and plays…awesome." Billy smiled, and despite the no-smoking sign clear on the wall behind him, lit up another.

"And it's got an 'awesome' history," said Billy. "That baby was played by Elvis himself. You hold in your hands one of the King's very own."

"You're kidding me?" I said. "This guitar? He played it? Fuck."

My good fortune continued when I went to see if the teenagers I'd heard playing earlier outside might be interested in having a bit of a jam inside. I found them sitting on a bench, having a smoke and discussing whether Johnny Cash could beat Billy Ray Cyrus in a fist-fight (we unanimously decided he definitely *should* have.) They almost coughed out their lungs when I asked them if they wanted to be my rhythm section for the night.

"Shit, yeah!" said the tall and skinny bassist, popping to his feet.

"Fuck, yeah!" said the slightly taller drummer, punching his friend in the arm as he jumped up too.

Less than an hour after arriving at Sun, I had a new guitar to play, a new (lanky) band to play it with and a sound engineer (with attitude) ready to record it all. Like me, Billy had hooked up the boys with some A-grade instruments, and their raw talent was shining even brighter under the studio lights.

I could hardly believe it was my songs getting all the magical treatment.

There were only four of us in the whole place but the air was electric. With Billy in the control room, me and the boys cut loose in the soundproof studio, a shrine to the sounds of a bygone time. I'd gone retro back to my roots; back to the very beginning. It felt like a dream.

The last song I taught the guys was one I'd written at home on the morning of the anniversary of Mum's death, the same day I told Hank I was finished being his roadie. I hadn't been able to finish what was the least country and most indie-pop song I'd ever attempted back then, but at Sun I found the words I needed.

*The best laid plans are slowly swept away*
*You gotta make 'em new every day*
*And dreams can seem to be fading fast*
*When they are on their way*
*Everything you do is gonna change the world*

259

*You can put some wrong things right*
*Everything you do is gonna change the world*
*There's no time like today, tonight*

"Now, you guys are all warmed up and familiar with Angus's songs," said Billy, over the studio talkback, "I'm just going to run the tape and see if we can catch some fire." The boys looked to me, excited and ready to go at my call. "We're rolling now so anytime you're ready."

"Cool," I said. "Okay, guys, I want us to keep playing, even if we make the odd mistake. We're going for a real, live sound. Human, alright?" The drummer nodded and started to count us in but I waved my hands to stop him. "Hold on! Hold on!!" I held my new *old* Gibson up to my ear. "Just needs a little tune." The new strings I'd put on had stretched since we'd started jamming, but with a couple of deft string plucks and peg twists I was done. I gave Billy and the band a thumbs-up and take two was soon underway.

Except to change tape reels, we didn't stop again for the next five hours.

Still to this day, and apart from when I shared the room with Cherry at the Grand Canyon, and one other amazing night we shared, that night in Memphis goes down as the best night of my life.

# Part IV:
# Santa Claus is Coming When The Sun Goes Down

## TO BE TOUCHED

Later that morning, Billy dropped me off at Graceland. Finding myself back in Memphis, I thought it would be nice to personally say goodbye to Doris. I was probably on a bit of a post-recording session high too. And since I was already going to miss my flight out of Nashville, I figured I had an hour or so to spare before I needed to organize a new flight to New York.

Arriving at Graceland before opening time, I sat down in the driveway, leaning against the famous gates. The early morning light had inspired me and I wanted to write down some new lyrics. They were less literal than I normally wrote, more poetic maybe, but I tried not to be critical, rather just let them flow. I'd learnt it was important to trust the creative process. You never knew what you might get or where your muse might lead you. Like all the way to Memphis, Tennessee.

> *Daylight brings its own kind of illusion*
> *Things might just get better*
> *Things might just get better*
> *Night sets in and dreams and prayers begin*

*For someone who's not there*
*To someone who's not there*
*The heart is for taking—give it up*
*The body is aching to be touched*

Doris was happily surprised to find me waiting for her when she came to start her shift. Once again, Doris escorted me to a more private part of Graceland for our chat. And though the Meditation Garden—a private cemetery where Elvis was buried alongside his grandmother, father, and mother—would be opened in a few minutes to the general public, for a short while at least it was nice being there alone. *This is my father's final resting place*, I thought, allowing myself the indulgence of one moment with no doubt of my paternity.

I realized too, if Elvis was my biological father then I was also visiting the grave of my grandparents and great grandmother.

*What a trip.*

"It's our address and phone number in Australia," I said, handing Doris our contact details. "I'm not sure how long we'll be at that exact residence but if you're ever up for a holiday, please look us up." Doris smiled.

"Thanks, Angus, but I don't think I'll ever venture that far down under. I'm a bit wary of snakes and umm…red-coated spiders? Is that what you guys call 'em? And all those other poisonous critters you got runnin' everywhere down there. They give me the willies."

"Kangaroos don't bite," I said with a wry smile. "Much." I nodded an acknowledgement to another tour guide waving *good morning* to Doris and me. From her co-worker's lingering stare, it seemed it was time for Doris to take her station.

"Looks like we're opening for business again," said

Doris. "I better get going."

"No problem," I said. "I've got a plane to catch too. But before I go, is there anything else you can tell me about Mum and me and…everything? I don't know when—or if—I'll get back here and I want to make sure I've turned over every stone."

"Well, since you mention it," said Doris, waving the busy-body guide away, "there was another little story I thought you might like to hear. I remembered it after you and your girlfriend visited the other day."

"Oh yeah? What's that?" I hadn't really counted on learning anything more about my murky past from Doris but I wasn't surprised she had something else to tell me either. She probably knew more about my mother than anyone I knew. More than I would ever know.

"What I'm going to tell you now isn't about Elvis and April, this is about you," said Doris.

"Really? I said. Doris nodded.

"Before you left Memphis, your family used to go to church with my family at the Pentecostal Assembly here," she said.

"I don't remember going to church," I said.

"Hmmm," said Doris thoughtfully, as though I'd given her the final clue of a murder mystery she was about to solve once and for all. "Hmmm," she hummed again.

"What about this church?" I asked.

"Well, sometimes your Mum used to get me to take you when she was too tired to get up early, you know, after being out all night playing a show with Hank or whatever."

"The Flying Flynns didn't play that many gigs together," I said, bending down to snap a red rose off a bush. "You sure she wasn't tired from all her stripping or whatever else she got up to?" Doris frowned.

"Your mother gave up dancing when she met Hank," said

265

Doris, disapprovingly. "Now I know you might be upset by some of the things you've learned about her, but you should know this—your mother loved you with—all—her—heart."

"I know she did," I said, tossing the rose onto Elvis's gravestone. "She loved a lot of people." I stood up. Doris gave me a stern, motherly look that spoke volumes. *Don't be mean about your mother, son.*

"Anyway, as I was saying, sometimes April couldn't make it to service but she always wanted to make sure you got your instruction. And also, sometimes you'd even ask April if you could stay over at ours—especially when you knew I was gonna be sittin' my nieces. You kids loved jamming on those damn pots and pans!"

"That's crazy," I said. "Why don't I remember that?"

"Who knows why we remember what we do," said Doris. "Or what we don't? But, wait—there's more. On one Sunday, after the sermon and almost at the end of the service, you were asked to sing a hymn. Like all the good young singers you were given a chance to do a solo, right up there on the pulpit."

"Was I?" I said. Doris nodded proudly, the memory seemingly still vivid and enjoyable for her.

"Yes. But on the day of your big solo, when it came time for you to sing—you wouldn't. You were standing there on that stage, looking so brave—but defiant with it—because you wouldn't sing. The preacher gave you a gentle nudge, but you wouldn't budge. The choir mistress pinched your cheeks—and you didn't blink. All the while you just stood there gazing out the open door at the other end of the church. You just stood there waitin', without making a peep."

"What for? What was I waiting for?"

Doris choked up with emotion. She looked away and waved a hand over her mouth as though she couldn't quite bring herself to finish the story.

"Your Momma. You were waitin' for your Momma, Angus. But she didn't come. Because, well…that was the day April died." She turned to face me. "That was the day Hank found her. You never came back to church again. And you never did get to sing your solo." I had no memory of what Doris was saying—but it felt true. The shiver up my neck and the clench of my heart told me so; Doris had a habit of knocking the wind out of me.

"I can't believe I've never heard that story before," I said.

"And *I* can't believe you turned out to be a singer! Eventually you had to be dragged off that stage. You was screamin' and hollerin' and you didn't want to go. Took four men to get you into my car. You were so traumatized that day—and in front of everyone too. It was like you already knew what had happened to your Ma."

"Might explain something about my stage-fright," I said with a wry chuckle. "I always thought I was just a big gutless wonder." Doris shook her head and put a hand on my shoulder.

"Just the opposite, Angus. You were always such a brave little boy. But all you wanted was your Momma to hear you sing. All you wanted was your Momma."

# VALENTINE

Doris was right. All I'd wanted was my mother.

And not just when I was a boy of seven but when I was a man too. It was as if part of me was still waiting for her to show up, still waiting for her to come and hear me sing. But that would never happen. And maybe I didn't need it to anymore.

What I did need, though, was the answer to a question. One that was on my mind the whole flight from Memphis to New York:

*Where to from here?*

As urgent as it was for me to come up with the money to pay off Hank's debts, I was also thinking about my life beyond this American trip. I was certain I wanted that life to include Cherry but what could I give her? I had no career, no savings, and soon—no home. I wasn't exactly the most promising prospect.

"Welcome to the Big Apple," said Cherry, planting a lip-smacking welcome kiss on me at La Guardia airport. "Where, it's been said, if you can make it here…"

"You can make it anywhere. But what happens if you *can't* make it here," I said with a smirk. "Does that mean you can't make it anywhere?"

"We're not even going to entertain the idea of failure," said Cherry. "Now let me look at you. Are you alright?" With all the excitement of the recording session, I'd almost forgotten all about my death-defying stunt crash.

"I'm fine," I said. "A few scratches, a couple of bruised ribs, but I'm not finished with yet."

"You're certainly not," said Cherry, leading us off straight to the taxi rank.

"Thanks for taking my stuff from Nashville," I said. "I didn't mean to lump you with my guitar and an extra bag to lug on the plane but I didn't know I was going to end up in Memphis again."

"Glad I could help," said Cherry. "But if your muse ever sends you off on another adventure, maybe just give me a call first? I was worried about you."

"Worried? Really?"

"Maybe you bumped your head worse than you think you did?" she said, pretending to knock-knock on my noggin. "Hello, Angus! Of course I was worried. I care about you."

Hearing Cherry say that made me smile. But I didn't say anything, just held onto the feeling. Then, on the taxi ride to our Manhattan hotel, Cherry and I held hands in the back of the cab, but didn't speak much. I was very glad to reunited with someone I couldn't imagine being apart from again.

After checking in, I was surprised when Cherry told me Slade was staying in the same hotel as Cherry and I. No matter how many messages I left on his cell and with reception, though, Slade wouldn't respond. I had little chance of convincing him to let me do the big final gig if I couldn't even speak with him, so I spent the next couple of days dropping off copies of my latest recording to various

New York record companies. I also found out where Gil Teaman was staying and left a copy for him at hotel reception; he had his own label and maybe his fears of working with me had died down since Nashville.

But unfortunately, after days of traipsing around New York, I still hadn't heard back from Gil and it seemed alternate-country ballad singers weren't high on the other record companies list of 'must sign' acts either; most of them wouldn't even accept my unsolicited material for fear of being sued should one of their own acts put out anything remotely similar.

New York was turning out to be a dead end.

So, on the day of the gig, after not hearing back from Slade or Gil or anyone, Cherry and I went for a walk in Central Park where we were due to meet up with Oli and Penelope. The crisp November air and autumn leaves made for a very romantic setting.

"Thanks for all your help," I said, tightening a woolen scarf around my neck and kicking a bunch of leaves. "I wouldn't have made it this far if it wasn't for all your encouragement. I owe you a lot."

"You don't owe me anything," said Cherry, with a smile, apparently amused by my enthusiastic leaf kicking. "I love your music and I want you to do well. You deserve it." Cherry and I continued our meandering stroll along a wide path lined by rugged-up bench-sitters.

"I just wish I hadn't been so impulsive in Nashville," I said. "It looks like that move has cost me everything."

"No, it hasn't," said Cherry. "There's still time to turn it all around. You'll see."

"Slade won't even take my calls. What else can I do? The gig's tonight!"

"You'll think of something," she said. "Don't worry. Let's enjoy this," she added, opening up her arms to the park surrounding us.

"So where are we meant to meet the guys?" I said, moving aside to let a couple of speed walkers fly by.

"Penelope said by the lake, over there," said Cherry, pointing the way, taking my hand and leading us off.

"What else did she say?" I asked. Cherry let out a chuckle.

"Well, apparently it's not true at all that Amish people never get angry. Especially when they find two naked lovebirds 'nesting' in their field."

"Oli and Penelope really like sex, don't they?" I said. Cherry smiled.

"I don't blame them. It's not everyday you meet someone you have that sort of chemistry with." We came to a natural halt in the middle of the path, ignoring some joggers now forced to dodge around us.

"What about us?" I asked. "How's our chemistry?"

"I'd say it's pretty good," said Cherry, wrapping her arms around me and hugging her body against mine. "There's a definite positive attraction."

"I feel the same," I said. "I have since Melbourne."

"It's strange," said Cherry, "but even when I didn't know it was you performing in Parkes, I had some weird attraction to that bandana-wearing outlaw I watched up there on that stage."

"That's such a spin-out that you were in the audience then. You saw my first-ever public performance."

"And your first ever Pipsqueak gig too. Though maybe we shouldn't bring up Albuquerque again. When we do, all I think about is those two sluts hanging all over you in the band room."

"Yeah, okay," I agreed, "let's *not* bring up Albuquerque." Cherry smacked me on the bum and I squeezed hers as we kissed. I was the first to break off and

271

Cherry looked surprised.

"What's wrong?" she said. "You look so serious."

"There's something important I need to share with you," I said. "And I'm not sure if you'll like it."

"What is it?" said Cherry. "What are you talking about?" I reached into my knapsack and pulled out something I'd been waiting for just the right time to give her.

"Smokey!" she exclaimed. "You got me Smokey the Bear!" Cherry thanked me with a kiss on the cheek. "I *so* wanted to go to that museum too. But I guess a souvenir from you is the next best thing," said Cherry, checking the tag then dropping her jaw open in child-like amazement. "You're kidding?"

"I know," I said. "Old Smokey was *'Made in America'*."

"Just like you," said Cherry.

"And you," I said, lifting her into the air and spinning her in a classic New York Central Park Lover's Twirl, landing Cherry standing on a bench. It was almost a moment worthy of a proposal. Almost.

"It's weird," I said, helping her down, "but even when I was just a roadie I never thought I'd get married—you know, living on the road and all that."

"Easy Crocodile Dundee!" said Cherry. "Where'd that come from? Pretty quick to be talking about marriage, aren't you?"

"What?" I said. "You think I'm getting a bit too 'When Harry Met Sally' a bit too fast?"

"A bit. Life isn't a romantic comedy."

"Well, I sure hope to fuck it ain't a musical," I said. "Otherwise I'll have to break into song." I started crooning my latest, a fifties-inspired love song, my first ever New York composition.

*"Will you be mine? Valentine?*

*On my lips, place a kiss, if you will."*

"What's that?" said Cherry.

"Another new one. It's called 'Valentine'. You like?"

"I do."

"It's yours," I said, theatrically handing her an invisible rose. Cherry bowed her head, taking the imaginary gift.

"Anyway, don't you at least want to take me home to meet Ma and Pa first?" Realizing what she'd said, Cherry instinctively covered her mouth.

"Might be a bit difficult," I said. "On both counts."

"Sorry," said Cherry. I shook my head, *don't worry.*

"But you can definitely meet Hank," I said. "And I know he'll love you." We walked on a bit until coming to the edge of the lake, where Cherry stopped to admire her new stuffed toy.

"So," I said, "as someone who knows this great city a whole lot better than me, can you tell me how I can get to Madison Square Garden?"

"Be really good at basketball," joked Cherry. "Why do you want to go there?"

"I've got one more thing I want to try," I said.

"Oh, yeah," said Cherry. "What's your big idea?" Before I could explain further though, a couple of familiar figures emerged from a nearby bush. For some reason I wasn't at all surprised at seeing Oli leading Penelope back onto the path, both of them still in the process of adjusting their disheveled clothes.

"Hey, partner!" exclaimed Oli. "Imagine bumping into each other in the Big Apple!"

"Hi, Cherry," said Penelope, before casually explaining why she was buttoning up her jeans. "We got bored waiting and decided to have a little cuddle." Cherry laughed.

"You guys never stop! Seriously? It's freezing. And what if someone saw you. Do you really think the middle of the day in Central Park is the best time for a randy romp?"

"It's always time for *love*, partner," said Oli.

"Let them watch," said Penelope. "We've got nothing to be ashamed of."

"Though you're right, Cherry," said Oli. "It is a bit on the shrinky-dinky-winky chilly side. I wouldn't mind if it was a bit warmer. Especially if people are wanting to watch." Oli winked at Cherry, who motioned with her finger in her mouth, *sick*!

"Whatever," said Cherry, smiling and rolling her eyes. "Now do you guys want to come with us? Angus wants to go to the garden."

"We never left," said Penelope, placing a leaf in front of her crotch.

"Well, come on then, Adam and Eve," I said, pointing to a distant cab rank, "let's share a taxi." Oli and Penelope followed Cherry and me as we headed off to catch our ride.

"Oohhhh," cooed Oli, "it'll be just like how we all got together in Los Angeles, when we shared a cab from the airport to West Hollywood."

"Oh, Oli, you're such a romantic," said Penelope. Breaking into a fast run towards the taxi rank, I yelled out with the self-assured confidence of a true New Yorker.

"Taxi!!"

Gil Teaman had had plenty of time to cool off since Nashville. And if he thought those songs I recorded at Sun were even half as good as I did, he'd have no option but to help me get that album to the world.

It was too good not to share.

# GIL TEAMAN AT THE GARDEN

The Garden.

Besides Carnegie Hall, Madison Square Garden is New York's most prestigious concert venue. When we arrived at the enormous auditorium—famous for having hosted everyone from Elvis to the LA Lakers—a vast crew of technicians and hired helping hands was busy at work. Lightning technicians scurried up ladders, sound techs tested leads for life and microphones for tone, and stagehands pushed amps on wheels and unopened flight-cases in and around all the pre-show action, deftly weaving through the organized chaos.

The stage was being set for one big show.

Backstage, I pleaded my case with Gil while the others waited in the empty V.I.P. area being set up front of stage.

"Ahh, fuck it!" said Gil, as I followed him up the stairs from side-stage to main. "Too early again." Gil was as jittery as an eighteen-year-old bomb-detector in Afghanistan. "That's the problem with those uppers," Gil said, showing me a handful of blue pills. "They get me *up* too early. What I really *needs* is some 'on-timers'. What color pill you reckon they'd be, Angus?"

"I don't know," I said, with a wave back to the gang waiting expectantly. Cherry, Oli and Penelope smiled as Gil paced back and forth across the stage, testing and marking out how much room he'd have that night to shake his country thang.

"Green? *Lime*? I think lime. Lime is an 'on-time' sort of color. Maybe I should do a side-line of prescription drugs. 'Gil Teaman's On-Timers: a safe way to balance out your act.' What do you think?" I shrugged and laughed which only made Gil's mood and expression more serious. "No, really," he said. "What do you think, Angus?"

"I wanted to ask you the same thing," I said. Gil frowned.

"You wanted to ask me whether or not you should branch out from music into pharmaceutical manufacturing?" he said.

"No. About my record. What do you think about my record? Is it good enough to put out on your label?" Gil grimaced and then drew a slow breath, a forced meditation to calm his jumpy self.

"Sure it's good enough," he said plainly. "*Sure*. Why I'd go so far up that baby's dress as to say it's fantastic, even. You say you did all those songs in one night?"

"Yep. One session," I said. Though I was still waiting on a final mix from Billy, I had a rough mix I'd given Gil to listen to. It wasn't perfect but it definitely had a vibe; those Memphis boys and I *had* caught some magic.

"And you ain't done no overdubs or Pro-Toolin'."

"No studio tricks at all."

"But it sounds pretty slick—how'd ya do it?" Gil flashed paranoid looks over each shoulder—*who was watching?* "You been into my uppers, boy?" I shook my head to confirm I hadn't.

"No, I wasn't on drugs and yes—it was all live." Gil seemed put at ease. Suddenly he became utterly joyful.

"Fantastic!" he screamed, before coming over serious again. "But no. I ain't puttin' it out on my label. No way, *mate*."

"Why not? You seem to love what you've heard. I think Pipsqueak can be huge, Gil."

"Maybe, but not with me. Thing is, we only do straight country on my label and your stuff is a bit 'alternative', innit? You're mixin' blues and folk and rockabilly—hell, you even got some soul in there."

"Heaven forbid," I said drolly.

"Look, your music is too 'eclectic'," he said, making air quotes around eclectic. "Ya got too much goin' on. Are you country? Are you rock? Are you blues? Are you coming? Are you going? Are you staying? Are you leaving? Look at me, I'm simple. Simple, simple, simple. I play country songs about trucks, girls and gettin' wasted—'The American Way'. Bang! Maybe they mixed you up down under?" Gil stopped dead as suddenly as he'd exploded. He scratched his chin. "Still, that 'So' is a great song. I'd love to record it—if the heat ever cools on you. Maybe one day I will?" Gil shrugged resignedly. "Could be a while though. You really pissed those Nashville sons-a-bitches off good—bad."

"Please, Gil. You don't know what this means to me—to my family. I can't go back to Melbourne with nothing. You don't have to give me a big advance or anything; just give me a chance to get my record out to the people. I think they'll love it as much as I do, as much as you seem to."

"I'd like to help you but—like I said in Nashville—it's putting my image in danger just hangin' with you like this." Gil spooked himself back into his pill-induced paranoid frenzy. "There could be paparazzis—countryazzis—fuckin' Nazis—anywhere!"

"Maybe there's something else you could do instead then?"

"What? Where?" Gil's eyes peeled off into every corner of the shadowy auditorium.

"Slade's cancelled my appearance tonight but…"

"He's cancelled you?" said Gil. "Oh, that's too bad. Why'd he do that? That's cruel. You come all this way from Melbourne to do this show and he goes and blows it out on ya. That's just cruel."

"He says it's just business," I said.

"Well, I guess you did kind of throw him over the metaphorical chair and ass-fuck him—without so much as spittin' on his ring," said Gil. "It is just business though. It can be cruel, to both the giver and the getter. If you know what I mean?"

"Maybe?" I said.

"Though on the other hand, you were just putting on the best show you could, you didn't mean to piss Slade off, did you?"

"No. Well, I mean, I thought me doing my own thing would probably drive him crazy but it wasn't my intention. I wanted to share that song about Elvis and so that's what I did."

"So what are you going to do next?" asked Gil, momentarily at ease with the seeming absence of unauthorized photographers lurking behind the stage curtains.

"Since Slade's cancelled my spot," I said, "I was thinking maybe I could come on and sing with you in yours?" Gil's face dropped from happy content to deadpan droll again.

"You're kiddin'?" he said. "Ain't you been listenin'? You got the Nashville heat on you right now. And not the *good* kind of Nashville heat—not the 'he's-one-of-us-white-guys-beer-drinking-n'-tractor-driving-on-a-summer's-day' heat but the 'brand-on-his-ass-says-he-thinks-he's-too-good-for-country' *bad* heat. Why on earth would I invite you up to sing with me and risk being tainted with the same branding iron that's seared your cheeks?"

"Well, it might actually be good for your image? I think some of the younger audience might relate better to one of the 'Nashville Establishment'—like your good self—showing he's not afraid to mix with an alternative 'eclectic' like me. Whatever those Nashville cats thought of my rockin' up the country awards with my unscheduled Elvis tribute, the truth is, Gil—controversy sells." Gil considered my angle for a moment then gave an encouraging nod.

"Hmmm. I ain't thought about it like that. Hmmm." Sensing an opportunity, I struck quick.

"We don't have to do any of my songs. I'd just be happy to share the stage with you. I want to finish what I started and do this final show." Gil nodded, still thinking; I could almost hear the manic mental wheels turning over in his mind.

"It might help convince Nashville you ain't such a Godless wild card too?"

"Exactly."

"Then, if you can be seen to have redeemed yourself in the eyes of the record-buying public I might be able to do 'So' just like I wanted to," said Gil more excitedly. "Without fear of any professional reprisals?"

"How about it?" I said, smiling back. Gil looked torn again. I thought he was going to pull the pin.

"Fuck it!" he screamed, scaring a nearby lightning technician halfway off his ladder. "Let's do it! See you tonight, Angus the Pipsqueak Hank Flynn Junior." Gil stopped and shook his head disapprovingly. "Hey, you really gotta come up with a better stage name one day. You don't want to be somebody's 'Junior' all your life, do ya?" Gil winked.

"Thanks, Gil," I said, shaking his hand. "You are an absolute life saver. See you tonight."

"Sure," said Gil, bending over to check a guitar amp for a hidden spy-camera. "Life saver, hey?" he said, standing up and taking a reverential tone. "You know I did save a life once? It was a pregnant horse back on my ranch in Dallas. If I hadn't a put my arms deep into her nether regions she and her slippery little little fella woulda both been summoned up to that great stable in the sky." Gil teared up as he struggled to finish telling his amazing tale. "I get emotional just thinking 'bout that night. The night I was blessed with the honor of saving that baby horsey. Jeepers. I love my ranch."

Leaving Gil to reflect on the spiritual experience of horse birthing, I went to tell the gang the good news: I was going to get a chance to perform in New York after all—with America's biggest country star's stamp of approval. And, with no sign of Slade yet getting in my way, maybe I could salvage the Hank Flynn dynasty; and maybe even kick-start Pipsqueak's plans to conquer the world of music.

Whatever was going to happen, at least I had one more chance before heading back down under.

# SANTA CLAUS IS COMING …

That night, after picking up tickets Gil had left for Cherry, Oli and Penelope at the ticket booth, I kissed Cherry goodbye and made my way to the artist's entrance of Madison Square Garden. The heavy door was guarded by a bunch of black, mountain-sized security guards, each menacingly shadowing the other in identical suits. Their leader held a clipboard in one hand, his other fingering a spy-like transmitter stuck in his ear. The stony expression on his otherwise unreadable face clearly indicated a problem.

"Your name's not on my list," he said, in the hushed tone of an overly self-important CIA agent. He checked his ear-transmitter was in place again while looking me up and down disapprovingly, perhaps looking for signs of a concealed weapon in my cowboy boots.

"Are you sure?" I said. "But I *am* performing tonight. Gil Teaman invited me as his special guest." CIA checked his clipboard again. He shook his head.

"Doesn't look like you're anyone's guest tonight. Please move aside." CIA moved his finger from holding his ear-piece in place to jab me in the chest. I stepped back, stumbling slightly at the force of his prodding. Two heavily made-up ladies wearing impossibly high heels walked past me with a flutter of fake lashes. Immediately I recognized them. What was better—they recognized me.

"Angus Flynn!" exclaimed the tall leggy blond I'd met at the Peabody Hotel. "What are you doing here? Shouldn't you be inside?" When her brunette friend (with impossibly perfect augmented breasts) turned around, there was no doubting it: these were Gil's gals, the party girls from Nashville.

"Why aren't you backstage and ready to go?" asked my new best bosom-buddy. "Gil told us you two have a special surprise for everyone tonight."

"Yeah," said the blond. "Why aren't you inside already?"

"Seems I'm not on the door list," I said with a shrug. "When you go in, do you think you could maybe let Gil know there's been a mix-up?" The blond smiled and lent down to whisper in my ear.

"No need, handsome," she said.

"We'll get you in," whispered the brunette. With that, the two sexy girls went into flirt mode, flanking CIA and whispering in *his* ear in unison.

"He's with us," they purred. And before you could say 'open Sesame Street', CIA had stepped aside and waved me through with his clipboard.

"If these fine ladies vouch for you," he said with a wink to Blondie, "that's enough for me."

I thanked the girls, and knowing I didn't have long until showtime, ran down the hall towards backstage. The show was about to begin. But with no sign of Gil, I waited patiently in the black-curtained dark space of the artist's holding-pen, alongside a few Santa-helper dancers also waiting their cue.

"What are you doing here?" said Slade, emerging from a dark corner like the malevolent spirit he is.

"Waiting for my invitation. Gil has asked me to join him tonight."

"You're not going on that stage," said Slade angrily.

"Yes I am. Gil has invited me. I'm his special guest."

"There's nothing 'special' about you, Pipsqueak. You had your chance and you blew it. All you need to be worrying about now is how you're going to pay off your rather expensive coast-to-coast tour. You didn't really think I was going to pay for *my* band to do *your* songs, did you?"

"I don't know what I expected from you, Slade. But I know what I'm doing now. I'm going up there and I'm singing with Gil."

"You're not singing with anyone," said Slade, stepping between me and the stage and crossing his arms. "Your career is finished before it began. And just like your old man's sad story, of him running away to Australia when things dried up for him here, you're going to go back down under with nothing. Like father like son, hey?"

"You're an idiot," I said. "My dad's life isn't a sad story. He was—he is—a great songwriter who made some bad business decisions, that's all." Slade moved his hands to his hips and tilted his head with a curious expression.

"Yeah, he made some bad decisions. My publishing company will make more off Hank when's he's dead. You didn't know that did you? You didn't know I own 'My Best Present Ever' did you? And the good thing is, we probably won't be waiting long to put out a posthumous 'best of' package. No doubt the stress you caused old Hank—by fucking up his chance to live out the few remaining years of his life in his own home—will be enough to push him over the edge." I shoved Slade hard in his chest. He stumbled back, falling on his ass.

"If you're lucky," said Slade, scrambling to his feet, "you might make it home in time for your old man's funeral." With a short step and a quick long hook I landed a punch square on Slade's jaw. The cracking sound it made caused the stage manager to gasp and the dancers to look away in horror—then quickly back in fascination. But as Slade crumpled to the floor, nobody moved in to help him. It seemed everyone knew the guy had it coming.

"I'll be at *your* funeral before his," I said. Slade pulled himself to his knees, spitting out another threat.

"You'll be in jail before you can get to the fucking airport! Nobody fucks with Slade Gaitlin. Fuck!" I stepped forward ready to finish Slade off with another one-two (three-four?) when the M.C. began his introduction for the first performer, the 'legendary country treasure, Gil Teaman'. On cue, Gil ran out of the hallway, through the holding pen Slade and I had accommodated as a boxing ring. Doing a double-take as he passed Slade on the floor, Gil propped himself momentarily on the stage stairs, surveying the scene.

"I love show business!" he said. "Folk are so passionate!" Gil turned and ran onstage just as the curtain opened and his band fired up with the opening number. "Woo-hoo!!" He screamed and the crowd went wild.

The big show had begun.

Christmas-colored red and green lights flashed off giant brass baubles hanging all around the arena. Sparkling silver stars dropped down from the ceiling. Oversized bails of hay, prop tractors parked around the stage, pantomime painted pitchforks and randomly tossed cowboy hats completed the picture of a Christmas country hoedown. A spotlight flashed on Gil's face and he smiled comically: a kid in a candy shop. Gil took the mic and gave a big old Texas welcome.

"Hey, everyone!" he said, waving gleefully, like a desert island mad man spotting a plane. "So tell me," he said in a deep voice, calm and conspiratorial, close to the mic.

"When—is—Santa—gonna—come?" Then, half-leading, half-following, he joined the audience answering as one:

"WHEN—THE—SUN—GOES—DOWN!!"

The guitarist played a familiar low-down riff.

"And please welcome with me out onto this stage now a fine man of my acquaintance—no, my *good friend*, Angus Flynn!" Gil stepped back from the mic, offering the stage theatrically to me. I bounded up the stairs to the second mic.

"Thanks, Gil," I said, turning to the packed house. "G'day New York! I've come a long way from down under and it's a real pleasure and a genuine privilege to share the stage with a country legend such as Gil Teaman. I'm especially honored to be invited to sing with Gil on his country classic, the song he made famous around the world. Whichever hemisphere you're from, chances are—like me—you know every word." Gil sang the melody and I took a harmony. We both gave it our all and everyone sang along.

In the front row, Oli and Penelope cheered me on while Cherry smiled behind her video camera, capturing every moment of my Big Apple debut. I flashed her a smile as Gil put his arm around me and the two of us took his classic country song home.

*Santa Claus is coming*
*Santa Claus is coming*
*Santa Claus is coming when the sun goes down*

I hadn't given too much thought to it before coming up on stage, but now that I was in the middle of a rip-roaring show at Madison Square Garden, I knew what those other songwriters meant when they'd said that stuff about if you could make it here, you could make it anywhere. This was New York City.

But it felt like the whole world was watching.

# THE NATURAL ESCAPE

The morning after the triumphant gig at Madison Square Garden, Gil woke me up, phoning me to make sure I was watching the morning news. Every major station was running the same story: *the Gil Teaman Christmas Spectacular.*

"Congratulations," I said. "That should help you move a few units this Chrissy."

"Chrissy? Who's that?" said Gil.

"It's what we call Christmas in Australia, Gil. *Chrissy* is Christmas."

"I knew that," said Gil. "I *also* knew all that Nashville shit'd blow over on you. Didn't I tell you?"

"You did,' I said, not seeing any point in correcting him. "And you were right."

"I was?"

"You were."

"Good. Great. You know what this means, don't you? Now I can do 'So'," said Gil. "Probably not until next year sometime, though. But I'll definitely be giving that ballad of yours a whirl. I might even like to see what else you got up your songwriting sleeves?"

"There's plenty," I said. "I'll send you some more demos when I get back to Melbourne."

"You do that, boy. You do that. I'll be at my ranch, takin' care of my horsies, waitin' for the latest new country sound to come up from down under. But don't make me wait too long, boy. I get bored waitin'. Doctors say I got attention deficit disorder. If I don't get me a heap of attention I go crazy."

"I won't forget you, Gil," I said. "I couldn't." Before I hung up I thanked Gil again for the chance to play New York, and he offered me a support slot next time he toured Australia.

*Cool.*

Later that day, I returned from the counter to our table at Rosario's New York Pizzeria with an extra slice of pizza for everyone.

"You shouldn't have," said Cherry, taking off her latest souvenir purchase, an 'I Love NY' baseball cap, "but I'm glad you did." Oli and Penelope were just as appreciative.

"Nice one, partner," said Oli, as I handed him his Pepperoni.

"Thanks, Pipsqueak," said Penelope, taking her Veggie Special. Penelope moved her laptop aside, being careful, as were the others, not to get any greasy hands on the pile of blank postcards, collected on our travels, and now scattered across the table. An assortment of scenes from Hollywood and Santa Monica Pier and everywhere from 'Las Casuelas Bar and Restaurant', Palm Springs to Niagara Falls were all represented. I had about a dozen from Memphis (Sun Studios and Graceland mostly), and like everyone's, they were all blank. We'd been so busy having fun we hadn't had a chance to write to anyone.

"Sorry I can't afford something more flash for this 'thank you' dinner," I said, "but I really appreciate everything you guys have done in helping me along the way."

"It was fun," said Cherry. "And now I can say I've finally seen the Grand Canyon."

"Don't forget Albuquerque," said Oli, moaning as he chewed his hot and spicy. "That was my personal favorite."

"I bet it was," said Penelope.

"Yes, Albuquerque was fun—even for me," said Cherry. "Besides, if I hadn't taken off then, Angus would have one less song in his songbook. I think 'When You Left Me in Albuquerque' could be one of his best ballads yet." She turned to Penelope who was now captivated by her laptop screen. "Watcha surfin'?" Penelope looked up long enough to take another bite of pizza.

"Just checking out where Oli and I are headed next," said Penelope, turning to Oli. "This place is fantastic, Oli. We're going to have so much fun there." Penelope swiveled the computer around so we could all see the screen. "What do you think?" A tree-trunk font proclaimed the official website of *The Natural Escape: a nudist colony for nature lovers.*

"So it's official?" I asked with a smile. "Are you going legit? Have you two streakers crossed over from 'Experimental Wild Alfresco' to your everyday standard nudist?" Cherry laughed as Oli and Penelope nodded enthusiastically.

"Yes, partner," explained Oli. "As a matter of fact we've not only crossed over but we're taking over as well." Penelope grinned proudly.

"You're looking at the new managing couple of America's most popular nudist resort," she said. "Well, at least *North Carolina's.*"

"As long as the face-to-face interview goes as well as the Skyped one, we'll be running our own nudie park in a couple of weeks."

"You're kidding?" said Cherry.

"Nope," said Penelope. "I've spent more than enough of my life in a closed cabin. This trip across country, from LA to—here, reminded me how much I love the great outdoors, and how I'm ready for a change." Penelope turned the computer back her way, closing it conclusively.

"Are you staying in the States then, Oli?" I asked. "How can you do that? Don't you need a green-card or something?" Oli nodded as he moved the postcards aside to find a cardboard frame with 'Remember Las Vegas With Love' printed at the top. He and Penelope gazed at it lovingly as he held it up so we could see the picture inside the cut-out love heart.

"We got drunk," said Penelope.

"And we got married," said Oli.

"In Vegas," they said together. Oli kissed Penelope, who playfully pushed him away to explain.

"We both forgot all about it until I found this stuffed in the bottom of one of my bags. We were going to tell you guys before but thought we'd wait until after your big gig, Angus."

"Didn't want to upstage ya, partner," said Oli.

"You should have," I said. "Congratulations. That's cool."

"It kind of is, isn't it?" said Penelope.

"Definitely," said Cherry. "It's exciting."

"This calls for more than lemonade!" I said. "Anyone want a beer?" Amidst the laughter, everyone raised their hands. As I started to dig through my pockets for change, Penelope grabbed me by the arm.

"You should stay too, Angus," said Penelope. "You were born here so you guys wouldn't even need to get married."

"We wouldn't *need* to," said Cherry. 'But what if we wanted to?" She raised her eyebrows playfully and I felt a strange sensation in my chest. I think my heart skipped a beat. *Was Cherry just kidding around about wanting to get married?* Penelope smiled conspiratorially. She opened her laptop back up and typed in a new search.

"And here's another reason why Angus should stay in America," said Penelope. Oli moved close to Penelope's side and Cherry and I moved around behind her so we could all see what she was talking about. "Look how many hits that YouTube video Cherry did for you already has." Cherry had uploaded the video she'd taken of my Nashville performance of 'The King'.

"Ten thousand and six?" said Cherry. 'That's pretty good for a home video."

"No," said Penelope. "Look again."

"Wait," said Cherry. "*One million* and six?" She hugged my waist tight. "Angus, your video has already had over one million views! I told you! 'The King: Live in Nashville' is a hit!"

"Really?" I said, looking closer. "Has it? Jeez, you're right. Maybe we should stay?" Penelope nodded.

"You should. You could work for us," she said.

"As much fun as that sounds like," I said, "we've got to get back and make sure Hank is okay." Cherry took my hand.

"Angus is taking me home to meet Daddy," she said. "You guys aren't the only ones getting serious."

"And even with the good news my song is proving popular on the internet," I said, "whatever happens, I won't have enough money to pay back Max in time. Hank and I are going to have to sort out something else." I turned to Cherry. "Better pack a tent. It looks like you might get to see more of the Australian bush than you were counting on."

"It's not over yet," said Cherry. "But don't worry, whatever happens, I love camping out under the stars." I gave her a wry look as the others went back to inspecting the homepage for their new home.

"Might be our only option?" I said. "Better bring your sleeping bag too."

## TAKING CARE OF BUSINESS

The morning of our flight out of New York, the street outside our hotel was as busy as usual with the morning peak-hour. Loading Cherry's last bag into the trunk, then my guitar on top, I felt a little sad to be leaving New York so soon—and without Oli. Sliding into the backseat to join Cherry I felt happy though, knowing my old partner had, in Penelope, found someone to continue a whole new adventure with. I gave Cherry a kiss, knowing I'd found the same thing too.

We arrived in Los Angeles a few days ahead of our long-haul to Melbourne. At Cherry's suggestion, and between visits with Cherry's grandmother, we decided to visit with Ginger to share tales of our adventures. Back at Elvis's old Beverly Hills home, our favorite sexy septuagenarian was loving hearing all about our trip across America.

"So you found out what you wanted to know," said Ginger, returning from the kitchen with a tray of piña coladas, each cocktail complete with pink paper umbrella. "I hope seeing Roy was helpful? I really must head out to the springs and share some beans n' rice with that old boy.

It's been too long."

"He was a great help," I said, taking my drink. "And so was Doris White, one of Mum's old dancing friends Roy told me to visit."

"Doris! Yes, I should have told you to find her too. How is Doris? Boy, I miss our old gang. We had some great times together."

"Doris is just like you," said Cherry, moving her drink's umbrella aside so it wouldn't poke her eye out, "she looks amazing for her age too." Ginger smiled then frowned.

"I'll take the 'amazing' and leave the 'for her age'," she said with a wry grin. Ginger stepped forward and kissed Cherry on the cheek. "You're too kind."

"Doris gave me this," I said, showing Ginger the photo of Elvis with his arm around Mum in front of his favorite roller-coaster, the Zippin Pippin. "It's not exactly a blood sample but it's close enough for me. Look how happy Mum is."

"Elvis had a way of making girls happy," said Ginger. "If you know what I mean?" Suddenly distracted, Ginger peered through a floor-to-ceiling window towards a large swimming pool on the other side.

"When's he coming?" I asked, remembering Ginger's penchant for home visiting handymen, giving a wink to Cherry.

"Who?" asked Ginger innocently.

"The pool man, of course," said Cherry, playing along. Ginger shook her head disappointedly.

"He's not," she said. "I fired him. Couldn't keep up. No, I'm waiting for a new helping hand. The fumigator."

"Sounds painful," said Cherry.

"Oh, darling—he's got a hose and he knows where it goes." Nursing my cocktail, I ambled over to an upright piano, scratched and worn with who knew what history.

Ginger noticed I was wearing my Elvis Presley TCB buckle, the one Mum found after Elvis lost it riding the Zippin Pippin.

"Angus, that is a beauty," she said, pointing to my buckle (I hoped she was pointing to my buckle).

"Doris gave it to me," I said. "Yeah, it's a bit flash for every day wear but when in Beverley Hills…"

Ginger smiled. "At least you got something out of the estate," she said. "And if you ever need a little extra cash to kick start your music career—or whatever life you and Cherry might be thinking about making together—you've got a nice head start there. Thanks to ol' Pretzel."

"What do you mean?" I said. "Is this worth a lot of money?" Ginger's eyebrows popped, almost off the top of her forehead.

"Do you know how many rich and crazy people around the world collect rare Elvis memorabilia? And I can't be certain but I'd say that buckle has never come up for auction before. It's probably a one-off too. Angus, you've got a house holding your jeans up."

"But that buckle is all Angus has to remember Elvis by," said Cherry. I smiled knowingly, running my hand over the piano.

"It's not *all* I have to remember him by," I said. "I've got this too." I waved the hand wearing Roy's TCB ring and sat down at the piano. I flipped the lid and began to play the song turning out to be, thanks to Cherry, a YouTube sensation.

*He made his name by singing, love and pain*
*Rock and roll*
*He made his name by singing, love and pain*
*Rock and roll*
*And they took all of his possessions*
*Thank God they could not take his soul*

I stopped singing as Ginger put her hands on mine.

"Now, don't think I'm a crazy old woman—especially the 'old' bit—but I just got a chill up my spine when I remembered you were born on the same day Pretzel left us, weren't you?"

"Yeah," I said, "same day."

"What if he left us but his spirit never did? What if part of Pretzel—like his soul, I guess is what I'm talking about—zoomed over from that Graceland bathroom and wiggled into your baby body for another go on this roller-coaster ride of life? Do you believe in reincarnation, Angus?" I looked to Cherry, shrugged, and was about to try and come up with an answer that didn't make Ginger feel either crazy *or* old, when the sound of car brakes squealing out front broke up our impromptu séance. Ginger's eyes lit up and it was clear she had another, infinitely more pressing question on her mind now: *was that Mr Fumigator in her drive?*

Ginger started clapping her hands in front of her chest, running out of the room to the front door. Cherry grabbed me by the hand and led me over to look out the window, so we could both see what all the fuss was about. Seeing the catchy slogan on the side of Ginger's pest-control professional's van we both started laughing:

*We go in where others fear to go.*

# CHERRY

Cherry and I spent the remaining few days in LA back at the same West Hollywood hotel Oli and I had shared when we'd first arrived.

Cherry didn't have a flat of her own (having moved in with Penelope before heading to Australia) and the Saharan was in a good location to serve both of our purposes: Cherry wanted to visit with her grandmother in the nursing home and I was hoping to get in some of the sightseeing I'd missed out on during my first visit.

From The Whiskey A Go Go bar (where The Doors used to play) to the famous Chinese Theatre (where movie stars still came to put their hands in concrete) Cherry and I hit all the tourist spots. Then, on the morning of our flight back to Australia, I surprised Cherry by taking her somewhere extra special, somewhere she hadn't even heard of, a place called Hot Pawn.

"I don't know if I feel like hitting a strip joint today," said Cherry, as we pulled up in her Kombi to the address I'd got off the internet. "You know I'm not a prude or anything but some things are better at night, aren't they?"

"It's not *porn* porn," I said, smiling. "It's *pawn* pawn.

Look." I pointed to the pawnbroker's shop I'd come to do business with. Its window was full of electric guitars, a testament to the financial hardships faced by many a musician before me, whether outlaw country or LA glam rock. "I phoned around almost every auction house and antique dealer in town and the guy here offered me the most. If he likes what he sees." Cherry frowned.

"If he likes what?"

"The buckle," I said, pulling it out. "I'm going to do what Ginger suggested and sell Pretzel's TCB buckle."

"You don't have to do that," said Cherry. "I'm still more than happy to ask Mum for a loan." Cherry touched the turquoise studs and fingered the diamonds adorning the shiny buckle. "It's a pretty impressive souvenir. You don't get more rock n' roll than Elvis's long-lost belt buckle either?"

"Except maybe Elvis's long lost son?" I said with a smile.

"Except that," agreed Cherry.

"Thanks again for your offer, but no thanks. All I want to do is pay off Flynn Station. Thanks to Elvis, and this, I can do just that."

"But wouldn't you like to keep it?"

"It's just a buckle," I said. "Besides, I've got the ring Roy gave me."

Inside Hot Pawn I met the owner, a sly looking fellow of about sixty, with a handlebar moustache. He seemed surprised I actually had what I'd said I had: the original Presley buckle.

"I've only seen photos before now," he said, as the expert he'd brought in to inspect it gave it a thorough going over. "Now here it is in our hot little hands." After verifying the buckle's authenticity, the guy came good on the tentative offer he'd made over the phone: one hundred and fifty thousand dollars. With such a large sum he had to wire it though, so I had him send it directly to Hank's account instead.

*Elated? Happy? Relieved?* The emotions I felt at the moment I realized Flynn Station was safe were many. And knowing I hadn't needed any of Slade's money at all only made the deal that much more sweeter.

"What about that?" said the owner, twirling his moustache, and pointing to my TCB ring. "You want me to take that off your hands too?"

"No thanks," said Cherry, answering for me. "That's not for sale."

"She's right," I said. "I'm keeping this." The owner pursed his lips.

"You sure? Could buy yourselves a couple round-the-world trips with what I'd offer you for that."

"Like we said—no, we're sure," said Cherry. "And, thanks anyway, but our travel plans are all taken care of." Cherry led me out as I thanked him, and we were on our way again. Back in the Kombi, Cherry let me drive as long as I promised to stay on the right side of the road.

"Literally, the *right* side," she reminded me. With my experience of driving a fair part of the way across the country now, I managed to get us safely to Pasadena and the nursing home where we'd already said our big goodbyes to Cherry's grandmother the day before. Before catching our flight to Melbourne, Cherry wanted to see her grandmother one more time. She'd also made a deal to sell her Kombi to one of the male nurses at the home, so after this last stop, all our loose ends would be tied up.

Arriving at the home, Cherry jumped out and kissed me through the open window.

"I feel a bit guilty running off to Australia again," said Cherry. "But I guess I shouldn't. Grandma really loves you. She said as soon as she saw us together she knew."

"Knew what?" I said. "What does Grandma know?"

"Beats me," said Cherry. "Something about us being 'meant for each other'. Apparently she's never seen me so happy."

"That's good, isn't it? Anyway, she's only a plane trip away," I said. "A fourteen-hour hop, skip and jump, long-haul flight. That's all."

"Thanks for reminding me," said Cherry, rolling her eyes. "I won't be long. Just wanted to drop these off too." Cherry held up a bag of souvenirs and pulled out a baseball cap from the Grand Canyon and another from New York. She walked off with a spring in her step. "I'll have to get Grandma a Melbourne one next."

Cherry disappeared inside and I waited a while, feeling quite content just sitting in the Kombi, reflecting on the great fun we'd had in it over the past few weeks. Remembering I hadn't yet told Hank about the cash on its way, I went and found a public phone to call him and let him know our financial troubles were no more.

"They just sent through the whole amount, Dad. You should get it in a day or so. I wanted you to know so you can stop worrying. There's plenty to pay off Max with a bit left over."

"That's darn good news," said Hank. "I don't know how to thank you, son. We won't have to move your mother's ashes now. I can stay in this place until I die."

"It is good news, isn't it? But go easy on the 'til I die' talk, will you? You've got a few good years yet. Your heart's okay, isn't it?"

"Yeah, as long as I keep eatin' my greens, apparently. You comin' home now?" asked Hank. "I got a call from the music director at the Elvis Festival. They want you to take the main stage at Parkes this year instead of me. Your stunt performing 'The King' at Nashville has paid off big time, boy. You done put your old man out of a gig!"

"Yeah, I'm coming home," I said. "We're leaving today."

"We? You mean you and Oli?"

"No, as it turns out, Oli's staying on here. He met somebody. And so did I. Her name's Cherry."

"Well, I can't wait to meet her," said Hank. "And I can't wait to see you too. I love you, son."

"I love you too, Dad."

It felt good knowing I'd come through for Hank and I decided then wasn't the time to have the "so how about Mum and Elvis?" chat; when we hung up it was on good news: Flynn Station was safe and I was coming home.

Strolling back to meet Cherry, a Mercedes convertible drove by with 'My Best Present Ever' playing on the stereo. The old guy driving had a bald spot he checked as he waited, singing along, at the stop sign. With his suit, flash car and obvious follicle challenge I thought how different Hank was to this guy, a man of about seventy who, if he'd been spotted coming out of a 7-11, could easily have been mistaken for Elvis.

Or maybe it was just me.

Back at the Kombi, I waited for Cherry by flicking through all the lyrics I'd written since coming to America. I was amazed with how much inspiration I'd found in such a short time. My little book of lyrics was returning to Oz packed full. I read a verse to myself of the latest, a love song for a real person, something I swore I'd never do again after having my heart broken by Honey Rose as a teenager.

*When I look at you I smile*
*Feel like life's worth living*
*When I look at you I smile*
*Feel like life's beginning*
*You are the one, Cherry*
*You are the one I see*

Cherry came back to the car with the new owner in tow and I closed the journal on my yet unfinished song. As she went over the van's personal idiosyncrasies with the new owner, I wondered if I'd ever get the courage to sing a love song for Cherry? *After all,* I told myself, *maybe she'd react a lot better than Honey Rose had all those years ago?*

After Cherry handed over the keys of the Kombi, and we'd unloaded our luggage onto the sidewalk, we waited for our taxi to pick us up for LAX. Cherry seemed to go strangely silent and I started to worry she was having second thoughts about coming with me.

"Are you alright?" I said. "What's up?"

"You know, it's something I've been thinking about a lot," said Cherry. "Almost since we met."

"You're not going to bring up those damn pink socks again are you?" I said, nervous that what was bothering Cherry was much more serious than that.

"No, I've come to terms with those," she said, with the first signs of a cheeky smile. "It's something even more likely to upset you."

"What?"

"I really don't like the name Pipsqueak," said Cherry plainly. "I know it was a pet name your Mum had for you, but as a stage name I think it…well…sucks." Instead of being offended I was relieved.

"To be honest," I said. "I kind of agree with you. I just haven't been able to think of something better. Pipsqueak does sound more like a name for a pet piglet than a country balladeer, doesn't it."

"Phew," said Cherry, theatrically dropping her head into her hands. "I thought you might hate me for hating it."

"Oh, you *hate* it, do you? I thought you said you just didn't like it?"

"I hate it," said Cherry. "You definitely need a better

stage name than that."

"Okay then," I challenged, "tell me. What could be a better name than Pipsqueak?"

# ZIPPIN PIPPIN

*Z*ippin Pippin.

Cherry was right. My new stage name had practically been staring me in the face all along—the name of Elvis Presley's favorite roller-coaster. And by the time I got to Australia's biggest Elvis Festival for my first ever headline slot, that name was on a banner stretching across Parkes' main street.

*Zippin Pippin.*

Backstage preparing for the closing night finale, I thought my new name looked pretty good on the flyer promoting my appearance too.

*This year's VERY special guest: ZIPPIN PIPPIN. Performing his smash hit tribute song to the King.*

My stage persona was complete.

Opening up my guitar case, I flipped the flap on the compartment where I kept my plectrums, capo and other accessories. Inside, under a couple of coiled guitar strings, was my favorite photo of Mum—the one she'd signed 'with all her love' to her little 'Pipsqueak'. I slipped out Mum's picture and put it in my pocket. Then I placed a very happy snap of me and Cherry at the Grand Canyon into the empty frame. The place where we'd first made love. I smiled, reading to myself what Cherry had penned on the picture, over the blue sky above our heads:

"With all my love, Cherry. XXX'"

I put the new photo—in the old frame—back in my guitar case. Cherry stepped in front of me and began fumbling with my belt and the buckle she'd had custom-made for me.

"I love it," I said, planting a big kiss on her big beautiful lips.

"Good," said Cherry. "Because I do too. I think it's perfect." While Cherry adjusted my own version of a TCB buckle, a ZP buckle complete with two lightning bolts either side of the monogram, I thought about how much change the previous year had brought. A year ago I was preparing to stand in for Flynn, and now I had created my own act on the back of a whole new batch of my own songs. Cherry seemed to read my mind.

"You've come a long way, baby," she said, patting me on the back. I opened a flap on our green room that led to a larger adjoining tent, and ushered Cherry through to where Hank was there to meet us.

"So you reckon my son's got what it takes?" said Hank, slapping me on the back too. "I always said Angus had talent in his blood." Hank winked at Cherry, who looked awkwardly at me.

"In my blood, hey?" I said, distractedly re-checking my buckle. Since getting back to Melbourne I'd been so happy to have Cherry there, and to have saved Flynn Station, I hadn't felt the need to bombard Hank with questions about Elvis and Mum and him—and everything I'd learned in America. Cherry's look, though, seemed to suggest she thought now might finally be the time for that chat.

"I'm going to go and make sure I get a good position out front," said Cherry. "I don't want to get forced to the back of the crowd by some boozy floozies. Break a leg, Zippin!"

"Thanks," I said. "I couldn't have gotten here without you." Hank and I watched Cherry leave. When she was gone, Hank picked up a bottle of scotch from on top of an esky full of beers. "And I couldn't have gotten here without you either, Dad," I said.

"So," said Hank, pouring some scotch into two disposable cups, "you're still gonna call me 'Dad', hey boy?"

"Of course I am? Why do you say that?"

"Well, you must have found out what I told you about your Mum and Elvis was the truth?" said Hank, screwing the top back on the bottle. "I wasn't just high on drugs, was I?"

"Apparently not," I said. "But I don't care. Yes, I did find out a lot about Mum I didn't know but it hasn't changed the way I feel about her. Or you. I still love her the same and I love you too. You'll always be my father."

"That's good," said Hank, picking up the cups. "I'm glad you feel that way. It never meant any different to me who spawned ya, I loved you from the moment I laid eyes on you in hospital. Now I'm not saying what she did didn't hurt me, especially at the time—and maybe for sometime after too—but what is most important is how much we both loved you. Look, Angus, the seventies were a crazy time. Believe it or not, life today is a lot more conservative by comparison. I mean, even us country singers didn't miss out on the free-love thing. Bet you never thought of your folks as hippies though, did ya?"

"Not really," I said, strapping on my guitar. "Then again I grew up thinking Mum was a school teacher not a stripper."

304

"You found that out too, huh?"

"Doris White was very helpful."

"Yeah, well, whatever Doris told you about April you can take as gospel. Doris wouldn't lie about April. She loved your Mum. And she's as honest as my hair is long, grey and…dry, actually. I need to see about a new conditioner." I chuckled at Hank's attempt to lighten the weight of our deep and meaningful.

"You loved Mum too, Dad. It must have been really hard for you when you found out what she did?"

"I survived," said Hank, skulling one cup of scotch. "Besides, I got a song out of it. What do you think 'Killer' is about?" Hank offered me the other cup and I waved my hand, *no thanks*; I didn't need a drink to get on stage anymore.

"I thought so," I said. "But you always told me you made that song up?"

"Well, it wasn't a complete lie when I said that. I mean Elvis and me weren't exactly *best* friends, like the guys in that song are," said Hank. "Besides, when you first asked me about that you weren't ready to know the truth." Hank finished my serve of scotch too. "Actually, no—that is a lie. It was me. I wasn't ready to tell you the truth. I wanted to be the only man you ever called Dad."

"You are. And like I said, you always were and always will be."

"Good," said Hank, wiping his lips. "Now before we need to dig out a box of Kleenex, give your old man a hug and go get this show on the road. Those good people out there are waitin' for you!" I moved my guitar aside for our embrace. Hank slapped me on the back then went to join Cherry as I opened the final tent flap leading me to the stage. From the bottom of the stairs I watched the festival MC—dressed in a pristine and starchy Elvis jumpsuit—

introduce me to the capacity crowd milling around expectantly under the athletic-field lights outside.

"It's a hell of a story," he said, "and one I know you are all well familiar with—well, any of you who read the paper, watch the news or surf the net. Elvis may have left the building but his legacy continues. Here with us today to perform his worldwide smash hit tribute to the one and only Elvis Presley is…the one…and only…ZIPPIN PIPPIN!!"

The crowd went wild. I ran up the stairs, slinging my guitar around to my front as I went. With a wave to the audience and a thumbs-up to the drummer, I counted the band in. Saving 'The King', I launched straight into my second song to have gone viral on the internet, one that Cherry and I had edited together and uploaded just a week before the festival; a song called 'Zippin Pippin' that told the whole Zippin story. Well, most of it.

*Zippin Pippin is my name*
*I ride my motorcycle through a flame*
*It's been my life, to entertain*
*Come shine or rain*
*See I was born inside a travelling show*
*And all the wild places we did go*
*Filled up my heart with a gigantic dream*
*And so it seems…*
*Life goes on*
*Life goes on*
*Life goes on—just like a song*

I spotted Hank and Cherry in the V.I.P. audience pen at the front. With them was Franny and Guitar Joe from Green Onions, the two of them now apparently an item. I kept singing, marveling to myself at how everything had worked out so well.

*Mistakes? I might have made a few*
*Did my own stunts and once I paid for two*
*But what is life, if you don't take a risk*
*And live a bit?*
*Regrets? I guess I could have one*
*But then again I know that don't help none*
*And all I did I'd probably do again*
*Right to the end*
*Life goes on*
*Life goes on*
*Life goes on*

Cherry looked up, smiling and singing along. I blew her a quick kiss and she caught it smack on the cheek. Bullseye.

*Just like a song.*

The clouds parted and the full moon seemed to light up Cherry's face like a spotlight upon it. It was almost as if someone up there was trying to tell me something.

# I DO

"**W**ill you mabby me?"

Walking back to our hotel after the gig, we'd ended up in a park on the edge of town when I was overcome with the urge to pop the question. Under the stars, on a cool summer evening, in a quaint country town, it seemed like a romantic enough moment to ask Cherry to be my wife. The truth was I couldn't wait any longer.

"Will I what?" asked Cherry, with a bemused smile. "*Mabby* you? What does mabby mean?" She laughed and looked up to the pitch-black sky, twinkling alive with the universe's fairylights. I was still on a high after the gig, but all those nerves I'd thought I'd conquered had quickly returned when I'd decided that was my moment; I was so nervous my lips had stuck together.

"Will you *marry* me?" I said again, partially deafened by the sound of my pulse in my neck pumping at a dizzying pace. I looked around, trying to gain some composure. I couldn't see straight either.

"Yes, I will," said Cherry. "I accept your berry bro-mantic bro-posal." Cherry didn't seem flustered at all. Just happy. She pulled me to my feet, hugged me tight and kissed me.

"Well, that went better than I expected," I said.

"What do you mean?" said Cherry. "What did you expect?"

"I don't know. I've never done this before."

"Neither have I, handsome," said Cherry. "Don't worry, I'm sure we'll figure it out together. Why are you so nervous? You must have known I would say yes. Why else would I come all the way back here from America?"

"The scenery?" I said, pointing to an old wooden see-saw. Cherry smiled and led us over to get on.

"Nothing like it," she said. "Now be careful. You're bigger than me."

"I'll be very gentle," I said, holding the plank horizontal, so she could get on the other end. "But I can't promise there won't be a few ups and downs."

"Very clever," said Cherry, pushing herself down and indicating for me to climb aboard the high end. "I see what you did there."

"Guess my inner poet has been unleashed and there's no turning back now," I said as I got on, using my weight to send Cherry a foot high into the air. "Sorry."

"Hey!" screamed Cherry. "I thought you said you were going to be gentle?" We laughed like little kids and I kicked off the ground to bring Cherry back to earth. After exhausting ourselves with a midnight playtime, we continued our walk back to the hotel, already making plans for our big day. Neither of us wanted a long engagement, and the only thing Cherry was adamant about in terms of wedding arrangements was the '50s wedding dress she wanted to have made. And that sounded just fine to me.

A couple of months later, and without too much hullaballoo, Cherry and I were standing in our wedding best on the edge of a huge red carpet in front of my shack on Flynn Station. With what seemed to me like even more stars in the clear sky than there had been on our proposal night, and with sparkling lights hanging from gum trees all around us, we were getting ready to start our lives together.

Wearing a classic black twopiece suit, and some new black leather shoes instead of my cowboy boots, I think I scrubbed up alright but Cherry looked absolutely stunning in her bespoke dress: a fitted lace bodice; a small bow accentuating her slim waist; and a full skirt falling just below the knees. Cherry looked truly elegant.

Holding both of each other's hands, we smiled up at our wedding celebrant, a Vegas-suited Elvis lookalike (a nice man we'd met in Parkes) standing on the steps leading up to the porch. With Flynn Station decorated in New-Mexican piñatas, fairy-lights draped from my shack to the main house, and a new, Cupid water fountain (especially bought to mark the day) gurgling soothingly in April's Garden, I imagined it was quite a unique view for the friends and family gathered behind us. Though when I looked across to Cherry I knew I had the best view of all.

"And do you, Angus Pippin Flynn, take Charlene Stephanie Ockham to be your lawfully wedded wife?" For some reason I hadn't counted on the celebrant doing an Elvis *impression* while he took us through our vows—but it only added to the fun. "To have and to hold and to let go of whenever she wants to go a little wild? Uh huh?"

"I do," I said. "I do very much."

"And do you, Cherry *baby-cakes* Ockham, take Angus *hound-dog* Flynn to be your lawfully wedded husband, to love and to cherish like a big old home-made apple pie fresh outta the oven?" Cherry laughed, stopping herself in time from completely losing it.

"I do," she said. "I do very much too."

"Then, by the powers invested in me by the Colonel—and the state of Victoria—I now pronounce you husband

and wife. Angus, you may now kiss, cuddle and do the Watusi with the bride, uh huh." Cherry and I kissed our first kiss as husband and wife. Turning to face the guests (seated in fold-out wooden chairs arranged in neat aisles), our loved ones greeted us with a big cheer, applauding as they rose to their feet. Hank caught my attention first, clapping madly above his head and looking very smart in a tuxedo and bow-tie (red, of course, to match his bandana). Surrounding him were all his old friends—and mine and Cherry's new ones— Ginger, Roy and Doris. Hank's old gang had surprised us all by arranging a trip down under together and it must have been fate they'd arrived in time for the wedding.

Walking down the carpet, headed for the reception tent next to the main house, Cherry and I dodged confetti and fielded kisses and hand shakes from all. Even Cherry's mum had taken some time off from her company's Asian expansion (jetting in on a private plane from Tokyo that morning) to be at our wedding. Cherry's father had made the trip too, apparently sucking up his pride enough to let his ex-wife buy him a plane ticket.

Hank patted me on the back proudly, happier than I'd seen him in years. Ginger stepped forward to be the first to kiss me good luck. She planted a wet one on my mouth and I was grateful—though not a hundred percent sure—not to feel any tongue.

"Didn't think we'd miss this, did you?" said Ginger. "April's boy tying the knot?" Roy stepped out from behind Ginger to shake my hand vigorously, the strength of his grip belying his age. He looked to Cherry.

"Your turn in the spotlight, hey?" said Roy, leaning past me to give her a kiss. "You look spectacular, girl." Doris slapped Roy on the back.

"Well, of course she does, Roy!" said Doris, turning to Cherry. "With that figure you were always gonna look amazing."

"And it's amazing how all you guys made it all the way here," said Cherry. Oli and Penelope stood next in line, grinning ear to ear to ear to ear.

"Couldn't keep us away, partner!" said Oli, coming in for a kiss—on my cheek.

"We wouldn't miss this wedding for anything," said Penelope. "It was bad enough we were so drunk we missed ours."

Eventually we made it to the reception tent, where we had a sit-down dinner that included yam pie, Hank's—and apparently now Cherry's favorite—for desert. Before coffee and chocolates, and after Hank, Cherry's mother and Cherry's father had said a few words, it was my turn to speak. I'd written something especially for the day and surprised Cherry by moving to the microphone in front of the band to deliver my wedding speech as a song.

Roy led the band in a sweet version of my latest completed composition. It was easily the most sentimental song I'd ever written but I'd figured if you couldn't wear your heart on your sleeve on your wedding day, when could you? However vulnerable I was feeling, only one thing really mattered anyway: whether Cherry loved it.

"This is for my wife," I said over the music and looking to Cherry, the immediate cheers reminding me I was surrounded by loved ones who were probably going to love whatever I said. Or sang. "I think this best explains how I feel and how lucky I am to have found you. It's called 'I Do'." Cherry smiled and raised her champagne glass. I took a breath and sang my heart out.

*I never thought I would get married living on the road*
*But I've never been so happy or felt so at home*
*Now I've got more than a song and sadness in my heart*
*Ready to start a new story, do you think this is the start?*
*I do*

Cherry covered her mouth and I watched as she tried—and failed—to stop herself from crying.

*I do take you to be my wife*
*I do know I'm one lucky guy*
*I do choose to share my whole life*
*I do promise each day and night*
*I do*

Next to Cherry, Oli was filming everything on his phone. I wondered if he had plans to upload it to YouTube before Cherry and I had even boarded the plane for our honeymoon in Paris.

*Maybe it is kind of funny making my speech a song*
*But it seems to be a way to make this day go on*
*Into the future where we'll live through*
*Some highs and some lows*
*But doing it all together, don't you think we'll grow?*
*I do*

By the end of the song, Cherry had left the wedding table and was already by my side, ready to kiss me. When we were finished smooching, and at my signal, the band started up again and Cherry and I danced our wedding dance to a music-only version of the first song I'd written for her, 'Treasure'. After a couple of twirls, Cherry whispered in my ear if I was ready to invite everyone else up, and we waved everyone to come and join in the fun. Slowly the dance floor filled with other partnered guests, including Oli and Penelope, Franny and Guitar Joe and a very jovial Hank following Ginger's lead.

"You look beautiful," said Ginger, giving Cherry a wink as she and Hank danced up alongside us.

"That's my wife!" I said proudly.

"'Trouble and Strife' they say around here," said Hank.

"Trouble and Strife? That's cute," said Ginger, rubbing noses with Hank. "I like a bit of trouble. I think I might like it *down under.*"

"Well, you always did," said Hank, squeezing Ginger's waist.

"You are a devil, Hank Flynn," said Ginger, feigning shock at my old man's double entendre. "Though I must say, you do have a good memory." We all laughed. "But can you walk the talk," challenged Ginger. "I want to know how's your stamina, old man?"

"This heart is better than ever," said Hank, smiling and fisting his chest. Ginger slid her hand down Hank's arm.

"Is it as strong as the muscle pulsing in my hand?" she asked, squeezing his bicep.

"Maybe we should go some place and find out?" suggested Hank.

"I was wonderin' if you'd ever ask," said Ginger coyly, before Hank swept her away for who knew what. Cherry and I were alone again in the middle of the bustling dance floor. Suddenly Doris almost bowled us over as she ran across the floor, screaming all the way from one side to the other.

"Snake! Snake! I saw a fat fuckin' snake!" Doris crashed into the arms of a local ex-farmer, a widower friend of Hank's who'd made his money sub-dividing and selling off many of the properties around Flynn Station. Doris smiled and composed herself, putting on the bravest face she could. "Maybe it wasn't a snake?" she said. "It might have been a goanna. Isn't that what you call a big lizard here?" The rich old guy nodded.

"There's many breeds of what you might call 'varmin', Miss," he said in a friendly tone, giving a tip of his old Akubra hat. "But I would be honored to offer what little

314

protection I might. Perhaps we could dance? At least that'd make it harder for the snake to get an easy bite on you." He offered his hand and Doris smiled at the eccentric farmer.

"Why, yes," said Doris, fluttering her eyelashes. "If you promise to *protect* me? All these strange critters make me nervous as a little girl."

"Do you think Doris will survive in this wild country?" asked Cherry.

"Sure," I said. "Doris made it out of the mean streets of Las Vegas alive. I think she can handle the odd reptile or two." I gestured to Doris, who was now go-go dancing to the delight of everyone watching.

"Yeah, you're right," said Cherry. "I'm sure she can handle them."

And the band played on.

Cherry led us over to the bar and another bottle of champagne on ice. She took two glasses, holding them out for me in the same way she had at the Grand Canyon when we'd shared a beer. As I poured our champagne, it occurred to me what a great tale our love story would make: the road-trip we took across America, the glamour of the Hollywood gigs, the romance of our desert camp-outs, and the hi-jinx of our journey to discover each other, all with the guidance of a kindly, benevolent spirit, the ghost of a rock n' roll legend who'd come back to live again.

Such would be the story of Zippin Pippin.

"I've got a couple more surprises for you," I said, resting my champagne glass on the bar so I could pull my pant legs up above my ankles. Cherry screamed with laughter, almost spitting out her bubbly.

"Pink socks!" she exclaimed. Then between laughs, "What's the other surprise?" I kissed her, ran over to the band and took the mic.

"Hello everyone, hope you're having a great time.

Before my wife and I get too drunk to thank you each personally, I just want to say how happy we both are to have you all with us on this very special night. And if you'd all be so kind to indulge me, I've got one more song I'd like to sing for you…"

"'My Best Present Ever'!" screamed Ginger.

"'The King'!" yelled Oli.

"No," I said plainly. "This one is named after the love of my life, the women I travelled the globe to find and bring home to my shack. This is a simple love song called…

…'Cherry'."

## ABOUT THE AUTHOR

Benjamin Grant Mitchell published his first novel, *The Last Great Day*, in 2011. One critic described his 'autobiographical' debut as 'a compelling tale of faith and family' (Inpress Magazine) while others called it a 'fascinating' and 'amazing' read.

Previously to beginning his career as a full-time writer, Mitchell worked as an actor and musician appearing regularly on Australian television and releasing the critically acclaimed indie album, *The Stars Can See*, in 2006. Americana UK described Mitchell as 'a major talent' saying "It's his song-writing skills that put him in a league above the litany of anonymous singer-songwriters vying for attention."

Zippin Pippin is Mitchell's second novel.

www.benjamingrantmitchell.com

CPSIA information can be obtained at www.ICGtesting.com
Printed in the USA
LVOW131935071012

301815LV00017B/161/P

9 780987 380319